Death at Cherry Tree Manor

An English Village Cozy Mystery

Tannis Laidlaw

Forth Estate Books

Copyright © 2020 by Tannis Laidlaw

All rights reserved.

No portion of this book may be reproduced in any form without written permission from the publisher or author, except as permitted by copyright law.

Chapter One

*I*T WAS RIDICULOUS. *I mean, we were just having a chat. And I was merely making a friendly business proposition. Yet she reacted like I'd become Public Enemy Number One.*

Honestly, old ladies!

One minute talking and the next she's waving an old rifle around like Amateur Night at the Little Theatre, her voice all squeaky, spittle flying, and yelling at me to get off her property or whatever. Oh, I don't know; it is all just so silly. Even that ludicrous gun.

Still, nobody likes having a gun pointed at you, right? So, I calmly walk over and take the stupid thing away from her. I decide to show her how it feels.

At first, I honestly didn't know what's happening. An ear-splitting noise and – well, once I get my senses back, I have a problem. She's lying there and she's far too still. I drop the stupid gun and watch an ever expanding puddle of red spreading out.

Utter silence.

I stare at her. Push at her hip with the toe of my shoe. One arm flops into the puddle. Splashes. I leap back. No way I can have any splatters on me.

A problem alright. A bloody problem.

Bother.

Chapter Two

MADDIE PARKED HER CAR close to the front door of Cherry Tree Manor on a weed-encrusted pea-gravel drive. She looked out at some impressively large trees and a green sward of unkempt lawn, the house hunched like a brooding angel in a neglected churchyard.

She stood in the morning sunshine for a moment mentally writing the copy: 'Late Georgian manor house, private location on spacious grounds. Ample opportunity to create a warm and stylish countryside milieu...'. She grimaced and looked more closely. Georgian? Maybe, or early Victorian. She presumed this sort of knowledge would come with experience. The house was constructed of large stone blocks, interrupted by mullioned windows. Three stories, facing south-east with extended views over the undulations of pastoral Oxfordshire. Quite a pile, all in all, but the neglected grounds probably indicated some unpleasant surprises inside.

A car crunched onto the drive behind her. This must be the former owner's nephew, now officially her client.

"Ms Brooks?" the man said as he opened his door.

"Madeleine Brooks," she said automatically, pushing down her nervous excitement, "and you're Mr Fanshaw?"

He unfolded his lanky frame from his low-slung car and headed up the steps without replying, hunting for the key in a pocket and unlocking the front door.

So, it was going to be like that, was it? She kept the smile plastered on her face and thought, 'Fluffy, fluffy, fluffy', her antidote to the severity of expression and body language demanded by her former profession as a Probation Officer. No more. She was now an estate agent. With a smile. And her new profession demanded a light and confident presentation to her clients. So she supposed. This was, after all, her first real client.

The cool interior contrasted pleasantly with the heat of the June day outside.

"The hallway," Douglas Fanshaw said as he strode across it to fling open a couple of French doors, "and the main drawing room."

She followed him across the dim hallway clutching her clipboard tightly to her chest. She loosened her grip on it when she was struck with the beauty of the drawing room, tall with light flooding in through the windows, turning the wooden floors mellow and warm. Large pink and green chesterfield settees and shabby Persian rugs made up the main furnishings, although spindly chairs were set at various places along the walls, most with small tables within reach.

"A nicely proportioned room," she said with what she hoped was estate agent-y aplomb.

He shrugged. "I suppose."

"Your great-aunt lived here a long time?"

"I've told the whole sorry story to Neil Black." He spoke to the room, not her. "They tell me you're new."

"Yes, new." She didn't tell him how new. Or that this was the first house she'd entered as an estate agent. Or the list of recommendations Neil Black had left for her. "Mr Black is ill. I'm the replacement for some of his clients. Will that be a problem?" Poor fellow, he was off having chemotherapy in London.

Douglas Fanshaw turned his gaze onto her for the first time since he had entered the house. He had pleasant hazel eyes, she noticed.

He glanced at his watch. "Sorry, but my time is limited today. Something has come up in Liverpool and I can only give you a quick tour."

"How about you show me the highlights then leave for your trip? I can wander around afterwards at my own pace. I'll lock up when I have a good idea of which features to emphasise when we have potential buyers. And I'll jot down a list of what's needed to be done." She waved one hand vaguely in the direction of the lawn and drive. "Like some basic garden work. I can organise that if you want."

He hesitated then nodded. "You were told the situation here? I can't sell until my legal problems are resolved?"

Maddie nodded. "My boss at *Green Acres* explained it to me. You're in the process of applying for a death certificate for your great-aunt. And you're applying to be considered her heir."

"Making a complex and uncertain story very short, yes." He shoved his hands into his jean's pockets. "The court has questions about her death and they seem to be stalled. My lawyer thinks it will all turn out fine but I'm too much of a realist to believe that wholeheartedly. I have waves of pessimism." He shrugged. "What will be, will be."

Maddie's heart sank. This was worse than her boss had said. He'd been burbling on about how the commission for selling the Manor would be significant. Motivating her by visions of easing her financial concerns.

"So we need to concentrate on planning but no spending yet. Have I got it right?"

He flashed a short-lived smile, the first Maddie had seen. Momentarily it transformed his face before it fell once more. "Fine. But there's just too much to do."

She nodded. "We'll need advice, which will lead to an evaluation." All of this was on Neil Black's file about the house, a list which was already proving to be invaluable. "Eventually, the house has to be dressed for sale. That is, if you want to get a top price."

He made a noise Maddie interpreted to be a sardonic laugh. "Dressed? If you say so. Better to be empty than with this old junk."

Enough of this negativity. "My recommendation is that we get people in to assess the basics, at least," she said in her old Probation Officer's voice, one that brooked no argument. It startled him and she mentally slapped her wrist. The voice had been effective with her crims; that was why she used it. All an act, of course, so she was disturbed it had popped out unintentionally.

"Yes, well," he said, "I imagine you'll want to 'dress' it differently, that's all." He made 'dress' sound like a swear word. He shook his head. "Sorry. Perhaps you could let me know which people and how much they'll charge."

"I'll start with the charity shop people. They come for free. They'll advise on which bits of furniture are charity shop giveaways and which discards. Maybe they'll be some things you'll want to keep?"

"You can dispense with the entire lot, if you want," he said with a shrug. Maddie was pleased about the carte blanche, but irritated that Mr Fanshaw was rooted in today's throw-away society. Obviously he thought the way to clean up was to hire a large skip and toss everything in it, an attitude which offended her basic eco self. She recycled whenever possible.

After a whirlwind tour, Maddie waved him away and was relieved to do so. Tall and thin. Dark hair. At first she'd thought him attractive. He would be if he had any manners. You'd think he'd be more pleasantly disposed with someone who would be working on his behalf.

She wandered back to the sitting room, an elegant space with a large fireplace and marble mantelpiece. The floral couches and well-worn rugs were homely and definitely brought to mind that rather overused phrase, 'shabby elegance' rather than cheap and nasty. Anything more modern would highlight the deficiencies in the décor. All in all, these furnishings would do.

The dining room housed an enormous table with more of the same spindly chairs she'd seen in the sitting room which must be the spares for when the table needed to seat twenty or more. Surely this stylish and well-designed dining suite was from an earlier era than the heavy Victorian furniture her grandmother had owned. She frowned. So much to learn. The sitting room was dusty and she'd seen a few cobwebs corresponding to the neglect she'd noticed outside but the dining room smelled of furniture polish. Strange, but good.

The morning room, furnished with old wicker furniture and a built-in dining nook, was also flooded in light from windows on two sides. It led to the kitchen which was straight out of the 1950s with pitted terrazzo benches and a badly chipped enamel sink. Maddie sighed. She wondered if she could persuade Mr Fanshaw to upgrade. Or at least to have the benches cut and polished. Stone benches were all the rage again. The difference in the selling price could be considerable. The bathrooms too. In fact ... her mind spun on the possibilities the house presented.

After locking up and turning her car around on the gravel, she wondered again about what had happened to the owner, Mr Fanshaw's elderly great-aunt. Apparently, she had simply disappeared a couple of years ago. Rupert Woking, Maddie's boss at *Green Acres Estate Agents* in Goring-on-Thames, had told her about the long and tortuous court case to establish Beryl Fanshaw's presumed death.

The police had determined, subject to corroboration by the coroner's court, that the octogenarian Beryl Fanshaw, crippled with Alzheimer's, had wandered off and died, probably in the extensive woodland nearby or possibly drowned in the nearby River Courtney which emptied into the Thames. Whatever, neither she nor her body had been seen in a couple of years.

Although Douglas Fanshaw did not yet have the official nod to put the house on the market, Rupert had told her a death certificate for Beryl Fanshaw was to be issued anytime soon. Once in hand, Douglas Fanshaw, as her only living relative, could apply to inherit her estate. According to Rupert, Douglas had been told the legal decision had been made to the effect that Beryl Fanshaw was now officially deceased although the paperwork had not yet been completed, which was why Maddie had been asked to get onto the preparations for sale straight away.

So why was Mr Douglas Fanshaw so negative?

Chapter Three

Back at Briar Cottage, Maddie rang her friend Caroline. "I'm settled in and I saw my first client today," she said to her old friend. "I am so grateful you've let me stay in your cottage. It's wonderful."

"The pleasure is all mine," Caroline said. "Any news about the Philanderer?"

Maddie laughed although she found nothing funny in the question. "Jade keeps me informed about her dad. I think she gets a vicarious pleasure telling me all about the new girlfriend. You know she's only a year or two older than Jade?"

"You've told me," Caroline said, "several times, my friend."

"Okay. Sorry. Anyway, I get a bit from her – even though I have to filter what she's saying." She kept her voice light. Jade was a problem. Maddie felt guilty she'd abdicated her mothering role for this daughter who had not yet found her way in the world. Was it abdication when a mother moves from London to Oxfordshire?

"And Olivia?" Two daughters, two completely different characters: Jade, always the rebel, difficult; Olivia, almost too conventional, sweet, easy. They'd been like that since they were babies.

"Zilch," Maddie said. "She thinks not saying anything makes her neutral. Ha. She's devastated at our separation, at the new girlfriend in the house. My daughter might be twenty-five years old and a mother of two but she's reacting to adversity exactly as she did when she was five." Maddie sighed. Olivia was more settled than Jade, always had been.

But she was upset by her parents' separation, no question about that. Maddie resolved to ring Olivia. Then berated herself for preferring to talk to Olivia rather than Jade who needed her more.

"You okay?" Caroline asked.

"Mostly," Maddie answered with honesty. "It's much better now I've moved in. You know how I've always loved this place. Thank you again for letting me stay." Maddie told her about her first day on the job, the large house she was handling and her brusque client.

Caroline laughed. "I have no doubt you handled him with aplomb after a lifetime of handling crims."

"I didn't have to make-nice to my crims."

"Come on, Maddie," Caroline laughed. "You had your favourites. You always said, 'Not all crims are grim.' It wasn't all bad."

"I had my fair share of charmers, certainly," she said. "But I can't believe I woke up every morning dreading going into work. For over twenty years."

"Because of working with the crims?"

"That's part of it. They were forever letting me down," Maddie said. "But mostly because of the repercussions when they did. From the powers-that-be in the Probation Service to politicians. Then whenever the newspapers got hold of something … huge pressure." She sighed. "The problem is, it's impossible to be right with every decision, especially when dealing with that lot."

Later as she prepared for bed, Maddie assured herself that her recent momentous decisions were opening a door for re-defining her life. Her separation, once she'd learned of her husband Wayne's infidelities, plus the unrelenting pressure of her Probation Service job had caused a minor melt-down and she was the first to admit it. But quitting her career and separating from a much loved husband were both one-way streets. No going back. She still had the occasional panicky reaction when she thought about it. But here she was, on her own, close to being totally broke, dealing with her daughters' distress by telephone, with not only a new job as an estate agent but living in a country village as different from London suburbia as could be.

Why did she pick a new career of selling houses? Happenstance, actually. As she had told Olivia, "I was looking up how much money it would cost to move to a rural location. Lovely old villages, stately homes, cute modern cottages overlooking fields of waving hay – maybe I could afford a little tract house, and some were definitely out in the countryside. That thought segued into how much I loved houses. All houses. Especially when I could see potential to improve them for sale. Maybe this could be a ticket to living and working in the countryside." That led to her estate agent's internet course and here she was.

As Maddie went through her nightly regime, she found herself bothered not only by her dire financial status but also by her loss of stature, that sense of authority when dealing with her clients, and, she had to admit, by her loss of self-esteem. Would things right themselves? Could they?

As she drifted off to sleep, she visualised herself at the door of some modernistic million pound dwelling, welcoming a crowd of people into an Open Day. She hoped and prayed this new life she'd designed for herself would work.

Fingers crossed.

Chapter Four

THE NEXT DAY MADDIE dressed in one of the new summer dresses she'd bought for the job, different prints but all pastel florals, dresses she privately called her 'uniform', but as different from the power-suits worn in her previous life as could be.

She and daughter Olivia had chosen her new wardrobe to be dressed up or down depending on the circumstances. This uniform was the last of her purchases; her new circumstances would be quite straitened. Today's temperatures were forecast to be warm, so she'd worn the sleeveless beige and blue with a gold chain, no jacket or scarf. Open toed sandals.

Dressing for this unfamiliar role, she felt uncomfortably 'fluffy' in the floral print, but, she had to admit, still smart. It was vital she felt good in her new job. And 'fluffy' was totally appropriate, according to Olivia.

Maddie was determined to make a success of her career change. She had to. She had slammed the door behind her when she'd left the Probation Service, especially given she'd resigned during a particularly stressful staffing crisis. And she'd slammed the door on her marriage, more because of the sickly sweet and impossibly young Chrystal – with an 'h' – than anything Maddie had done or decided. That still galled her.

She had completed a correspondence course in *Property Management: Sales and Practice* during the worst of her stress – and could hardly remember a thing – so she was a bit wary now she'd been taken on by *Green Acres*. But, she reminded herself, she had Neil Black's notes and a willing resource in her boss Rupert. Her appointment was strictly commission, no salary. At the moment, she was eking out the last of her savings which meant she had to get her act together and smartly. She either sold a property soon or she'd be forced into pressuring Wayne to sell their family home and divide the pathetic profit after the mortgage was paid off. She'd much rather sell a property for *Green Acres*. For many reasons. Selling the Manor would solve so many problems – she would be able to go into the supermarket without counting pennies; she would gain in stature within the estate agency community and most importantly, she'd still be with *Green Acres*. If she didn't contribute to the office by selling, she was out on her ear. She must never forget that.

Maddie knew and loved Woodley Bottom. A few years ago her friend Caroline had inherited her grandparents' country get-away and the two of them had spent many girly weekends here since. And it was here Maddie was now camping. Pro tem, of course. She badly wanted to search for a place of her own. But that dream had to be shelved. Hopefully, temporarily.

As always, when she thought of her ex, her heartbeat rose to send a tattoo into the very core of her being. She couldn't be honest with anyone about how she felt. The truth was, she didn't want this separation. Not at all. She'd secretly hoped he'd tire of his bit-on-the-side now it was out in the open and want her back. She and Wayne had twenty-nine years of history after all, most of it smooth with many highlights. They'd had their moments, but the companionship was first rate and the sex always good. She'd continually felt a little smug about how they had made it when so many of her friends' marriages had faltered. Now, she had to admit, the friends were on their second, or even third, time around and settled into quiet domesticity. Even Caroline.

Sometimes Maddie still awakened believing Wayne's philandering and their separation were only parts of a bad dream. She still cried sometimes, not that she admitted it to her daughters or even Caroline. Even now she found herself asking, how *could* he?

Maddie picked up her hairbrush and attacked her hair vigorously, concentrating on her brush strokes, banishing from her mind any thoughts of bloody Wayne Brooks and his dolly-bird. Brushing away her grief at a future now denied her.

Her cell-phone rang. The office. Someone had heard the Manor was up for sale and that someone was in the office. Could she come as soon as she could as this may well be a hot one.

Driving through the country lanes towards Goring, Maddie couldn't keep a smile off her face. A buyer? And someone who must already know the property if it was word of mouth that brought him along? She put her foot down and flew over the back roads towards finding out.

She and daughter Olivia had discussed how she could soften the severe and authoritarian manner she'd developed from her years as a Probation Officer. 'Fluffy' was their joint decision. She'd repeat 'fluffy, fluffy, fluffy' to herself to signal switching to this different persona, that of a feminine, slightly daffy sales person who had the common touch. She hadn't tried it properly yet. Did it count that she kept an artificial smile on her face for Douglas Fanshaw? No, not really.

The potential buyer was a balding fifty-ish man with dark eyes under brooding eyebrows. He was wearing a countryman's clothes and his face was weather-beaten. Maddie put him down as a working farmer. As soon as he opened his mouth, she revised her mental description. An educated working farmer.

"Thought I'd drop in to see if the Fanshaw place is on the market," he said. "My wife noticed activity over there yesterday."

"Not officially," she said smiling into his eyes. "But we can talk about it." She remembered to keep her voice light and her smile in place.

"What brings you to our part of England?" he asked as she shepherded him into the private interview room the sales staff could access. At least it gave some respite from the constantly ringing telephones in the shared office area.

She was prepared for this question. "Couldn't stand one more day in London," she said. "This job came up. And here I am." This was the truth, albeit this version was economical.

"South Oxfordshire will blow some country air into your lungs," he said as he sat down. "Problem is, we're quite a stable area, not many people moving either in or out. I hope you can make it as an estate agent in these circs."

"I do hope so, too," she said as she spread out a few official looking papers on the table in front of her. Window dressing.

His face sobered as he switched to the matter at hand. "Our business is called Cherry Tree Farm," he said. "My father bought more than half of the land and the right to retain its name from the Fanshaws years ago and I've added the rest to our holdings since. They kept the house and a couple of home paddocks and we have the acreage. We also bought the old workers' cottages on the northerly edge of the land, where we now live. But my wife...."

Maddie smiled at his pause. "Your wife?" she prompted.

"My wife would like to reunite Cherry Tree House with the farm," he said stiffly.

"Yes, well, let's merely say Cherry Tree, erm, *Manor* could well be on offer in the near future," Maddie said.

Cherry Tree *House* indeed. "Would you like to leave me your contact details and I can be in touch if it does go on the market. I might be able to give you a nod before it becomes public knowledge."

The man stared at her. "Uh, yes," he said. "Yes, a call would be appreciated."

There was an awkward pause. To fill it and hopefully bring back a sense of polite calm, Maddie asked, "So you knew Mrs Beryl Fanshaw?"

"Everyone knew the Fanshaws," he said, "They lived in the big house for the whole time I've known them."

"Do you know anything about her disappearance?" Maddie asked. "Just curious."

"The official line is that she became confused. Wandered off. Probably one day we'll find her bones out in the woods somewhere." He looked directly at Maddie. "She was very old. Early Alzheimer's. Bad memory, confusion, that sort of thing."

"I suppose that's one explanation," Maddie said. "But maybe she met a dashing young man of, say, seventy, and went off with him!" She flashed what she hoped was a semi-flirtatious smile with the aim of appearing light-hearted and slightly silly. A fluffy statement if there ever was one. Something no Probation Officer would ever say.

He smiled but the smile didn't reach his eyes. "Well, thank you for your time. And I'd appreciate your giving us a bell when you have some news."

She saw him out, wondering why she felt disquieted. She glanced at the contact details the man had given her. Somehow Mr George Higgins hadn't come across as totally straight. You didn't work for the Probation Service for a quarter of a century without being able to smell that sort of thing from a long way off.

Chapter Five

MADDIE RETURNED TO THE Manor the next day to formulate some idea of upgrading the house without spending a fortune. Costs were going to be a factor, unfortunately. The charity shop people were due to arrive in a day or so but she needed time to figure out what basics needed to be done. She again parked on the weed-infested drive and opened the massive door. She liked the door. And she liked the silence of the big house as she closed it behind her. She stood for a moment then headed for the stairs which wound up from the entrance hallway. Every step creaked like the sound effects for a ghost story, but that was part and parcel of a house of this age.

Upstairs, she cautiously stepped into the first bedroom, pad and pencil at hand. It smelled slightly musty and she noticed black mould on the windowsill. But spacious. A threadbare rug covered painted boards. She figured they'd come up a treat if sanded and refinished. She noted it down. The wallpaper was not fashionable, but it was muted and in good repair. It would do. But the overly fussy curtains could go. New window coverings added huge cachet and were not expensive. The bed was a single with a faded bedspread. No other bedding. Somehow its narrowness illustrated the spaciousness of the room, so it could stay. She'd add a plain duvet and some brightly coloured toss cushions. Maybe a comfy chair and a large painting above the head of the bed?

Perhaps picking up some of the colours in the toss cushions. Or maybe buy a painting and take the colours for the cushions from it. She'd have to think about that. But first, the mould would have to be scrubbed out and a mould-repelling paint applied. First things first.

The second and subsequent bedrooms, some singles, some doubles, could have much the same treatment as the first. The wardrobes in all of the rooms were freestanding, not built in, but they were substantial and relatively attractive. Victorian, she was almost certain. They could stay. She'd opened the doors of one of them only to be confronted with more strong musty smells. After that, she opened all the wardrobe doors in all the bedrooms to air out years of being shut up. She wrote 'Air freshener' on her list. Next time she came, she'd open all the bedroom windows.

The master bedroom had obviously been inhabited in recent times. A corner room, it had windows on two sides with extensive views over a rolling rural landscape. The bed, a double, was made up with a large candlewick bedspread on top. A glass on the bedside table, given the residue, must have contained milk. Interesting. Aunt Beryl either left in a hurry or didn't complete her morning chores before she went out to her death. Or disappearance. It all pointed, Maddie thought, to Aunt Beryl dying at the time she went missing. Could she have been abducted and murdered? She shook her head to clear it of such thoughts. It probably was just standing here alone in a bedroom which belonged to a woman who hadn't come back.

She noticed a bulge in the middle of the bed and pulled back the covers to find a long-cold hot-water bottle. The bedding was unpleasantly odorous. She quickly stripped it off the bed. Maybe throw it in the wash before giving it to the charity shop people? Or she could simply leave everything as was. Maybe that was for the best; after all, it wasn't her job to do this sort of thing. On the other hand, she wasn't exactly overly busy. Yes, she would wash it. She hated waste. She wouldn't take the chance the charity shop people would sniff it and dispose of the lot.

Maddie continued her snoop. The dresser drawers were full of clothes. If Aunt Beryl had gone off with a fancy-man, she hadn't taken much of anything. All Aunt Beryl's underwear was old and tatty. Her woollen cardigans were full of moth holes; her nightgowns heavy flannelette; her stockings cotton lisle. Maddie couldn't remember anyone she knew, old or young, wearing lisle stockings. Not for decades.

The wardrobe contained dozens of dresses, all having seen better days but needing sorting. On the top shelf of the wardrobe, Maddie found a fur stole packed in a moth-proof bag and a case full of silk and satin evening gowns in brilliant colours. That meant Aunt Beryl wasn't always old and dowdy. But today, what on earth could anyone do with them? They were rather attractive. She put them to one side to show Douglas Fanshaw. Maybe they could go to a retro clothing shop. She figured the styles looked about fifty years old. Plunging necklines, sweeping long skirts and bare backs. A flattering era, and, she remembered her mother saying, a godsend for those with big hips.

She found shoes, all leather and all misshapen, most likely conforming to the old lady's feet. Maybe they should be binned. She shook her head at the waste. These had been good quality shoes once upon a time.

All in all, these garments suited a bag lady. Was it that Aunt Beryl in her old age just didn't care any more? Or maybe she was as poor as only a formerly wealthy old woman could be and fancy clothes eventually meant little to her.

Maddie peered under the bed and disturbed years of dust by doing so. She sneezed violently several times, wrenching her neck in the process. But while there, she glimpsed a flash of colour. Something was sandwiched between the mattress and the old fashioned wire-wove springs. She heaved the mattress up enough to see. A cardboard folder tied with a bright pink cotton ribbon was lying on the wire-wove, its thickness intriguing.

But all that dust. Time for a break. Maddie took the folder down to the morning room intending to look at what she'd found in a relatively dust-free environment over a cup of tea. A cuppa. The perfect antidote for a dry throat.

The kitchen kettle worked; teacups were in the cupboard and soon Maddie headed for the morning room dining nook with a milkless cup of tea in hand and the folder tucked under her arm. She slid onto the built-in leather covered bench and untied the pink ribbon.

Inside were several documents, the first of which was the last will and testament of 'Mrs Beryl Gladys Fanshaw'. Possibilities flashed through her mind. She hesitated a second or two but curiosity consumed her. She opened the will. Douglas Fanshaw was the heir, thank heavens. Maddie let out a sigh of relief. The will was simple and straight forward. Everything was left to her grandnephew. Lock stock and barrel.

How had Douglas Fanshaw not found this document? If he had found it, he would have saved himself a heap of trouble – and money – going to court to prove he was the likely heir. Thus, he hadn't discovered it, couldn't have. Of course, if the old lady had left the property to a cat charity or some such, he could have destroyed it. Or, Maddie reminded herself, presuming he was an ordinary person with few criminal tendencies, he could have presented it to the authorities with a sigh of regret. She reminded herself of one salient fact: the people in her life now were most likely law-abiding. Her Probation Service days were well over. Ordinary adults don't lie. At least about the big things. Maddie figured Mr Douglas Fanshaw would be extremely pleased with her find.

Chapter Six

EARLY THE NEXT MORNING, Maddie packed a hamper full of milk, tea bags and a bag of cream buns from *Jenny's Kitchen*, the local bakery, before setting off for the Manor where she was to meet up with Douglas Fanshaw. He was anxious to see the will, as well he should be. She hadn't kept him in suspense. As soon as she'd returned home, she'd rung him on his mobile phone – he was in Liverpool – to give him the good news. The will was found at the Manor and, yes, he was named as heir. They agreed to get together in the morning. She'd put together a morning tea to celebrate his good fortune. Besides, she wanted to get his agreement about spending a bit of money on updating the place and this was a golden opportunity. They had a lot to do.

She arrived at Cherry Tree Manor early so she could collect the bedding from the clothesline. She touched it. Still a little damp from the morning dew, but sunshine would soon fill the courtyard.

She set up their celebratory picnic in the breakfast room. The teapot (pink roses, fine china) was ready with its teabags before she heard his car on the gravel out front. At the first crunch, she re-boiled the kettle and arranged some of the cream buns on a floral plate. She'd even found a little milk jug to match. It did look inviting.

Douglas Fanshaw came into the house as she set it out. She ushered him into the breakfast room but he refused tea, rejected the cream buns, didn't smile. Maddie gritted her teeth and poured tea for herself anyway after producing the will and leaving him to read it. She nibbled at a cream bun as he slowly went through the will, still standing, a frown on his face. He re-folded it and put it into his briefcase. Some celebration.

"Anything else you have to give me?" he asked, his voice as cold as the bottom shelf of a refrigerator.

"These," she said, thinking 'fluffy, fluffy' to relax her facial muscles. She managed a smile with what she hoped was a pleasant creasing of both mouth and eyes as she passed him the other documents from the folder. One was a certificate for a new roof from 1989; one a document for insurance purposes certifying that a registered electrician had checked and updated the wiring in 1995 and the third was a bill for putting insulation into the roof using a special 'seniors' discount, dated 2001 and guaranteed for ten years.

"Well, well, well," he said under his breath.

"All selling points," she pointed out. "Even if the insulation guarantee is now out of date it testifies some insulation is in the ceiling, which is more than a lot of houses this age."

He nodded. "But," he said with an icy stare, "why, may I ask, did you read them? These are papers belonging to my aunt. Private papers."

Maddie felt a wave of dismay. She knew she shouldn't have peeked, but once the damage had been done, she'd been honest about it. "I'm sorry but I could hardly tell if they were private without reading them. You did say to bin the lot," she said as mildly as she could. She stared back. "How did you not find them?"

"Ms Brooks, I have to tell you I scrutinised everywhere possible in this house. You say you found them in the bed. I looked there, especially under the mattress. So where did you find them? They certainly were *not* under the mattress."

Her inner dismay at being taken to task evaporated. She stared him down. Crusty crims were her speciality. "You didn't look far enough. I saw the folder from below, tied with pink ribbon, resting on the wire-wove springs in the middle of the bed. Above a great deal of dust."

"It was not there." He stared right back at her. "Nothing was under the mattress. Not a thing. Lots of dust under the bed, I agree, but no will."

"Then we have a problem, Mr Fanshaw, because that's where it was found. By me." She had the voice but cursed her lack of real authority. "Just appreciate getting the will, please. Remember, I have nothing to gain by lying."

"That, Ms Brooks, remains to be proven." He took a deep breath, shook his head and turned to her. "Look, I'm at the end of my tether. I don't know what happened to my aunt. I don't even know if she's alive or dead. The police say she's dead, but is she? Did she become lost or, God forbid, someone killed her?" At that, he walked away. Maddie heard the front door open and slam shut.

She let out a lungful of air she hadn't been aware she'd been holding, picked up her teacup and swallowed the remaining tea, the cup clattering against her teeth. She must be losing her touch. This type of confrontation used to leave her unscathed and here she was, thoroughly rattled. What a strange reaction to what should be the answer to his prayers.

And he'd thought about his aunt being killed as well. Killed or more specifically murdered? And, who, Mr Douglas Fanshaw, would benefit from her death? Answer that?

She noisily tidied away her little 'celebratory picnic' and recognised her stress was morphing into anger. How dare he yell at her? Especially given how much she was doing, well beyond what most estate agents would do, for heaven's sake.

She let herself outside through the utility room backdoor and felt the bedding on the clothesline. Almost there. A good drying day, as her mother used to say, with a stiff breeze and full sunshine, even if the temperature was not yet very high. She took a lungful of fresh air. Clearing her head.

Back in the house, she examined the utility. What a useful room. As large as the sitting room at Briar Cottage and twice as bright. Cupboards lined the inner wall leading to the separate backdoor which she had unlocked earlier to get out to the washing line. Under the windows on each side of the old washer were long wooden benches with more storage underneath. An ironing board complete with ancient iron stood to one side.

The corner boasted a broom cupboard and in there she found cleaning materials. In one section, a chain dangled with a padlock attached. What was it for? Maddie stared at it for a few moments but her mind was a blank. Who would chain up a broom?

She shrugged and opened the first of the lower cupboards next to the broom cupboard and found it full of Wellington boots. Several pairs, all large. Green, black and grey, some still caked in mud.

The next cupboard held other footwear. On the lower shelf were an assortment of shoes, all very old. Every pair a throw-away. She stepped outside and headed around the house towards her car. As she approached the corner, she heard voices.

"Only a tiny snip?" said a woman, her voice flirtatious. "Please? Pretty please?"

"At the right time of year," a man said. Not just any voice. Douglas Fanshaw's.

Wouldn't you know.

Instead of heading back inside, she paused in the shadows. The woman was one of those gorgeous creatures who either garden or golf all day, with a suntanned skin, a tawny mane of hair that owed much to an expensive hairdresser and long, long brown legs. She'd dressed to show off her figure in white form-fitting shorts and a skimpy sequinned pink and white tee-shirt.

Maddie could hear them clearly.

"Promise me you'll give me the cuttings before the others?" she asked, her voice still teasing.

"What others?" he asked.

"At the Gardeners Club, of course. They'll have their hands outstretched if you're offering bits from this garden."

He laughed. "But you've told me most of them wouldn't know a cutting from a seedling, much less know what to do with one."

"They're all right," the woman said. "Come along on Tuesday. I'll have fun introducing the handsome new owner of the Manor. You'll meet them all. It's the one place you can put names to faces all at one go. It's the social centre for all three villages." She paused. "What a dreamy white hibiscus. Does it grow from cuttings too?"

Maddie slipped away. She walked quickly to the outbuildings across a brick-paved yard. She'd meant to have a look at them anyway. Besides, she had no desire to talk with Douglas Fanshaw again today. And even less desire to meet his flirtatious companion.

The voices faded as she entered the first of the outbuildings. It had obviously been a potting shed at one time, complete with high wooden benches and masses of earthenware pots on a shelf underneath. Someone had been a gardener, or, more probably, this house employed its own gardener or even gardener and staff. It only needed a thorough sweeping. Outbuildings were a selling point.

Through an archway was a storage shed for lawnmowers and other equipment. She exited from a second door into the courtyard and peered into the next outbuilding which seemed to have housed chickens at some point in its lifetime judging from the still pungent odours. Yes, roosting boxes extended from the back wall. She walked from the door around to the rear along a brick path. Sure enough, a hinged lid exposed the nesting boxes where staff could harvest fresh eggs. Once upon a time, anyway. The Manor, way back when, must have been a lovely country retreat.

Maddie crossed the yard with quick steps. Douglas Fanshaw would have seen her car and knew she was still around. She'd avoid him if she could, visitor or no visitor.

She turned to her laundry, *his* laundry. She hastily gathered in the now dry sheets. The benches in the utility were perfect for folding them and a good spot to leave them for the charity shop people. Why was she being shy about seeing him again today? He had given her permission to get the house ready for showing, but, after their recent confrontation, she felt awkward.

As she gathered her things to leave, she went over in her mind what she knew about Douglas Fanshaw. Liverpool, he said. What was happening up there? And that was about it. Douglas Fanshaw, nephew of Beryl, heir and he had business in Liverpool.

She wasn't too sure about Mr Douglas Fanshaw. Like, the plain fact was that he didn't find the will. Her discovery of it irritated him no end because he'd just wasted hundreds of pounds (if not thousands) going through the courts to have some access to an inheritance that was his all along. So, yes, exasperated if not incensed. She had no doubt he was totally convinced he'd given the house a thorough going over and had not found the will. Nevertheless, the hiding place seemed very old-lady-ish. Strange that he was convinced he'd checked there.

She had a thought. Did that mean someone else placed it there after he made his search but before hers? But once the thought was formed, she dismissed it as far-fetched.

• • • • • • • • •

Maddie went home to shower and change into her working 'uniform'. In her days as a Probation Officer, she would never have described herself as a 'softie', although not 'hard', especially surrounded as she was by others much tougher and more careworn than she could ever be. Even so, she'd become inured to dramatic tales and, over time, ceased to be curious about anyone. She figured she'd heard every story possible from her wayward clients. They'd described emotional outbursts of horrific description in graphic detail to her; she'd heard protestations of innocence from the most violent of offenders and hard luck stories of every variety from all and sundry. Her brain had finally said, 'Enough'. Years in the past she'd stopped feeling sympathetic.

This job was to fulfil a need. She wanted to deal with ordinary uncomplicated people from now on, people who didn't lie. Mr Fanshaw was ordinary. Mr Higgins was ordinary. She'd have to keep reminding herself of that fact. The only violence or major dishonesty these people had contact with was through television dramas and the occasional news report. It was unlikely she'd ever again have to agonise over yet another disastrous decision made by a client, thank goodness. She'd never again try in vain to persuade her constant recidivists that living simply was possible and they might even find life pleasurable on the minimum wage, purely because they'd be free, at last, of their ever present anxiety about being caught.

She was tired of drama, tired of suppressing her own emotional reactions to tales of horror or stupidity. She no longer would have to deliberately shrug off the disappointment of a favourite client turning up in the system yet again. From now on, she'd only have to think about houses, interior decoration, and loyalty to her vendors. And concentrate on helping buyers visualise a bright future in one of the houses she wanted to sell them. A relief. More than a relief. Freedom.

She dressed with care and savoured the pleasure of looking forward to her next appointment. She'd assumed responsibility for three properties listed by poor Neil Black, who had taken the trouble to leave extensive notes for this newbie estate agent. The first of the two smaller properties was a terrace house constructed in the 1960s (70s?) located in nearby Courtneyside. Somewhat modern looking from the outside with beige render and a tiled panel fronting the gable and a tiny front garden. Parking was some distance away on the small estate. The vendor had told Maddie on the telephone they wanted to sell and buy in the same area, something bigger with a garden for the children.

Maddie knocked on the door. "Hello, Mrs de Mille," she said with a smile to the young woman with a baby on her hip. "Madeleine Brooks from *Green Acres Estate Agents*, We have an appointment?"

"Yes, of course. I was expecting you," the young mother said. "You're going to give me some advice about marketing the house."

"More presenting than marketing, Mrs de Mille," Maddie said. "And please call me Madeleine." She decided 'Madeleine' was a suitable half-way point between 'Mrs Brooks' and 'Maddie'. Perfect for clients.

The young woman smiled. "Louise. And this is Master of All, Lord Anthony, commonly referred to as Tony," she said nodding to the baby in her arms.

"I well remember," Maddie said, smiling at the baby, "how littlies rule the roost. But we'll have to put him in his place if we want to sell this house."

She meant it. The front door opened onto a miniscule sitting room which was wall-to-wall with baby paraphernalia, from a tiny swing hanging from the rafters to a playpen. The floor was carpeted in toys. Neil Black's notes advised Maddie to do something about the 'baby junk'. Maddie knew now what he meant. 'Baby junk' festooned the place.

Where would the family put all the paraphernalia? There was no storage in this little place. She despaired for them. Good advice, but.... Her appointment with *Green Acres* depended on an ability to move property, to say nothing of needing an income to pay the bills. She inwardly shook her head and forged on regardless.

"Here's my first bit of advice. Baby things will have to be restricted to Lord Tony's bedroom. Sorry, but buyers are put off by this sort of thing. As mothers we know it's natural. Buyers, even if they are mothers, only want to put their own stamp on a place."

"I was afraid you'd say that," Louise said, rolling her eyes. "Okay, I suppose. Anything else?"

The sitting room was made even smaller by two over-stuffed sofas.

"Remove one of these comfy couches; it will open up the room. Maybe a couple of chairs instead? Smallish ones? With a little table between them?" She noted three studio shots on the wall of the two children, wee Tony and a pretty little girl of about six. Photographs of children were not good selling points, but that large wall would be intrusively blank without them.

Upstairs were two bedrooms, the larger given over to a single bed, a baby's cot and more toys. A double bed was crammed into the smaller of the bedrooms. There was no room for anything else.

"I see what you've done," Maddie said slowly, "but buyers will want to see the larger bedroom as the master."

"We swapped just recently," Louise said. "We can get the two beds in the smaller room, just, but where was my little girl going to play? To say nothing about this one." She patted the nappy of the baby who gurgled in response.

Maddie shook her head. "I can see the practicalities, but your potential buyers won't. Sorry, but my strong recommendation is to put it back to the conventional arrangement."

"You can see why we're desperate to move," Louise said as they walked back downstairs. "The sooner the better."

Maddie felt buoyed up. Carrying out Neil's recommendation was all to the good, but she'd spotted the bedroom problem on her own. Maybe she could become good at this new occupation of hers. All in all, the house merely needed cosmetic attention. The recommendations cost little and could be completed in a weekend. She left, quite hopeful this could be her first sale.

Chapter Seven

THE LAST HOUSE ON her list was a cottage much like Caroline's Briar Cottage, but located in the neighbouring but more upmarket village of Woodley Vale. Maddie headed there. It was owned by Mr William Dingle, an elderly man thinking of buying in an old folks' village. It, like the Manor, was badly in need of updating. No urgency about this one. Neil Black thought the old fellow was in two minds about moving.

On her arrival, Mr Dingle brought out a tray covered in a cloth with teapot, two cups and saucers and an almost identical plate of cream buns from *Jenny's*. His genial hospitality contrasted to Douglas Fanshaw's lack of it.

"Shall we get to business first, then dive into this lovely spread?" Maddie asked.

"If you mean, have I made up my mind whether to sell or not, then the answer is no," Mr Dingle said as he settled himself into his easy chair. "Should I sell and move to a modern little flat where some nice woman comes to clean up my messy living areas? Can I stand not having the peace and quiet I have here? And my garden?" He rolled his eyes. "I'm just hoping I'll wake up one morning with a crystal clear decision I've made in my sleep."

"No rush," she said. "But it's a charming old cottage, even nicer than the one I'm living in." She explained how a friend had inherited Briar Cottage and had made it available for her. The conversation eased into other directions. Her old job, her new one, her pleasure at living a village life. She told him she was handling the sale of the old Manor.

"Beryl's place," he said. "I knew her when we were young, you know. Our mothers were friends and we were shoved together a lot before we went off to school. She was good fun back then."

"Boarding school?" Maddie asked as she helped herself to another bun. At this rate, she'd soon put back the weight she'd lost on discovering Wayne's betrayal. They were in the sitting room, replete with chintz covered sofas and a large fireplace. She could see red roses surrounding the diamond-shaped window panes. The sunshine flooded in. The cottage, even though crying out for an interior update, was everything a cottage should be, brick fireplace with an oak mantle, beamed ceilings, roses around the front porch and creaky wooden floors. Also cramped rooms and a kitchen half a century out of date.

"It was what happened those days. State schools were considered to be inferior. Maybe still are."

"Tell me about her," she said, trying to keep her eyes away from the plate of buns.

"She was an ordinary child but she turned out to be an extraordinary woman," he said, gazing into the far past. "She had the uncommon ability to bewitch the male of the species and I was not immune. All of us worked for a smile, a touch, a bit of time spent in her company. Not just me. She had potential beaus in a queue from here to London."

"Here?" Maddie asked. "Was the Manor her family home?"

He laughed. "Far from it. She was the daughter of a travelling salesman. The family lived quite modestly in Woodley Bottom. The Manor did become her family home once she'd married Freddy." He looked at Maddie and asked if she'd like another cup of tea.

On her smile, he reached over and poured another cup for her. "Of course, she'd turned into a real madam before she ever married the old man. Shouldn't speak ill of the dead, but you'll be hearing about her from others, I have no doubt."

Maddie was surprised. A 'real madam' didn't fit with her image of the impoverished but genteel little old lady living in the Manor. She liked this old man. He was open and friendly. Charming. She could feel her old professionalism slipping away.

"You knew her a very, very long time," Maddie said, relaxing into her role of avid listener.

"Heaven's yes. But after she was married, we knew each other more to speak to at church or on the street. My wife and I were not in her rather grand social circle." He kept his head down as he was speaking.

Maddie thought of the silken evening gowns. "They were social people, were they? Mrs Fanshaw and her husband?"

"Until the old goat lost all his money." Mr Dingle snorted. "A fair few people had the last laugh on him, I can tell you."

"How did he—" She stopped herself. She was no longer a Probation Officer who needed to know all the details. But she was curious. Imagine, having curiosity rear its head after what seemed a lifetime where her curiosity had been blunted.

Mr Dingle laughed. "Worthless investments. Threw good money after bad. Couldn't tell which were safe investments and which were run by con men. He was funding one particular reprobate in Canada for years – supposedly in search of a 'sure-fire' gold mine, would you believe."

Maddie shook her head. "The land? I've heard the Fanshaws sold their farm to their neighbours."

"Bit by bit over the years. The high life was well and truly gone by that time, of course." He raised his eyes to Maddie's. "You could do worse than bang on Higgins' door and let him know the old place will be up for sale. He could still be interested. You never know."

Maddie knew enough not to tell Mr Dingle that Mr Higgins had already been in touch. That was a bit of business information and not part of this conversation. "Thanks, I'll bear that in mind," she said, finishing her tea. "And this cottage, Mr Dingle? Don't think when I ask you about it that I'm putting any pressure on you at all. But I would be remiss if I didn't ask if you'd made any decisions whenever I see you."

"You'll be the first to know. As for the immediate future, maybe I'll enjoy my vegetable garden one more summer," he said. "I'm a great fan of gardening. Real gardening, not like the poncey Gardeners Club."

"Poncey? What is the Gardeners Club? Is it a country club of some sort? I've only heard of it today."

"A social club, that's all. Gardeners? Ha. They meet in each other's houses and pretend to exchange plants for a few minutes at their so-called meetings. But that's the only time gardening comes up in conversation. They're far more interested in the sherry or the whisky and their particular brand of socialising," he said with some spirit. "No pub in these three villages, you see."

"Courtneyside, Woodley Vale and Woodley Bottom, yes," she said. "I realise they're almost one village."

William explained how Woodley Vale and its little brother, Woodley Bottom were almost continuous with Courtneyside. The original village was Woodley Vale which existed at the time of the Doomsday book. In the nineteenth century, Woodley Bottom was created for workers on the railway which was being constructed. Lots of little working class cottages, then rude and simple, now charming and perfect for weekenders. Courtneyside was the newest – several modern estates, all constructed in the twentieth century – with consequently a different atmosphere and facilities. All three villages benefited by the presence of the others.

"No pub in any of the villages? I suppose the nearest is in Goring."

He nodded. "I used to love going to the Catherine Wheel pub in Goring. Lovely place, very old, just the right size. But it's too far to travel at night. Don't like driving after dark any more. So I don't go unless someone gives me a lift."

Maddie laughed. "Was that a hint?"

He grinned. "Take it as you will, young lady."

Chapter Eight

THE PIERCING RING OF the telephone roused Maddie from a sound sleep. She'd dozed off watching television, exhausted from her day.

"Jade?" she said to her younger daughter's greeting. "You all right?"

"Dad came in tonight," Jade said, her voice hoarse with emotion. "And his bimbo."

"You're at work?"

Jade had recently landed a waitressing job working six to midnight, Wednesday to Saturday. "Just finished." Jade sighed loudly. Maddie braced herself. Something had upset her daughter, but then again, lots upset her daughter.

"She waved at me. Right there in the restaurant. What does she think I am, a friend?"

"I presume she's trying," Maddie said. "She'll want to get along with you for your dad's sake if nothing else." She glanced at the time. Yes, a bit after midnight. Jade must have rung as soon as she could.

"Of course they had to ask where my tables were. And of course they had to sit in my area."

Maddie steeled herself to a tirade. Jade had been using her mother to vent her spleen about the marital situation for months now. Maddie no longer tried to stop it – that only made it worse. She looked at her watch again. Only a minute had gone by.

"When Dad went to pay, you know what she said?" Jade paused.

"What?" Maddie asked obediently.

"She had the nerve to say she'd known Dad for five years!" Jade practically shouted down the phone. "Five years, Mum. That means she was a bloody teenager when they met! Hell, I was only sixteen!"

Maddie said nothing but fingers of icy cold spread from the centre of her being out to the tips of her toes. She couldn't have spoken if she tried.

"Dad would have been forty-nine years old, Mum! If that's not illegal, it should be!" Her voice rose even higher.

"I don't know what to say," Maddie whispered.

"What? Speak up, Mum."

Maddie took a deep breath. "I...I don't know what to say to that, Jade. Not illegal, no. But shocking." She could hardly get the word out. Shocking was such an ordinary word. It conveyed so little of what she was feeling.

Jade ranted on and on for another seven minutes. Maddie timed it. Finally Jade paused.

"Otherwise, you're doing okay?" Maddie asked. Jade usually rang when she wanted something.

"Not really."

Maddie shut her eyes. What now?

"I need some money, Mum. Dad's money hasn't come this month and I'm skint. I can't pay the rent."

Maddie suppressed a sigh. "I'm skint too, Jade. Honestly, I'm living on Chinese noodles half the time. Just ring your dad. He's probably just forgotten." Maybe. Or he'd decided he made a bad deal financially, bribing his daughter to move out so he could move his bimbo in. He seemed to have forgotten that his income as an itinerant musician paid for little. Their middle-class existence all these years had been almost entirely funded by Maddie's government-backed steady salary from the Probation Service. But with not much more than one income all those years, it left them, at this stage of their lives, with a large mortgage and almost no savings.

"What he spent at the restaurant would do me." Jade's voice was bitter. "He's not living on a waitress's part-time wages."

Maddie suggested they both should have a hot chocolate before bed and a read of something enjoyable.

"Hot chocolate? How can you think of that when we're talking seriously here?"

Maddie was so enervated by the time Jade finally rang off, she sagged back into her chair. She stayed where she was until she felt her knees had recovered enough strength to transport her up to bed.

It was Chrystal's youth that disturbed Jade but that was not doing the damage right now to Maddie's equilibrium; it was the period of time. Five years? Maddie had known something was wrong in her marriage for at least a year. But five? She was freshly devastated.

Wayne had kept his boyish figure and his looks. He was a composer and sometimes performer of his own avant-garde music, provocative compositions which pushed the boundaries but had little street appeal, little sales appeal. He wore his hair longer than most men who'd hit fifty and he had almost no grey. His face was soft, with what Maddie called 'bedroom' eyes, large and dark. She'd always found him attractive, still did, to her chagrin. Never much of a provider, he made up for it with charm and warmth. Until recently.

Chrystal, according to Jade, bore an uncanny resemblance to Maddie with shiny hair and big blue eyes. And a reasonable figure. Only Chrystal was a generation younger.

Maddie couldn't find cocoa in Caroline's kitchen so made herself a cup of tea. It was not the same. It didn't help. Nor did reading a cookbook, her 'recipe' for falling asleep. She tossed and turned uncomfortably until she gave up and paced around the little cottage in the moonlight. Finally, when she crawled back into bed, she turned her mind onto what she'd do to this cottage if it were hers.

When she awoke at eight the next morning, she remembered noting the red numbers of her clock every hour until four. Then blessed sleep until eight. She hoped a shower with copious amounts of scalding water would waken her enough to start the day.

• • • **•** • **•** • • •

In personality, Maddie's boss, Rupert, was as far from that of her former boss in the Probation Service as it was possible to be. Rupert was soft, artistic and gay while her former boss was hard, authoritarian and gay. Maddie knew whom she preferred.

Rupert wanted her to start slowly, thoroughly acquainting herself with the three houses passed on by Neil Black and he advised her to ingratiate herself with the owners.

"Go the extra mile at the beginning, Madeleine. Find out everything you can about your area," Rupert said. "Join the dramatic society or go to church. Maybe join a bridge club."

Maddie screwed up her nose. "Why, for heaven's sake? I'm so exhausted after rushing around all day, it's a wonder I can drive home."

"These are your potential clients, my dear," he said. "As soon as they think of selling, your face should appear in their mind's eye. You know the scene...that nice woman from the bridge club, whatshername? Oh that's right, Madeleine Someone."

She laughed. "Yes, I see the point. I'll give it a go. I've recently heard our local Gardeners Club is the place to see and be seen."

"You a gardener?"

Maddie shook her head. "But I have it on good authority having green fingers is not a prerequisite. It exists more for imbibing than imbedding, if that's what you do with plants."

"Wouldn't have a clue," Rupert said with a broad grin. "But the imbibing sounds all right."

"That I can do," Maddie said as she put down the phone. Bother. She'd just agreed to join the wretched Gardeners Club.

"So, you see why I should attend the Gardeners Club meetings," Maddie said to Mr Dingle. "If I do the driving, would you accompany me? Introduce me, that sort of thing? We don't have to stay long." She noticed his expressionless face. "In exchange, of course, for taking you out to the Catherine Wheel in Goring one evening," she added, "soon."

"Blackmail," Mr Dingle muttered, but he smiled as he said it.

Maddie thought it more *quid pro quo*.

• • • ● • ● • • •

That afternoon, Maddie felt waves of tiredness wash over her. How was she going to cut Jade off if she rang so late again? She had no answer. Jade was Jade. Maddie worried about her. Jade was trying to study part time, planned around her uncivilised hours of work at the restaurant. She had made what both Wayne and Maddie had considered to be good decisions when she decided to study, work and live at home more than a year ago.

The arrangement was shattered when Maddie discovered Wayne's infidelity. Maddie left home, a grand gesture that went pear shaped. Wayne didn't try to persuade her to come back; far from it. He revelled in her leaving. He then set to getting rid of Jade from the house by offering to pay a good part of her rent in a student flat. So much for the fresh start Maddie had hoped for. Instead, Maddie found herself supporting

Jade emotionally when she had little emotional reserves herself, and often supporting her financially.

Now she needed Wayne to divide their marital goods, to give her what she was entitled to, a realistic offer for her half of the house and their other possessions he was using. But she didn't want to pressure Wayne because, she hated to admit, she still had hopes he'd see the error of his ways, kick the young woman in an appropriate place on her anatomy and welcome his dear wife back home. Maddie sighed. Fantasyland.

She forced herself to concentrate on preparing the Open Day at the de Mille terrace house which was coming up soon. The very first Open Day for Madeleine Brooks, Estate Agent and she wanted everything to run like a well-oiled engine. She arranged to have the photographer drop by after this weekend, giving the de Milles time to make the changes she'd recommended. Meanwhile, she was supposed to be writing the copy for the brochure that would be both posted on the *Green Acres* internet site and printed on glossy paper for viewers at the Open Day. She'd been advised to advertise on so called 'property portals' on the internet and the de Mille place was now available to be seen by anybody doing a property search for a 'modern townhouse'.

By the time she arrived back at the cottage that evening, she only had energy to grab a simple supper of egg and toast before heading upstairs. She nodded off over her cookbook which gently slid to the mat by her bed, not awakening her. Luckily, no call from Jade.

• • • • • • • • •

Tuesday produced a perfect June evening, fine and cool. When Maddie picked up Mr Dingle, he was kitted out in cardigan, scarf and padded jacket.

"You're dressed for winter," Maddie commented as he settled himself in the passenger seat.

"You never know if they're going to force us to be outdoors," he grumbled. "I'm wearing layers." He glanced at Maddie. "You'll freeze later if we're in the garden."

Maddie had agonised about what to wear. How casual would this club be? Jeans casual? Good slacks and blouse casual? She decided to wear her white jeans, a bright pink and orange print silk blouse, sandals and a matching white denim jacket over top in deference to the temperature. She'd rolled up the sleeves of the jacket to elbow length.

Mr Dingle guided Maddie to the right address. It was an imposing new house with broad sheets of glass and walls rendered white, situated on a slight rise. Maddie hooked her arm through his – not for herself, but in case he found the going tough.

As they neared the front step, the door burst open and three young men dressed in black leathers rushed towards them, knocking Maddie sideways and dislodging her footing. She fell heavily onto Mr Dingle's arm.

"You idiot!" shouted one of them; to be fair, he was shouting at one of the other boys.

The third young man saw what had happened. He grinned as he swept past. "Sorryyyy!" he yelled over his shoulder.

Bloody teenagers up to no good, she was certain. She regained her footing and thanked her companion for preventing a nasty fall.

"That was Jenny and Gabrio's son and his pals, I presume," Mr Dingle said, his voice faint. "You all right?" The sound of three deep-throated motorcycles almost drowned out his words.

"Fine," she said as the sounds faded. "You?"

"Still on my feet," he said, holding her elbow as they ascended the steps to the impressive wooden panelled front door. They entered into a hallway tiled in shiny grey stone.

"Billy, darling," cried an elderly woman, kissing him on both cheeks. "Too long, darling. Too long."

Mr Dingle's old friend was joined by a middle aged plump woman with a face wreathed in smiles. "Lovely to see you, William. And who is this?"

"My new friend, Madeleine Brooks," he said, touching Maddie's arm. "Staying in Bob and Aileen's old cottage. A friend of their granddaughter's." He turned to Maddie. "I'd like you to meet, first my friend Mrs Cecilia Dennison, and this lovely lady is our hostess for the evening, Mrs Jenny Flores. You're partial to her cream buns."

"How do you do," Maddie said to the older woman who went off arm in arm with Mr William (or was it Billy?) Dingle. Maddie turned to their hostess. "Who wouldn't be partial to your cream buns?" she said, realising this was Jenny of *Jenny's Kitchen*. "Last Friday I had two lots and enjoyed every mouthful." She smiled without having to think about it. "Thank you for including me tonight. I hear the Gardeners Club is the place to meet all my new neighbours."

Jenny ushered Maddie into the room. "It is at that." Jenny had a local accent and a Spanish last name. And she certainly produced deliciously light cream buns. "Now what drove you to chose our little villages?"

Again.

Maddie smiled and trotted out her prepared lines. "Couldn't stand one more day in London," she said. "And this job came up."

"Smart lady," Jenny said, patting Maddie's arm. "Now it's our job to dispel the myth that country villages are unfriendly to incomers."

Jenny introduced Maddie to a welter of new faces and names, none of whom she'd remember. But, they were universally welcoming. It was a brilliant start.

Someone showed her the exchange table where early plums, radishes and lettuces were offered under a sign that said, 'Surplus to requirements'.

"For free?" Maddie asked him.

"We always try to produce a bit more than we need. Of course, we all have extras of the same thing at the same time but it feels good to share our bounty," the tall man said. "My plums. They're at their peak right now. Help yourself."

Jenny had disappeared to answer another knock at the door. She returned with two people. Maddie instantly recognised George Higgins and the leggy woman must be his wife, she who wanted the Manor.

Jenny brought them over to Maddie who was putting some of the extra produce into a bag. Excellent supplements to Chinese noodles.

"Well, hello again," George said in a somewhat forced way. He turned to Jenny. "We've met. Mrs Brooks is a new estate agent in Goring."

"But living here," Maddie said easily. "You're about the only local person I've met so far, Mr Higgins. I'd hoped you would be coming to the Gardeners Club."

"George, please. And this is my wife, Tina," he said.

"Very nice to—" Maddie started to say. She'd recognised her immediately. The woman in the white shorts talking to Douglas Fanshaw.

"You're handling Cherry Tree Manor," she said. Her mouth turned up at the corners as she extended a hand browned from the sun. Gold bangles tinkled as she moved and her sundress clung to her athletic figure perfectly. Maddie unconsciously pulled in her tummy and straightened her back.

"I am, yes," Maddie said. "I've taken over from Neil Black. Cherry Tree Manor was on his list."

"Dying, I hear," Tina said, "from the Big C." She shuddered. "Poor man."

Maddie felt her smile becoming fixed. She'd have to become a tad more fluffy with this woman. "Chemo, anyway. Although so many more people are surviving nowadays, aren't they?"

"Smoked like a blacksmith's forge," Tina said. "Those types don't survive long." Somehow the way she said it emphasised her own superb fitness. She tossed her hair. Maddie envied women who could get away with tossing their hair. If she did it, she'd look like a bad-tempered pony.

Douglas Fanshaw, ushered in by Jenny, was making his way towards them. Jenny introduced Douglas to everyone they came to as they made their way across the spacious room. But before they were half way, Tina had flown to his side and busily engaged him in conversation. Jenny smiled and left them to it.

"You're a gardener?" George Higgins asked Maddie, as much to fill a gap as for information, Maddie thought. She glanced at Tina and Douglas and looked down. She tried to keep her eyes away. She turned her back to face George.

"Not yet," she said to be on the safe side. "I've never had the space for a garden before. Where I used to live, we had an outdoor eating patio and a lawn given over to a kid's mini-playground. Somehow when the girls grew up, I didn't get around to putting in a garden for my own pleasure. Maybe someday soon, now I've moved to the country." She was distracted by the intensity of Tina's conversation with Douglas, not that she was listening in, but Tina's voice carried. George, too, was distracted by them. He muttered an 'excuse me' to Maddie and moved towards his wife.

Relieved to be free of him, Maddie unsuccessfully searched for Mr Dingle. William. They'd better get onto a first name basis now they were socialising.

Maddie turned to find Douglas's eyes on her once more. He excused himself from Tina and George and walked over.

"I tried ringing you earlier. On your way here, I suppose," he said. No smile. In fact, he seemed to be embarrassed. "Just want to...erm...to apologise. There was no need for rudeness this morning. You're doing a fine job. And you wanted to discuss things with me and I left before you could do so. Sorry."

Maddie smiled. "It's all been a bit much, hasn't it? But, yes, I do have some suggestions."

Tina left George and again approached Douglas. She flashed a smile at Maddie as she touched Douglas's arm. "No need for introductions here, I see." She beamed up at Douglas. Her figure, even though not overly tall, was that of a model. Maddie felt elephantine in comparison.

Douglas stepped back to include Tina in the conversation.

"Shall we grab ourselves some drinks?" Tina asked him.

He turned to Maddie. "I gather the choice is sherry or whisky. What will you have?"

Maddie was acutely aware of the by-play. "Whisky, please, equal parts scotch and water."

"And you, Tina?"

"I'll come with you and decide when I see what's on offer." She hooked her arm through Douglas's and they set off towards the serving tray.

Maddie was left feeling a little non-plussed. Now what? She decided to stay where she was so she could collect the promised drink then excuse herself to find William Dingle. She didn't know what to make of Douglas's change of attitude. Was he *interested* in her? She giggled to herself. With a creature like Tina on his arm, hardly.

A handsome man with a full head of salt-and-pepper hair was positioned at the drinks tray, acting as bar-tender. When Douglas and Tina arrived back with her drink, Maddie asked who he was.

"Gabrio, of course. Our host," Tina said, with an easy smile.

"Jenny's husband?" Maddie asked.

"He's our local carpenter," Tina said, sipping her sherry. "Very good, I'm told. I wouldn't know as George does all our DIY projects."

Maddie met Douglas's eyes. A local carpenter. The same thought must have gone through Douglas's mind. He nodded.

Maddie excused herself. She had been about to make an appointment with Douglas for going over her list of suggestions but instinctively she didn't want Tina knowing the time and place.

She moved towards Gabrio to introduce herself. She asked him about this wonderful house.

"It started as a small place we bought years ago, built about 1920 or so," he said in lightly accented English. "But you know about the shoemaker's children..."

Maddie gave him a quizzical look.

"Going to school barefoot."

"Oh, of course," she said. "So the conversion of your house took a long time? It's been worth it, though. It's beautiful."

"Come see the kitchen," he said. He ushered her through a door into a blindingly bright commercial kitchen of white and stainless steel. "Originally this was the sitting room in the old house," he said. "What used to be the kitchen is now our larder. The first stage was to get this kitchen up and working for Jenny. We used the dining room as a sitting room back then." He opened a door and showed Maddie a dining room. "It's now back to being a dining room, but it worked in the interim."

"I've never seen such an enormous kitchen in a private home," Maddie said.

"Jenny's bakeshop has no kitchen. She does the baking here," he explained.

"It's certainly beautiful," she said. And it was. It boasted large windows and excellent overhead lighting with miles of bench space, two commercial ovens and a couple of sinks.

As they re-entered the lounge, Gabrio said, "Finally I got around to our living room." He laughed. "We've lived here seventeen years and this room has only been finished for a year."

"Worth the wait, I'm certain," Maddie commented. "Gabrio, have you a card? Your skills may be needed in my line of work. If this is what you produce, you're a find."

"We'll exchange cards," Gabrio said. "You never know." Gabrio, A little like 'Gabriel', but not quite. Pleasant look to his face.

"I'm handling the sale of the Manor in my capacity as an estate agent. If there's a call for quotes to do some modernisation, are you interested?"

"Always," he said.

She took a deep breath. "Did you know Mrs Beryl Fanshaw?" she asked him.

"Of course. A local personality."

"I've heard she just wandered off."

He smiled. "Much more likely one of her many enemies topped her in utter frustration," he said. At seeing Maddie's concerned look, he added, "Don't listen to a word I say, Madeleine. She's probably in some tropical paradise sipping gin slings, if I know old Beryl."

Mr Dingle spotted Maddie. "There you are, my dear. Have you had enough socialising?"

Maddie got the hint.

In the car, he asked about Douglas.

"He inherited your friend Beryl's big house," Maddie said.

"I surely hope he's more pleasant than his aunt," Mr Dingle said. "Crazy old bat. She was impossible as she got older."

"So I gather. But what was she like when young?" Maddie asked.

"Pretty as a picture when she was a young thing. Maybe even beautiful."

"Were you sweet on her?"

He sighed. "We do have a history, I have to admit. My first love. She was the most attractive, accomplished, witty, lovely looking – but impossible – young woman I ever met."

"Whoa, Mr Dingle," Maddie said. "A sweetheart of yours, you say. So what happened?"

"Once upon a time she did the dirty on me," he said. He muttered something under his breath and Maddie wondered if he had said, 'bitch'. Maddie's eyes widened. Had nice old Mr Dingle really called Beryl Fanshaw a bitch? Time to change the subject.

She stopped the car in front of Mr Dingle's cottage and told him how much she'd enjoyed the evening.

"Not bad," he said, "But, Mrs Brooks, you noticed there was not much conversation about gardening, didn't you?"

"Maddie."

"William," he said with a smile. "Not, definitely not, 'Billy'. Those who call me that have almost all died out by now, thank heavens."

"William, it is. A friendly bunch here, though."

'Harrumph," William said as he levered himself out of the passenger seat.

* * * * * * * * * *

Maddie knew not to leave the pub visit for too long. A couple of days later, William was back in the passenger seat of her car and they were on their way to the Catherine Wheel.

"It's probably the smallest pub in Goring," William said. "Maybe the oldest too."

He was dressed in a tweed jacket with a maroon silk cravat at his neck. Maddie had changed from her 'uniform' into casual beige slacks and a scoop-necked green knit top. She had a cardigan in the car in case the evening cooled off too much.

"You used it as your local?"

"Always. For fifty years, or more."

They parked in the car-park behind the pub and walked around to the entrance.

"Dingle, you old devil," was their greeting. "Hey, you blokes, look what the cat dragged in."

William quickly introduced Maddie. One of the old fellows immediately rose not only to give her his seat but to fetch her a drink. She decided to relax, sit back and listen. As she had anticipated, the pub was warm, the volume of voices soft and the atmosphere congenial. Even though smoking had been banned for years in public places like this, she could still smell the remnants of centuries of tobacco use. It was part of the very fabric of the old pub, a pleasant beery scent with a hint of smoke from a by-gone era.

The old friends caught William up with what had gone on since he had last met with them. Maddie sipped her white wine and observed.

Like William, they were all probably in their eighties, with one aged fellow maybe even older. They all drank draft beer and its smell was delicious. But they'd not offered her beer. Wine or sherry. She smiled. Politeness, courtesy and pre-conceived ideas about what women drank.

"Maddie here's the estate agent for Beryl and Freddy's old place," William said, most likely to bring Maddie into the conversation.

"Did they ever find her?" one asked.

"Never," William said. "I expect one of these days someone will trip over her old bones deep in the woods."

"Unlikely," said the oldest man, white hairs waving in the breeze from the shakiness of his head. "Too many kids lark about under those trees. And joggers and dog walkers and people photographing the bleeding bluebells and the like. No, she'd have been abducted, mark my words. Probably killed when she wouldn't tell 'em where her fortune was."

"What fortune?" asked an old man with a beanie on his head. "She had no fortune. That old bugger Freddy saw to that."

William's eyes swept to Maddie at the swear word and she beamed at him over the rim of her wine glass.

"You'd never dare call him Freddy to his face, you old hypocrite," the oldest man said.

"Course I would have," the man in the beanie said, but even Maddie could tell he was denying it without any real force.

"Well, you're right about one thing. That la-de-da bloody Fanshaw was a right old bugger if there ever was one," the oldest man said. "He led Beryl a merry dance."

Maddie was all ears. She'd love to know more about Beryl's life, to say nothing about her death.

"He owed me money, you know, when he died," the man with the beanie said. "I'd just finished extending the chicken house for him. Good job too. Red brick with white trim. Never got paid. Beryl claimed she hadn't hired me. Shut her fancy front door in my face."

"You should have gone round the back," William said, lifting his beer in a silent toast to his friend. "You didn't know your place, you silly old buffer."

"I hear a relative inherited," the oldest man said. He turned to Maddie. "That right?"

Maddie looked at William for help. She shouldn't divulge any information. But William could.

"That's what the Gardeners Club goss says," William said, winking at Maddie as he raised his glass to his lips.

"Is it right he had to sue somebody so's he got his inheritance?" the oldest man asked.

"Not quite. He applied to the court. No will, you see," William said. "Until the other day. Will found; no further problem."

"Whoever inherited probably did her in," the man in the beanie said, moving his glass within its wet circle on the table. "Stands to reason. Follow the money, is what I say."

The oldest man drained his glass. "Sounds about right." He grinned at William. "Or *you* knocked her off, Billy-Boy. No love lost between you two."

"Wish I had," William said. "Only I'd have done it years ago, not wait till she was a feeble-minded old harridan." He didn't laugh or even smile as he said it. It was as if a cloud had obscured the sun.

• • • • ●•●• • • •

One morning a couple of days later, Maddie rang Douglas. "Shall we meet?" she asked, unsure whether his affability the evening of the Gardeners Club had been fuelled by alcohol and the convivial atmosphere.

"I have the gardening contractors starting this morning," he said. "I'll be at the Manor in about half an hour. Can you come out? I'll fetch some cream buns...."

Maddie laughed. "It's a deal. See you in about an hour." Gardening contractors? Actually spending money on some maintenance?

• • • • ●•●• • • •

Maddie left her car on the road as the front drive of the Manor was clogged with vans and machinery. Douglas met her on the front steps.

"Already it's looking better," he shouted over the din of men and machines. She nodded agreement; she could hardly hear him. At this point, mowers were attacking the tall grasses in what eventually would again be a lawn and the hedge cutting was progressing along the near side of the front garden. The hedges on the roadside were now noticeably shorter.

"You're so right. Street appeal is vital," Maddie yelled, remembering a snippet of her estate agent's course.

Douglas ushered her inside the commodious hallway and closed the heavy front door on the noise.

"You have an attractive façade here," Maddie said at a much lower volume. "I'm so pleased you're getting the front garden done. People will now be able to view the house from the road."

"You told me first impressions are important," he said. She followed him through the living room into the dining room. "But this is a celebration of sorts. I got a bit of redundancy and thought, what the hell, let's go for something that can really be seen."

"More than first impressions, Douglas," she said, "A messy view from the curb means people are primed to look for more work that needs to be done. We don't want potential buyers only seeing a gigantic project requiring time, effort and money, even when the Manor isn't yet on the market."

Douglas nodded. "Hadn't looked at it like that, but you're probably right," he said. "If I'd known about the will...." His lips made a thin line.

Maddie shot a glance at him. Their relationship wasn't out of the woods yet.

"I've had one inquiry.," she said to change the subject.

"Higgins, I bet. My immediate neighbour. He hasn't said anything to me about the state of things. Nothing about improvements. Maybe there's a chance I won't have to do much. Only more tidy up."

"'Maybe' is the operative word," Maddie said. "My boss was telling me that usually when someone buys a big project like this – kitchen needing doing, old fashioned bathrooms, that sort of thing – they expect to buy it cheaper than cheap."

Nonetheless, she made a mental note to contact George Higgins again. It wouldn't hurt to let him know she knew he was talking privately to Douglas. Not that she worried about her commission. Douglas's contract with *Green Acres* was tried and true. It ensured that no matter who sold the house, private sale or not, the commission was still paid to *Green Acres*. Estate agencies had learned that lesson decades before and built it into each contract.

Over tea and buns, Maddie put her suggestions forward, accompanied by the incessant noises of lawnmowers and hedge trimmers. "I'm not about to suggest you put in an indoor pool or redecorate from the bottom up, but I think a few improvements won't go amiss when marketing this place," she said. They were sitting at the elegant dining room table. "I can divide the list of suggestions I've put together into must-do jobs, like the gardening you're having done today, to popular additions which are certainly not necessary but can be specific selling points."

They went over the must-do list which included commercial cleaners. "For instance these gorgeous green velvet curtains," Maddie said. She pointed out the heavy drapery found in both sitting room and dining room. "I want to show you something."

She walked over to the curtain and lightly patted it. As she did so, clouds of dust billowed into the shafts of sunshine streaming through the window.

Douglas sneezed. She laughed; he frowned.

"Good demo. It's now on the to-do list," he said, searching for a tissue in his jeans' pocket.

"And worse, is this," Maddie said. She turned the curtain back to show its lining. "Come here, Douglas, so I can illustrate what I'm talking about."

She held a piece of the lining stretched between her hands. "Poke it here."

He touched it lightly and his finger went straight through the fabric. "Shit," he said then hastily glanced at Maddie. "Sorry. But this is another example of more hideous expense."

"I said the same when I did it," she said, choosing to react to his apology. She replaced the curtain carefully to minimise the dust. "The good news is the curtain fabric itself is in amazingly good nick. It's only the lining. We'll send them to the dry-cleaners, if that's okay with you – don't faint when you see how much they charge for heavy curtains like these – and we'll ask them to replace the linings."

"I presume that's cheaper than replacing the curtains themselves?"

"A fraction of the cost."

"What's next on your wish list?" he asked, with a half smile, more mockery than amusement.

"My biggest and most expensive suggestion is to build a Victorian conservatory."

"A conservatory? Like a glasshouse? Where?"

"Right here." She pointed out the dining room window. "It's a wonderful place for a sunroom, an orangery, in the parlance of the early nineteenth century. This aspect of the house is drenched in light. If you put in a conservatory, you can have wicker furniture for lounging in the sunshine and a small table too. I figure people use a conservatory about nine months of the year, autumn, sometimes in the winter and springtime. And during a cool summer. It's a huge selling point."

Douglas got up from the dining room table and moved to the window. "One thing I must emphasise, Madeleine, is that I'm not made of money," he said, "even when the will is through probate. I'll be asset rich but still cash poor." He leaned against the window sill, careful of disturbing the dusty velvet curtains. "My aunt Beryl was supposed to be the rich one in the family. But look at this place. Nobody knew the real story."

"I gather the house was the last of the family fortune."

He glanced at her sharply. Bother. This information originally came from William, not from Douglas. She mentally slapped her wrist. Too relieved to be talking with this more businesslike Douglas. Too relaxed, and now blurting out information. Rumour. Besides, she reminded herself, Douglas Fanshaw was a client, not a friend. She never had trouble with the distinction when she was a Probation Officer, but there, the gulf was wider and easier to see.

"Sorry, that's the gossip I'm hearing, tales from villagers who knew your uncle. They tell things to me because I'm the agent," she explained. True enough. She'd heard it from William. "Your aunt and uncle apparently used to throw fabulous parties here. They lived a very good life, I'm told. But your uncle started selling off the land to the locals. Then, eventually, no more land could be sold; it was all gone. He died and your aunt Beryl seemed to be struggling for years afterwards, I gather." She didn't mention the unwise investments.

Douglas nodded, still looking out over the sunlit view through the window. "The family thought Aunt Beryl had secreted money away after Uncle died; she was eccentric. Very eccentric. But I searched; I told you. No bank accounts. Nothing with a lawyer; they didn't even have a copy of her will. Nothing here. Not a penny for her to live on except her old folk's pension. Or not. It's one reason I still wonder if she's still alive. Taken her fortune with her and left this as an old dump that was nothing but a millstone around her neck."

Maddie stared at him. So he had misgivings she was still alive somewhere. What a spanner in the works that would be. "You didn't know your aunt very well?"

He shook his head. "Not really. Probably spent less than an hour a year when I was a child. None since. That's why the will was such a shock, a nice shock, of course, but still unexpected. I'd argued in court I was Aunt Beryl's only living relative and was entitled to at least part of what this house would bring once sold. My case was based on logic and a memory by the lawyer that a now-deceased partner in his firm had written a will years before for Aunt Beryl in my favour. They didn't tell me that until recently and even then it was a 'word to the wise', nothing official. I'd no idea she'd made me her heir. None at all. Besides, I wouldn't have gone through the court case without being shoved into it."

"Shoved?"

"Maybe too strong a word. A friend was keen I do something about the situation. Not let it ride." He paused. "I got kind of pushed into the court case. Damned expensive undertaking, as it turned out."

Maddie tidied up the tea things. She wondered if the 'friend' was Tina Higgins.

"Shall we go outside and see whether the conservatory idea is a good one?" she said.

He sighed. "Once the will is through probate, then maybe ... just maybe the bank will advance a renovation loan. Which means, from then on, I'd have to finance the loan." He let out a groan. "But you're going to tell me I need to spend money to make money."

"I won't tell you that," she said, "but—"

"You don't have to. I know it." He did give her a smile then. A crooked smile, but a smile all the same.

Soon they were standing on the gravel of the side path in front of the dining room window. The spot was out of the wind and they were bathed in morning sunshine, looking out over a sea of green that stretched to distant hills. The closest paddock was inhabited by a couple of horses.

"Takes advantage of this superb view," Maddie said.

"What advantage will it give when selling?" Douglas asked. "Someone falling in love with the conservatory, that sort of thing?"

"That's one aspect of it. And it does happen. Often one particular thing becomes the reason why a person wants to buy a house." She remembered this bit clearly from her estate agency course. "They then search for the other things on their wish-list. The other things have to get ticks too, but mostly there's not the same emotional reaction. At least, not like the bit they fell in love with. Make sense?"

He nodded. "You have another reason?"

"Speed of sale. As long as the vendors haven't ignored something basic when showing their house. Say, they haven't tidied their teenager's rooms or the back garden is a jungle, or the paint on the house needs redoing – stuff they no longer see." She took a deep breath. "Any of these things makes a house sit on the market without being sold. As far as the Manor goes, you want to do the fix-ups and get the place onto the market without delay. Take advantage of the summer weather."

"The weather? Surely that's irrelevant?"

"The more comfortable potential buyers are when viewing, the more disposed they are to the property. It's a simple fact of property selling."

He shrugged. "I can't argue I'd like it sold asap. I will listen to your advice; you're the one with experience."

Maddie didn't correct this inaccuracy. "Of course there can be problems with price. Sometimes vendors don't take a reasonable offer because they want a bit more. What they don't realise is that it costs money to maintain a house for several months." She looked at Douglas. He was paying close attention even though he was still frowning. "One exercise to do is to figure out your costs when the house is unsold. The overheads like rates, electricity, water, mortgage payments or any other monthly bills such as keeping the lawns cut or cleaners. Then figure out what the difference will be if you sold it in Month One compared to Month Two or Three or, yikes, even Twelve. You should actually mentally take that money away from any profit you're envisioning."

"Okay," he said. He was frowning again.

She ignored his expression. She had more suggestions she wanted to get on the table. "Something like a conservatory and a new kitchen can make the property more desirable, make it sell quicker."

He sighed. "New things and maintenance. Sounds like daft complexity but I said I'd at least listen to your advice. I'll do the maths."

"Maybe ask Gabrio Flores for some quotes? He's a builder. He constructed that superb sitting room we were in. I have his number."

"I thought about it, too, when I heard he was a builder. Let's have him quote on some of the more urgent things anyway. Especially the kitchen."

"He showed me the commercial kitchen he built for Jenny. Impressive."

"I don't need anything fancy. Just something a bit more upmarket than what we have here."

Maddie grinned but he wasn't looking at her. "A lot more upmarket," Maddie said under her breath. That kitchen needed yanking forward fifty years.

Douglas busied himself pacing out the dimensions of a conservatory.

"I can picture it," Maddie said. "Shelter when the sun is out but the wind is biting. Luncheons. Drinks in the evenings when the temperature goes down. A lazy autumnal afternoon with a good book and a cup of tea."

"Unfortunately, so can I," Douglas said. "All costing a pile of money I don't have."

Maddie was ashamed of herself. She wasn't listening to him. He had money problems. Her need to sell the Manor was interfering. "Wish list stuff, Douglas. This is low priority. It's a fun thing. Still, have you investigated paying for the improvements with bridging finance?"

"I've not talked to the bank yet, no. I can imagine they could be interested in funding a new kitchen, but this sort of thing?"

"If you go ahead with the improvements, we can value the Manor within our company or you can get an independent valuer to make an estimate," Maddie said. "Mostly, not always, improvements providing more living space are worth more than what you pay for them. Mind you, it's always a gamble." She remembered to say that. It was emphasised in the estate management course. Maybe more of that information stuck than she realised.

"This is all I have," he said, again staring off towards the horizon.

"You certain you don't want to live here?" Maddie asked.

"Me? Can't afford it," was the simple answer.

Chapter Nine

SOMETHING WAS NIGGLING HER. Something about Gabrio and Jenny Flores's front room. Something good. She'd had a fleeting thought when in their sitting room. What was it? Before being distracted by social th ings....she closed her eyes and pictured coming into the room with Jenny and William, being introduced...no, before that. She mentally took that first step into the large and airy room. What did she see first? Yes! At the far end of the room was a modern fireplace and above the mantle was a large painting divided into three. A triptych? Is that what it's called? A modern triptych of red poppies swaying in the breeze.

Now why was she thinking of that set of paintings? Then she got it. The three portraits of the de Mille children. If only she could have something like the painting of the poppies in the de Mille living room instead, smaller, of course, and a different colour.

On a whim, she rang the number Gabrio had on his card. "It's Madeleine Brooks speaking. We met last evening? Have I caught you at a bad time?"

"No problem," his accented voice said. "What can I do for you?"

"First, who painted that wonderful triptych over your mantelpiece? Is it a local artist?"

"Local to Oxfordshire, yes. It's by Kathleen Short, over Henley way. Splendid, isn't it?"

Maddie agreed. "Second, and more importantly, Douglas Fanshaw would welcome a quote for a new kitchen at Cherry Tree Manor. And some advice on a few other bits and pieces out there. Are you interested?"

"Of course," he said.

They arranged a time early in the following week. Maddie rang Douglas and told him what she'd arranged. He said he'd get another couple of quotes too; plenty of kitchen specialists around.

"We should sit down and figure out a budget," Maddie said. "Maybe you'd better find time for a visit to the bank."

Douglas sighed audibly. "It's on my list," he said.

She put the telephone away, reminding herself that she had better rein in her enthusiasm. She must not try to take over or act like a Probation Officer and, more importantly, never, ever act like a wife. Douglas was a little cooler again. She'd have to watch how far to push him.

Maddie looked up Kathleen Short online and found she had a studio and gallery less than an hour away. She glanced at her watch. She was itching to get outside. How had she worked eight hour days in a cramped little office for all those years as a Probation Officer?

She left Goring and headed east. The day was bright, the leaves an impossible green and the air coming through the window fresh. On a whim, she pulled over and rang William. "Are you busy this morning, William? I'm on my way to an art gallery near Henley. Want to come for the ride?"

"Sounds like fun," he said. "When?"

"Five minutes? I'm in the car already."

He laughed. "You're trying to wrench me out of my old man's routines, aren't you?"

"Nope. Only want you to navigate me to the right area."

"See you in five minutes, my dear," he said warmly.

• • • ● • ● • • •

They used the interconnecting network of country roads to work their way towards Henley. As they motored through shady lanes, William spotted a sign, 'Peppard Art Gallery and Studios'. "Will that be it?"

They crunched in over a pebbly drive. A small sign directed them along the side of an attractive Georgian house to the back where a substantial carpark was situated in front of an old black barn. A small sign indicated they were in the right spot.

Maddie pushed open the glass door which set a bell ringing. Within a few seconds, a blond woman dressed in a paint splattered smock came through an internal door.

"Can I help? I'm Kath Short."

"We saw one of your interesting paintings recently and we decided to have a peek at your gallery," Maddie said.

"Which one? Where did you see it?"

"The Flores house."

"The poppies. Yes," the woman said. "Glad you like it. But this gallery is not only about me. You'll find work from quite a collection of local artists here, paintings, sculptures and we also have a couple of glass artists who've produced these." She pointed to some glass mobiles catching the light from roof windows.

The space was impressive. High above, typical blackened barn rafters spanned the distance between side walls. Most of the gallery was painted white to show off the art. One enormous mural covered the back wall.

"If you're okay to have a look around here on your own, I'll finish what I was doing in the studio. Any time you want me, hit the teacher's bell and I'll be back." She indicated a small counter with an old bell in the centre.

Maddie and William spent an enjoyable half hour gazing and coveting. Eventually Maddie rang the teacher's bell.

"Do you ever loan paintings to anyone?" she asked Kath Short who entered wiping her hands and smelling of turpentine.

"Rarely," Kath said. "Why? What do you have in mind?"

Maddie explained her idea. What if a local artist like Kath was willing to loan art to a homeowner who was selling? For the privilege, Maddie would put a photograph of the room showing the painting in the sales brochure with contact details of the artist.

William and Maddie were invited into the studio in the other part of the barn. Over cups of tea, the two women came to a tentative plan involving insurance, transport, agreements and advertising.

"Fair enough," Maddie said to many of Kath's suggestions. "You know what it takes. We both want the same thing – using your art to enhance a house and thus enhance the chance of a sale, then the art can be returned to you intact. Meanwhile, you have a new venue where your art can be seen and appreciated in an appropriate setting. And your contact details will be there for people to take away." She stood up and extended her hand. "Think about it. My hopes are that we both benefit."

Back in the car, William was pleased. "I bet she'll go for it. How often do you get a new venue for hanging paintings? It's clearly a win-win."

"Maybe. It has to be a mutual thing. I'll have enough problems getting vendors to take down their own tasteless photos and reprints. They'll never agree to paying very much for insurance and the like." She sighed.

"Well, I think you're onto a winner," he said. "Who knows, maybe the deal can be extended to others in the agency."

Maddie drove along a road lined in copper beeches. "New girl's ideas? We'll see."

William beamed at Maddie. "You'll do all right in this estate business, young woman. Creative is what you are. Not just new girl's ideas. Original ideas."

• • • • ● • ● • • •

On Saturday, Maddie interrupted the de Milles while they were putting her suggestions into effect. Antoine de Mille was not French, as Maddie expected, but Canadian.

"I have another suggestion for you," she said. She told them about the painting on-loan idea. "I'd like to put a painting I saw in an art gallery on your front room wall instead of the darling photographs of your children."

"Anonymising again?" Louise asked. She turned to her husband. "Madeleine's idea is to have as little of our lives showing as possible so a potential buyer can picture their own life here and not be overwhelmed by ours. And that means very few personal effects." Her voice was strident. Maddie resolved to tread a tad more carefully.

"The other day I saw a stunning painting by Kathleen Short," Maddie said. "She's a local artist. I've now seen more of her work. She's one talented lady. I was particularly interested in a painting called 'Calendula'. It's of marigolds; we're looking up into a head of golds and yellows. Perfect for here," she said, pointing to the wall.

"That colour is called 'marigold'," Antoine said pointing to the paintwork. "Appropriate, I suppose."

Maddie explained the deal. It would cost them very little, as long as the painting was returned in perfect condition.

She rang Kath Short and confirmed the deal in front of the de Milles. Louise looked delighted at it all; Maddie was more than delighted. Something she'd thought up, a win-win-win.

On Monday two paintings were delivered and Maddie supervised their hanging after getting precise instructions from Kath. 'Calendula' looked as good as she had envisioned. Visitors would see the painting immediately when entering the front room. And it was hung well out of the reach of little fingers.

She also had the de Milles agree to a second painting for the dining area if one with the right colours could be found. The room was a pale grey, a much more modern colour than the marigold in the front room, in Maddie's opinion. When she visited the gallery to organise 'Calendula', she'd selected another flower painting called 'Woodland Violets', done in pale mauves and purples. Again, it was the first thing anyone noticed on entering the dining room.

The photographer carefully included both paintings in his shots for the brochure. Maddie rushed back to do its final composition. By afternoon, she'd mocked it up and run it past Rupert's expert eye.

"Tell me the story about the paintings," he said, his finger on the paragraph Maddie had written with the Peppard Gallery details.

She did so saying she'd negotiated a trial run for the de Mille property's Open Day scheduled for the following weekend.

"Impressive," he said, rocking back on his chair. "Not just a pretty face."

Maddie smiled at the compliment. It would take some time to see whether any of her grand ideas translated into house sales. And she knew Rupert was thinking the same thing.

Chapter Ten

GABRIO TOOK ONE LOOK at the kitchen and laughed. "Okay. Here we'd have to do a whole new kitchen from the top to the bottom. Except for the terrazzo. I wonder if we can use that."

Maddie fingered the roughness of the old stone bench top. It was a green-grey colour and deeply scratched and indented. Food scraps most probably would have been trapped whenever it was used; for years the top must have been highly unsanitary. Re-using it seemed unlikely.

Douglas was watching the two of them from the doorway where he was propped against the door jamb. "Can the bench-top be resurfaced?" he asked, joining them to look closely at the well worn surface.

"I wouldn't know about that," Gabrio said. "But I might be able to turn the whole terrazzo over. It all depends how they finished the underside." He opened one of the lower cupboard doors and manoeuvred his head inside. He felt the area with his fingers. "It's possible," he said. "I'd hate to throw it out. If we can salvage this stone for part of the bench top, the pastry cooks will love you. Nothing like stone for perfect pastry."

Maddie figured he was married to *Jenny's Kitchen*, so he should know. She nodded. Her recycling self was pleased.

"You'll need new kitchen cupboards, new bench-tops for the rest of the kitchen. New cooker, fridge, range hood, tiling for the splash-back and the floor surface," he said. "It won't be cheap, but you don't have to spend excessively to make this kitchen look fantastic, not with that terrazzo as a feature."

"Before we decide on anything, maybe you should see what else needs doing, Gabrio. I'm suspicious the floor in the utility room is rotten," Douglas said. "And I'd like you to check the outbuildings to see they're safely built." He turned to lead the way outside.

"And, I hate to remind you, Douglas, but we agreed there's a need for new plumbing," Maddie said, "maybe new loos and bathrooms. Only one inside loo in a house this big? And that one is big but hopelessly old-fashioned." She glanced at the two men. Both had nodded. "Still, I did have a couple of ideas. The front hall coat cupboard? Can we change that into a powder-room toilet with wash-handbasin? It's big enough, I think. Then you could put in a pole for coats and an umbrella stand in the hallway itself. Second, how much will it cost to turn the small bedroom beside the master into an en suite bathroom? That would be such a selling point."

"Removing a whole bedroom? Seems extravagant," Douglas said, a familiar frown again appearing.

"An en suite and walk-in wardrobe?" Maddie asked Gabrio.

They trouped upstairs and Gabrio eyed the possibilities. "The walk-in wardrobe on the window side and the bathroom on the inside. I have a feeling this bedroom used to be a servant's room, maybe for a nanny. Or it was a tiny nursery? You can see where a door used to be." He indicated how the skirting board to the wall had an insert cleverly slotted in. "We could open up that doorway again. It's a good idea, Madeleine." He turned to Douglas. "What do you think? I can price it up, if you want."

Douglas didn't look overjoyed, but he agreed.

Back downstairs in the dining room, Gabrio pointed to the window. "You do that repair yourself?"

Douglas shook his head. "It was like that when I took over. My aunt must have hired someone to do it for her. What do you think caused the problem?"

Gabrio examined the piece of new wood. "I'd say someone smashed the bottom pane of the window sometime. But the repair has been done by what I like to call a 'good DIY'. Not all that bad but still an inexpert job for a beautiful room like this. I'd re-do it."

Maddie remembered her first visit to the Manor when she noticed the polished dining room table. "You could tell someone cleaned up in here after the window was fixed. I bet that means the break and repair were fairly recent. Do you remember, Douglas, the dining room table was polished?"

He frowned. "Not relevant. We're talking about the window repair."

Damn the man. He was again on the edge of being rude.

Douglas took Gabrio to examine the floor of the utility and the outbuildings. Maddie, in a minor surge of pique, excused herself. She went back up to the bedroom where she had piles ready for the charity shop person. It was too quiet; she found herself going over and over the conversation. But eventually the silence of the old house calmed her. She sat back on her heels in the middle of the floor in front of her pile of 'possibles' for the charity shop and pulled herself up short. Who was she to push Douglas into her own way of thinking? Pure Probation Officer arrogance. She took a deep breath and let it out slowly.

She heard voices at the front door and came back downstairs. Gabro was off to prepare the estimate leaving Douglas and Maddie standing on the front step in the sunshine.

"We're going too fast," Douglas said, staring at the retreating car. "My biggest priority is finding out what happened to Aunt Beryl."

She glanced up at him. "I thought the police are certain she wandered off. To her death."

He nodded. "That's what they say. But, I don't know...it seems facile to say the least."

"Too easy? Little old lady wanders off?"

He turned to her, his eyes as bright as she'd ever seen them. "Precisely."

"Presumably the court case needs to know?"

He shrugged. "No, with the will now found, it'll just take the time it takes. There's that other reason." He took a deep breath and looked out over the long front garden. "I feel bloody guilty thinking about doing things to the Manor without knowing where she is. Alive or dead. Whether she wants me to interfere or not. And I've got to go up to Liverpool again. Dammit, I wish she'd left some sort of clue where she was going that day."

This man was full of surprises.

He went on, "If I really thought she had ended up in the woods, I'd be scouring every inch of it."

"Or the river?"

"Damn right."

"So you think neither of those possibilities are likely."

He turned to her. "You're a naturally nosy person, aren't you, Maddie?"

She bridled. "Hang on—"

"Sorry. There I go again. Blurting out stuff which comes out all wrong," he said. "I mean you've heaps of curiosity. Not afraid to ask questions. And quite creative when you're problem solving. Me, I'm just a plain engineer. I can fix things when I know how they work. But the human mind?"

Maddie let out the breath she'd been holding, her umbrage collapsing like a punctured beach ball. He wasn't putting her down. Stop. Take a deep breath. "Did you want me to help you nut out the possibilities about Aunt Beryl's disappearance? Is that what you're asking?"

"Would you? I talked to the cop in charge yet again. They've accepted she wandered off and died someplace they haven't discovered yet. But they've devoted as many resources to the case as they can. They expect her body will turn up someday. But you know ... I know and they know ... too often that just doesn't happen."

"Did you like her? As a little boy?"

"I did actually. She gave me things I absolutely adored – a jack-knife, a realistic looking ack-ack gun, a drum set that made the most tremendous noise – all the things my mother forbade me having." He smiled a little boy's grin. "Now I can see she did it as much to get up my mother's nose as to please me. Back then, I looked forward to Christmas and seeing what she'd bring me. Wonderful Aunt Beryl."

Maddie shook her head. "She was a complex character, no question. I haven't a grip on her personality yet at all, much less her death."

"Say you'll help out with this problem I've got. Please. Your type of mind will be much better at it than mine."

She looked up at him. It would be arguably easier for her to ask questions than for him to do so with his frequent trips away and no solid contacts except for Tina and George. Besides, it was enlightened self-interest to have things neat and tidy when selling a property. Especially a big property like this one. And she was nosy. Curious. It's part of what had attracted her to a Probation Service career.

She nodded. "Okay, I'll do my best ... at asking questions and noticing things, at least."

Douglas left to see about prices. Before any decisions could be made, he needed some idea of what it would set him back. Maddie suggested he concentrate on the bathrooms and kitchen but he was now keen on the conservatory.

"It's just a quote, not an order to buy," he said. He needed estimates before his all-important appointment with the bank.

"Fingers and toes crossed," Maddie said to herself as she watched his car turn from the now smart looking pea gravelled drive. Douglas had eased up somewhat, thank heavens. She was inordinately pleased he had asked for her help. But better and more experienced minds than hers had been flummoxed. Where are you, Beryl Fanshaw?

She reluctantly went back inside the house, carefully noting the sound of the creaking floor as she walked along the length of the utility room. Yes, it did sound different at the area near the washer. She opened the lower cupboards. Still musty smelling. She felt the floor boards at the back behind the old shoes. Slightly damp.

The day was lovely with the promise of a hot afternoon again. She couldn't remember such a long spell of settled June weather for years. But the shadow had moved and her car was now sitting in the sunshine. When she opened the car door, the escaping hot air hit her like a blast furnace. No way should she have to subject herself to that on an increasingly warm day. She decided to roll down the windows and wait until the heat dissipated. A walk? Why not see where George and Tina Higgins lived? It must be close by.

She shifted the car into the shade and left all windows open before walking down the shady drive towards Tick Lane. She breathed in the scent of the woods with delight and turned onto the road. Cars did use it but only very occasionally; none since Gabrio and Douglas had left. It was so quiet, she could hear the rustle of leaves in the woods and the soft sound of her shoes on the gravel edges of the tarmac.

She strolled past the trees on the other side of Tick Lane; nobody was about. A small side road labelled 'Cherry Tree Farm Lane' branched to the right. Bushes and trees lined it for a hundred yards or more before she came upon what surely must be the Higgins' place. 'Cherry Tree Cottages' was a row of three, probably sixteenth century or earlier, rendered in a pinkish terra cotta. It had probably been thatched once, but now boasted a slate roof that sloped from a roofline that was far from straight. The cottages were utterly charming. But when a car turned from Tick Lane into Cherry Tree Farm Lane, Maddie resumed her stroll by walking along the verge. She didn't want to be caught gaping.

She watched the car carry on past the cottages. Maddie slowed her pace. She could hear some noises. The lane ended in a wide carpark containing several vehicles in front of a substantial set of modern steel clad buildings, the noise now identifiable as a mix of animal sounds, men's shouts and machinery. George Higgins emerged from the car and walked towards her.

"Hello, Madeleine," he called with a broad smile. "Come calling?"

"Stretching my legs, actually," she said as she walked across the carpark. "Is this Cherry Tree Farm?"

He waved at the sign she hadn't noticed. 'Cherry Tree Farm, G Higgins. All enquiries to

Cherry Tree Cottages.'

"This is the working end of rural Oxfordshire," he said.

"Impressive," Maddie said looking at the array of tall barns. "What do you do here?"

"We're breeders. All sorts of farm animals, but we specialise in heritage breeds. Cattle mostly."

Maddie could see and hear the place was humming with activity. She could also smell it. The rich odours of farm animals. She took a lungful. "Smells ... erm ... almost good."

He smiled. "Tina doesn't agree with you. But I do. A good honest stink, especially in the sunshine." His lowering look vanished with the smile and Maddie had a flash of a possibly handsome youth in the distant past.

"I'm pleased to see where you work. And the cottages I've just passed? Your offices? But where do you live?"

"There, as well. Someone a century or two back knocked the three cottages into one. But I needed office space that was a bit more upmarket than these barns. This just doesn't cut it," he said glancing at the industrial looking buildings. "Originally the living area of the left hand cottage, the sixteenth century one, was my study which I had to give up for our business office. Now I can meet clients in some comfort. I converted the large bedroom upstairs into the general office. Conveniently, the ancient stairwell was still in place."

"You have quite a setup here," Maddie said.

"Pretty small, really, in the grand scheme of the business world," George said. "I have an assistant who oversees the office, helps me with the day to day running of the business and takes responsibility for staffing, then a bookkeeper and her assistant. Three in the office. Ten in the messy side of our work in the barns. Plus a few consultants, the vet, for instance."

"Lucky you had room in the cottages for the office," she said. "It's a lovely spot. Ticks all the right boxes."

"Lovely, as you say, for my clients, yes. And for me. But not for poor Tina. Whew, did she have a go at me for daring to even suggest it, much less make the move. Still, I have to acknowledge she's lost a third of her home plus there is the not inconsiderable problem of eating and, well, peeing."

Maddie looked at him in some surprise.

He laughed. "The girls take coffee breaks and have to have a place to eat lunch every day. We had no space for a lunch room so they use our kitchen. Altogether it's only an hour a day, Tina is not impressed. You can understand why. But I can't ask them to troop over to the barns. The loos. Not too salubrious over here."

"I guessed about the toilet situation," Maddie said with a smile. "I can also see why Tina would love to leave you to it at the cottages and move into the Manor instead."

"She's always wanted the big house. Always. But since I've brought the office to the cottages, it's become a driving force."

Maddie thought 'obsession' might be the word, but she didn't say it aloud. "Great for you, too, I suppose, if it works out with Douglas Fanshaw."

"Better dealing with him than the old lady," George said. He paused. "You know we have a track between the house and the barns?"

"The Manor and here? Where?"

He walked over to the right hand side of the carpark. It gave onto a wide swathe of ripening hay. Between two hedgerows a footpath led towards what was probably the back garden of the cottages.

"Come this way. It's an old cart track for the farm, part of a public right of way. I keep it mown."

They walked towards a stone wall with a gate in it. "Tina decided she wanted extra room in our back garden so she's appropriated this part of the track. Now the public path officially goes through our back garden, but because nobody knows about it, it's essentially part of our living space. Of course, someday someone might surprise us by walking though the gate, across our lawn and out the other side. It's their right." George's heavy eyebrows were back in place. Maddie had to remember this was merely a trick of physiognomy, not an expression of distaste or disapproval.

He ushered Maddie through the gate and into the garden. The cottages, with their warm colours, glowed in the morning sunshine. A large patio stretched along the entire back wall furnished with outdoor chairs and a big table.

"What a lovely entertainment area," Maddie said.

"It is. And we do use it a lot this time of year. The back garden is a liveable space now. All due to Tina."

She had removed the two banks of hedgerow for the width of the cottages, replacing the far side with a low wall of grey stone. Immediately in front of the wall was a long bed of roses stretching the full width of the garden. They were of different varieties but all were a variation on yellow ranging from cream to the deepest gold. The rippling field of hay came to the other side of the wall drawing the viewers' eyes to the trees in the far distance.

"What a show," Maddie said. The blooms were prolific and the yellows stood out beautifully against the wall and the field behind.

"It's the first good flowering since she put them in a couple of years ago," George said. "She had it done as a surprise for me when I was away on a business trip. She was actually in the process of planting them when I returned. The new wall was already in as well as the new gates to the track. I told her not to spend good money on planting at the beginning of summer, but she went ahead anyway. What do I know? She's the one with green fingers. And she was right."

"Delightful," Maddie said. She wouldn't know when to plant or when not to plant anything that grows in a garden.

They walked along the double row of roses, their scent permeating the air. Maddie stopped to drink in the perfume of the individual varieties. Mid-way along so that the path went between it and the rose garden was a garden feature, a picturesque well with peaked tiled roof and a winding rope complete with wooden bucket. Privately, she thought it a bit twee. With so many genuine historical features in the cottages and Tina's good taste in the stone wall and rose garden, this jarred. But it probably looked charming when seen from the terrace. When they came to the opposite gate on the other side, George opened it for her.

"This takes you around the field of hay to the back of the big house, maybe five minutes walk," he said pointing the way. "Forget what I said about people not using the track. Feel free to use it whenever you want."

"Thank you, George. It was fortuitous meeting up today. I've really enjoyed the guided tour."

"Do you like barbecues?" he asked her as he latched the gate after her. "We're entertaining in the garden this Saturday, weather permitting. We'd really like to see you here. I'm given some quality meat from time to time. Satisfied customers, you see, and I celebrate with a barbecue. This time I have some especially succulent steaks to throw on the fire."

"I love barbecues," Maddie said. "But I've an Open Day this Saturday, so I'm afraid—"

"We're telling people to arrive after five sometime," he said. "Will that give you time?"

Maddie thought about how long she'd require for tidying and reporting to the vendors after the Open Day itself, then the paperwork it would generate, plus getting home to change. Then, knowing nobody. "There's one other problem – I'm a stranger here. I won't know your friends."

"Jenny and Gabrio will be here. You'll have probably met a few others at the Gardeners Club as well. And I know Tina has invited Douglas Fanshaw." He laughed. "She thinks buttering him up will result in a lower price for the House."

Maddie laughed with him. "I wish her luck."

"Do come on Saturday. It should be good fun."

Maddie thought of Rupert telling her to become involved with the village. And, besides, she loved the casual atmosphere at barbecues.

"Okay," she said with a smile. "I'd love to. Maybe closer to six than five?"

"See you then," he said with a cheery wave.

Maddie followed the track to the back of the Manor. She'd have to look it up, but the file she'd read at work called it Cherry Tree *Manor*. George kept referring to it as Cherry Tree *House*. Of course she knew it wasn't a medieval manor; it was probably early Victorian built in the style of. But it piqued her innate curiosity; she would check the deeds.

• • • ● • ● • • •

On Saturday morning, Maddie awoke with fresh anticipation about the coming day. First she had the Open

Day for the de Mille property and after that, the Higgins' barbecue. Other than the Gardeners Club where she'd turned up unannounced, this was the first social event to which she'd been invited since she moved into Caroline's cottage almost a month before.

For her estate agent duties, she dressed in a summer dress of muted blues with a matching jacket. She put on stockings and beige shoes and took care as she applied her makeup so she'd look as professional as possible. She ate a muffin mid-morning before leaving for the Goring office because she was highly unlikely to have lunch given all that she had to do, and when. She reminded herself not to drink too much tea.

But first she needed to talk to someone about what to wear at the barbecue. She hunted for Gabrio's card. It contained a landline, so she rang it, not to ask him (obviously no man would know), but to ask Jenny.

"That white denim trouser suit looked lovely on you," Jenny said. "But, come to think of it, white at a barbecue?"

"What are you wearing?" Maddie asked.

"With my hips? Always a summer skirt. I'll take a cardie in case it cools off. And flat sandals for walking on their lawn. But you're so slim, you can wear trousers with élan."

"I'll have a rummage. My skirts tend to be too business-like. Would jeans do?"

"Lots will wear jeans, certainly. And some will be wearing long shorts or those trou that are cropped somewhere between ankle and knee."

"You've given me an idea," Maddie said. "I do have some cropped trou. They must be hidden somewhere in my wardrobe. Thanks, Jenny. You've been a great help."

Maddie laid out the outfit on her bed. She had mixed feelings about wearing it. It fulfilled the suggestions made by Jenny. Both the trou and the jacket were of a beige poplin and both were cropped below elbow and knee. She could wear her blue and beige sleeveless top, then put on the jacket if needed.

She well remembered when she'd worn it last, and that was the problem. Olivia had invited her friends over to farewell a couple who were moving to Australia, hosting it in her parents' garden. Chrystal was there, brought along by a mutual friend. Maddie had always thought it was that occasion when Wayne had first met her. She remembered watching the young people milling about, drinks in hand and Wayne commenting on the rising noise levels.

"If I didn't know you were standing right beside me, I'd swear I could see you down there," Wayne had said, pointing towards a knot of giggling young women.

She couldn't make out anybody in particular, but she answered anyway. "A generation younger, of course."

Wayne had slid his arm about her waist. "You look pretty damn good for your age," he said into her hair. But that young woman he had spotted was Chrystal.

The thought hurt. She missed him. She missed those moments. Gone forever, now. He had chosen the younger version.

That was only two years ago, not five. She pushed the thought away.

Chapter Eleven

MADDIE WAS NERVOUSLY EXCITED about her first Open Day. To start with, she went into Goring where Rupert gave her some last minute schooling on both the duties of the agent and the pitfalls that can happen. He had her in stitches describing one disastrous Open Day which was held for a house being sold due to a marital breakup. People came and went rather quickly. After the Open Day, the agent checked through the house, as usual, only to find a message – an explicit message – written in lipstick on the mirror in the master bedroom. Maddie laughed, but it brought to mind the five years Jade had talked about. The thought was like a bucket of cold water. She managed to respond appropriately to Rupert but she kicked herself. She needed to forget about her own sensitivities. Drop them from her mind. Especially today.

Back at her desk, she became immersed in putting together her Open Day kit following a checklist Rupert had provided and including the all important list of appointments her advertising had generated. She shoved all she needed into a box she placed in the boot of her car. Still too early.

Instead, she looked up the history of Cherry Tree Manor in one of the reference books Rupert kept. Well, well. 'Cherry Tree Manor' was built in 1837. There. But it became 'Cherry Tree House' at the turn of the last century, well before the Fanshaws bought it. Someone not impressed with the pretentiousness of calling a large house a manor, she supposed. But the Fanshaws reverted to its original name in the 1960s. So, the 'Manor' it would remain.

She glanced at her watch. Time enough. After one last glance in the mirror on the wall of the staffroom, she headed to the estate where the de Mille house was located. Had Louise complied with the request to pack away all the baby paraphernalia?

• • • • ● • ● • • •

Maddie looked at the Open Day announcement on the For Sale sign. It had generated a fair few of the appointments for later, a tribute to the 'curb appeal' of the townhouse. Inside, too, she found the place immaculate with nary a toy in sight. Louise was polishing the kitchen bench and Antoine was running a Hoover over the stairs.

"Hello there," Maddie called over the noise of the vacuum. She glanced at Kathleen Short's painting of the marigolds. Yes, it would be the first thing anyone saw, grabbing visitors' attention as they come in. Then their eyes should wander over the two upholstered chairs (Louise had borrowed them from her sister) with their cushions that picked up the golds and greens of the painting. Sophisticated and perfect. And not a hint of babies, messy or otherwise.

"The children are with my parents," Louise said from the kitchen. "We'll be off there ourselves once Antoine finishes the stairs." She put away the cloth she was using and called to her husband. "Get a move on, Antoine. We have to go. Now."

True to her word, the vacuum stopped and they were about to leave.

"The place looks superb," Maddie said with her best estate agent reassuring smile. She meant it. Neat, clean and smelling good.

Maddie spread the shiny brochures on the kitchen bench and, beside them, she put a holder full of her new business cards. She kept the clipboard with her; she needed to keep track of the appointments, who showed up and when. That is, if anyone showed up. She glanced at the time. Ten minutes to go. Through the front window she saw a car draw up near her sign. The people inside must be reading the details. The car slowly moved away again. Maddie felt a frisson of worry which she shook off. She needed to keep good control of her emotions or she'd be a wreck well before she was due to arrive at the evening barbecue.

The time of the Open arrived and so did two families, one earlier than their scheduled appointment. She greeted them with a fluffy-fluffy smile and told them she was there for any questions but they were to feel free to wander wherever they wanted.

A few minutes later, the first couple came back to the door where Maddie had stationed herself and she asked them how they liked the house.

"Probably a little small for us," the woman said. "We have one teenager still at home and he takes up lot of space."

"I've seen slightly larger versions of this house on our books," Maddie said. "I'll give you a ring about them, if you like."

While the woman thanked her and was saying her goodbyes, the other couple came down the stairs.

Before Maddie could stop her, the woman reached over and touched the painting. "It's an original," she said to her husband.

"Wonderful, isn't it?" Maddie enthused, thankful the woman's hand had left the painting. "The artist is Kathleen Short from over Henley way. She also runs a little gallery for local artists from her studio. All originals, of course. If you're interested, I've put the details in that brochure you have there."

After a confused cacophony of comments, both couples left. Maddie looked carefully at where the woman had touched the painting. Still pristine, thank heavens. Before any more people arrived, she repositioned herself alongside the painting making it difficult for anybody else to finger it. She had not long to wait before another group came up the path. She turned on her fluffy smile and prepared to do her estate-agent thing yet again.

Sixteen 'parties', as Rupert called them, came through in the end. Essentially sixteen families. Three of them seemed quite interested in the de Mille townhouse and one other couple said something similar to the first couple to whom Maddie had spoken about needing a larger place. The exercise had resulted in five chances of real interest or for further contact.

She swung by the office. Maddie was glowing. Rupert was suitably impressed with her list of further contacts. After she tidied away the bits and pieces from the Open Day, she transcribed the contact details of the five and left to change clothes for the barbecue, feeling as if she had taken a gigantic stride towards success in her new career.

But the closer she came to Briar Cottage, the more exhausted she felt. Did she really want to go out again? Once home, she kicked off her shoes and collapsed into a chair. She sighed. Now home, the last thing she wanted to do was to socialise. But she couldn't not go. Not when specially invited by George Higgins.

She padded to the fridge in her stocking feet and poured herself an icy white wine and took it with her upstairs. Soon she was luxuriating in a bath, sipping her cold wine in the hope it would revive her. By the time she'd dressed, renewed her makeup and finished her wine, she was feeling substantially better.

Maddie turned into Cherry Tree Farm Lane and was immediately confronted by cars parked higgledy-piggledy along the verge, crowding the lane itself. She manoeuvred her car past, heading towards the barns where she found plenty of room for her car. She left it on the right side of the carpark in the corner near the gate so she could walk to the barbecue the back way along the farm track.

Sunlight slanted through the thick hedgerow; she could identify elderflower bushes, hawthorn, privet and that bush, whatever its name, which produced fruit for sloe gin. She only caught glimpses of the field of hay beyond the bushes but she could certainly smell it in the late afternoon sunshine. Lovely rural odours, somewhat more enticing than the smell of the barns back where she'd parked her car.

She could hear voices and other vague party sounds when she came to the gate that led into the garden behind the Higgins' cottages. Again, she was taken by Tina's vision in all that she'd done here: removing the hedgerows for the width of their garden, constructing the low stone wall and creating the rose-bed; this time, she even appreciated the little decorative 'well'. The blooming roses produced bright splodges of concentrated sunshine backlit against the green hayfield beyond.

As she pushed the gate open, she hung her jacket on the lower rung of the gate itself, half hidden by the first rose bush. She balanced the bottle of wine she'd brought as a contribution to the barbecue on the edge of the 'well'. She could fetch the wine later when she knew her way about the party. The evening was warm and having hands free at a barbecue was an advantage.

Maddie could see a goodly number of people producing the social buzz of conversation she'd heard, both up on the terrace itself and down on the grass. Was Douglas here? She scanned the garden and spotted Jenny with not a little relief. She walked over to join the group she was in.

"Maddie, you look lovely," Jenny said. "Yes, you do look good in a trouser suit. Sigh."

The others laughed.

One of the men, who introduced himself as 'Sebastian' said, "Let me fetch you a glass of wine, my dear. You have some catching up to do; we've been here for ages and we're making good inroads into George's wine cellar."

"You have met him," Jenny said to her as he walked off across the lawn. "The judge. Remember?"

Maddie did remember his face, if not his name, from the Gardeners Club. She also recalled his wife ran the local pony club. "I'm terribly afraid people will know me from the other night at your place and I'll be at a loss as to who they are."

"Stick with me," Jenny said. "I'll rescue you if you use the wrong name."

"I'll be struggling to remember any," she said as Sebastian shoved a brimming glass of red wine into her hand. "Thank you, Sebastian," she said, smiling at the little man. He was unprepossessing, but she guessed he would assume the dignity of his office when bewigged and gowned in court.

Maddie had consumed about half the glass when Tina appeared, having a word here, a short conversation there, working the gathering, all the while radiating glamour. "Nice to see you," she said with a brilliant smile as she topped up Maddie's wine. "Madeleine, isn't it? We must do coffee soon." She was dressed in a longish sheath that only someone with her figure could wear. Her mane of hair was hooked up to fall artlessly around her neck and shoulders, a look only achieved with great patience and skill. This was clearly Tina's party. It did cross Maddie's mind to wonder if George had remembered to tell her she was invited.

The conversation in the group ebbed and flowed along with the levels of wine in the glasses. It was only as Tina topped up her glass for the third time, Maddie reminded herself to go a bit more slowly. Time for those steaks George had promised. Or any food to soak up some of the alcohol.

Jenny had gone off somewhere, but Maddie was comfortable with the people she was with – Sebastian had been joined by his wife Simone, plus a couple named Roger and Wendy, also from the Gardeners Club, and a man she couldn't place. He was an older man with a full head of white hair. He introduced himself as Adrian.

"I work with George," he said. "I'm the vet. I hear you're the estate agent for whoever inherited the Manor – the place that belonged to the woman who was murdered."

"Murdered?" Maddie said. "Is that what you heard?"

"A couple of years ago it was," he said.

"Not murdered...there is no evidence—" Sebastian started to say but was interrupted by his wife.

"She disappeared, poor old dear," Simone said firmly. "No body was ever found. The police never talked of murder. So I don't think—"

"Maybe I got it wrong," Adrian said with an easy smile. "But I was working here at Cherry Tree Farm one day shortly before she was reported missing and the chap I was working with – a young fellow – swore he'd heard a gunshot. Not me. I was in the middle of a difficult procedure and I'm not that brilliant with high pitched sounds any more."

"So you didn't hear it?"

"Afraid not," he said.

"But the young fellow thought the old lady had been murdered because of what he'd heard?" Maddie asked.

"Because of that gunshot. And the timing. For a little while anyway."

"I heard it was murder, as well," Roger said. "That was the talk at the time, anyway. But nothing came of it.

Only an old lady who'd wandered off. Nothing about a shot."

"Did you tell the police about the gunshot?" Sebastian asked Adrian.

"Not my call," Adrian said. "I did advise the young fellow to ring the police when I heard the old lady was missing and us being so close by. But I think he decided it was someone shooting rabbits."

"No blood anywhere?" Maddie asked. "Nothing to suggest guns?"

"Depends which newspaper you read," Simone said with a raised eyebrow. "The tabloids would have it as a killer who stole her fortune from under her bed."

Maddie didn't mention the will had been hidden in that very spot.

"The regular papers hardly reported it," Simone continued. "It was only in the village that people still talked about it. Talk about it; here we are several years later, still at it. Truth be told, most people are far more interested if it's murder, don't you think? No matter the truth."

Maddie turned to Adrian. "I'm Madeleine Brooks, Adrian. Nice to meet you and, yes, I am the estate agent for the sale. I have to admit a morbid curiosity about what happened to old Mrs Fanshaw, like us all, I expect." She raised her glass in a mini-salute to the others.

"It's no secret that Tina and George have wanted to buy the Manor for ages," Wendy said. "I bet you'll be hearing from them." It seemed an open secret that the Higgins wanted the house. Maddie smiled and sipped her wine. It was a flavoursome Spanish Rioja, Sebastian had told her, and it was slipping down far too easily.

George shouted for people to come for their steaks and salads. Tina had arranged the food buffet-style and the terrace table was groaning under a wealth of dishes. Maddie followed the others, was given a plate, a steak and access to potatoes done in a dozen ways, and that was before she was expected to load her plate with salads.

Adrian waved at her from some chairs set out on the grass, indicating he'd saved a seat for her. She waved back and headed down the few steps to the level of the lawn. She kept her right hip sliding along the balustrade to help with her balance. Yes, a bit too much wine on an empty stomach. She'd better start eating straight away.

Adrian chatted about his work with rare breeds of cattle. He had a great deal of respect for George's father and George too.

"His father began the business," he told Maddie. "They started with fields and a barn or two over Gatehampton way, then when Cherry Tree Cottages became available, they bought them to live in. Being on the spot, they arranged to lease the barns. They nibbled away at the land, first leasing then buying bits from the old fellow, gradually, in the end, acquiring the lot." He paused as he sawed off a large bite of steak. "Except for the Manor, of course."

Maddie found the meat as good as any she'd eaten in a London restaurant. "Old fellow? Do you mean Mr Fanshaw?"

Adrian nodded and swallowed. "Fantastic meat, this. A satisfied client who sends George meat every year for the start of the barbecue season."

"Lucky George," Maddie said, digging into some coleslaw. "Lucky us to be invited to share it."

"That old bugger Fanshaw was difficult, to say the least," Adrian said, returning to his subject. "Don't know how his wife could stand him."

"People are quick to think she was murdered," Maddie said. "Do you think she had enemies?"

Adrian laughed. "I don't know about enemies, but I can imagine someone becoming totally frustrated with her," he said. "They both drove people bonkers. Freddy in particular. Arrogant and rude. However, you'd think murder needs a stronger motivation than that. Also, don't forget it was Beryl, not Freddy, who was murdered."

"You'd think, but that's only logic; murder is probably the least logical of crimes," Maddie said, putting down her cutlery. The steak was enormous and she wanted a little room for whatever sweet Tina would have – and she now anticipated Tina would serve up quite a choice. If only she had a 'doggie' bag to take the remaining steak home for the next day....

She brought her mind back to the matter at hand. "I watched a television series on serial killers last year. The reasons for murder were sometimes trivial, not like those found in fiction."

"I saw that series," Adrian said and they happily discussed murder cases until the sweets appeared, served with a dessert wine. Of all the whites, Maddie enjoyed late harvest dessert wines best of all. They tended to be pricey and she only treated herself rarely. Tina and George served only the best.

Maddie became aware of a disturbance in the ambiance of the party.

"George, for god's sake." Someone's voice was clearly audible. Tina. "You're not serving this?"

They all looked up onto the terrace. Tina was waving a bottle of wine. George hurried over and grabbed the bottle, saying something to her. She went inside, shutting the door behind her with a determined click. George poured himself a generous portion.

Adrian was grinning. "I bet I know what happened."

"And?" someone asked. Which one was he? Roger?

"Tina sees this ordinary bottle of wine some non-pundit like me brought to contribute to the party. But it's not up to the quality of what's in her cellar, not by a long chalk."

"Oops," Roger said with a chuckle. "Tina makes a fox's paws."

Difficult to imagine the Tina Maddie knew making any such faux pas.

Maddie thought about the bottle she'd placed on the well down in the garden. Maybe she'd just leave it there. A ten-pound bottle probably wouldn't cut the mustard.

"Go on," his wife Wendy said to her husband, "help old George out. Pour glasses for us out of that bottle."

He smiled, nodded and walked over to do so.

Maddie met Adrian's eyes. "Nice people," he murmured.

Eventually the sun was down, dusk was falling and people were saying their goodbyes. Maddie excused herself, thanking Adrian for the interesting conversation before making her way to her jacket hung on the gate railing.

"Maddie?"

"Douglas! I've been keeping an eye for you. I'm just leaving; glad you spotted me," she said. Bother. She'd said 'shpotted'.

"I was very late. Awful traffic coming south from Liverpool. But I got here in time for some steak and a taste of that harvest wine."

"So delicious," she said carefully, holding onto the gatepost. She saw his eyes flick to her hand.

"How about I run you home?" Douglas asked. "We can take the track to the Manor and I'll pop you back to your place."

Maddie flushed and hoped Douglas wouldn't be able to see it in the gathering gloom. But he was absolutely right. Emphasised by the fact he could tell. "I've brought my car," she said. "It's parked in front of the barns. I'm about to walk over."

"I think you'd better let me drive," Douglas said. "It's a Saturday and the cops are out in force at this time of year. And, my friend, you're over the limit."

Damn, damn, damn.

"Yes, well, maybe I'll take you up on your offer," she said with as much dignity as she was able to conjure up. "They're very generous with their wine here. I can walk back to pick up the car in the morning."

She found the growing darkness and uneven surface of the lawn underfoot contributed to her already evident balance problem. Douglas offered his arm and the two of them traversed the garden to the other gate and slowly walked down the avenue between the hedgerows towards the Manor. There, Douglas saw Maddie into the passenger seat of his car and he drove the few minutes to her home. She offered coffee but he refused, so she thanked him and headed inside with relief. All she wanted was to flop into her own bed and sleep away the long day, to say nothing about the excess of wine.

Amazingly, Maddie woke with a clear head and an acute embarrassment. Douglas seeing her like that? Hardly the image to display to a client.

In her bath, she remembered she'd left her contributory bottle of wine sitting on the garden feature. She smiled, imagining George or Tina gazing out over their back garden and seeing the wine in the morning sunshine. She hoped at least he would enjoy it – an Aussie shiraz, one of her favourites, although not exactly top drawer. She winced at the memory of Tina and the fuss she made about the bottle that was not up to scratch.

Maddie grabbed breakfast, looking forward to her walk in the fresh air to fetch her car. She figured it was probably a two kilometre walk, all in all, a good excuse to get herself outside, a good way to stretch her legs.

Somehow the world seemed bright that morning. She kept refilling her lungs with rural smells, a constant delight. Why had she waited so long to move to the country? Maybe she should have persuaded Wayne years ago. Oh dear. Would that have made a difference?

Wayne.

She honestly had not given him a thought for almost twenty-four hours, the longest she had experienced since their separation. Somehow that spurred her to walk more vigorously and she could feel her muscles responding to the extra demand.

As she turned into the carpark from Cherry Tree Farm Lane, she could see hers was the only car there. But when she drew closer, she saw something had been scratched into the paintwork on the driver's door.

'Your not wanted here. Go away, bitch!!!' Three exclamation marks.

Chapter Twelve

THAT DAMN WOMAN! SUCKING up to everyone. Batting her eyelashes and shepherding everyone like sheep to a dip. Swanning in with her citified ways. Pretending she's a decade younger than she is. She's got grown up children, for gawd's sake, and grandchildren, I'm told. Not that she talks about them. Or a husband.

Sneaky, sneaky, sneaky.

What happened to old fashioned English country reserve when strangers arrive into a village? Down the gurgler along with all the other time-honoured values of rural life. Making us have fake fox hunting. Selling green spaces for housing developments. Look at Courtneyside! Full of ignorant immigrants from the city looking for a 'rural lifestyle'. As if they get that when having to live cheek by jowl in row housing. And voting for wishy-washy liberals who want more of the same. And estate agents like Sneaky get to reign supreme. Ridiculous.

Something has to be done, even if small.

Watch this space.

Chapter Thirteen

MADDIE CLOSED HER EYES and reopened them. It was still there. 'Your not wanted here. Go away, bitch!!!' Her first thought was a case of mistaken identity. Maybe someone else had a car like hers?

No.

It was clearly meant for a newcomer to the area. Her.

With shaking hands, she pulled out her phone and took several photographs of both the crudely scratched lettering and the position of her car near the gate to the track. She then opened the door and started it up.

Who would want her out of their life? Who? So far, she hadn't met very many people. And who, of those she'd met, were at the barbecue? George and Tina, of course, Jenny and Gabrio, Douglas, Sebastian the judge and Simone, Roger and Wendy. Adrian she'd just met. She groaned. So many people who'd been at the Gardeners Club last Tuesday. But none she'd irritated, surely.

She arrived back at Briar Cottage and made herself a big cup of milky tea, taking it out into the overgrown back garden. Lots needed doing.

She sat on the old wooden bench and peered through the tall shrubs to the field next door which housed several woolly sheep munching the short grass. It was quiet and the air still smelled fresh. But her inner calm was gone. Who would vandalise her car? And why that ugly message?

Tears pricked her lids. What next? She was loving it here. What had she done wrong? Who would do such a thing?

Then another thought struck her. She could hardly drive clients in her car with such vandalism visible to all and sundry. She groaned aloud. She couldn't get it fixed right away; today was Sunday and car workshops would be shut.

She closed her eyes and leaned back against the old wood of the garden seat. Where was her customary resilience? She needed to get a grip, and soon.

She drank her tea. Thinking, thinking until she came up with first one, then another temporary fixes. The first required a bar of soap which she grabbed from the bathroom. She ran the soap over the scratches in the hope the words would recede. If anything, they stood out even more clearly. With a sigh of frustration, she went back inside for a bowl of water and a sponge to clean off the soap. After polishing it dry, she could try the second idea. She soaked a small piece of paper kitchen roll in olive oil and headed back to the car door and vigorously rubbed the oil into the scratches. Yes. They were certainly less visible. She backed off several metres and slowly walked towards the car. She couldn't read the words until she was about a metre and a half away. The oil couldn't render the damage invisible but the letters had faded enough to obscure the message. It would have to do. She'd call the insurance people first thing tomorrow morning. And maybe they could tell her where she could get a fresh paint job in a hurry.

The phone rang as she was washing the oil off her hands.

"How would my favourite estate agent like to be treated to a Sunday lunch at the Catherine Wheel?" said a voice that could only belong to William Dingle. "They're serving roast of Welsh lamb this week."

"William!" Maddie said. "You cannot believe how welcome that sounds. When should I pick you up?"

"My goodness, you forget easily," he said. "I don't drive at night anymore and you've driven me twice now. But this is the middle of the day. I'll pick you up."

• • • • ● • ● • • •

When they were seated in a booth at the pub, Maddie congratulated William on ringing ahead of time. The little pub was busy yet they were immediately shown into the booth he'd reserved, smiling a trifle triumphantly at the many people wandering around searching for a place to sit.

"You promised to tell me what's bothering you," he said. In the car he'd commented she was uncharacteristically quiet. She said she'd tell all when they were settled at the pub.

"When we have a pint in front of us," she said getting up to order at the bar. "I'll order."

"No you don't," William said, heaving his elderly frame up from the booth seat. "This is my treat. You sit down, young lady."

Maddie smiled at the 'young lady' appellation and obediently sat down.

Once they were sipping their pints, Maddie filled William in on the scratched car door and its missive.

"I haven't annoyed anybody that I know of," Maddie said in despair. "I have absolutely no idea why anyone would do such a thing."

"This harks back to my insurance days," he said.

"What did you do in insurance?"

"I was an investigator. This type of damage periodically occurred. Our first question was always whether the insured had done it himself and was blaming someone else to get an already scratched paintwork redone. If it was someone else, we'd go after their own insurance company. That sort of thing."

"So, Mr Retired Insurance Investigator, what do you think?"

"It has to be a local," William said. "Nobody but a local would bother saying that you're not wanted here."

"And an uneducated one at that." Maddie couldn't keep the bitterness out of her voice. She'd escaped to the country to avoid this sort of thing.

"Uneducated?" William asked, taking a long draught of his beer.

"Sorry, I've told you what it said, but not the spelling. He used 'your' not 'you're.'" She spelled out the words.

"A common enough mistake," he said. "But the important thing is to have it repaired before many people see it."

"Any idea who could fix it on short notice?"

William set his tankard down and wiped his chin. "I use a firm not far from here. In fact, one of those boys who almost bowled us over at the Gardeners Club works there. His father's firm. You remember, the young fellows with the motorcycles? Tomorrow I'll ask them about your car, on your behalf, of course."

The motorcycle boys. Motorcycles. Gangs. Wayward youth.

"You don't think..." she paused. "No. Not fair."

"Come on, spit it out," he said. "Something has occurred to you."

"The motorcycle boys. The Flores boy and his two pals...."

"I hardly think so," William said slowly. "But I'll do a little sleuthing if you want."

"It's just occurred to me...kids that age...you know. Sometimes they don't need motivation."

William shook his grizzled head. "I can see your point, but, I don't know...it's unlikely. How about someone from work? Anybody there who might have a grudge against your coming here? That fellow you've taken over from?"

"Very ill, I'm afraid. He's having chemo in London. No, he was grateful he wouldn't be letting his clients down. I'm 100 percent confident he has nothing to do with it."

"Did you say anything untoward at the Gardeners Club? Something someone might take the wrong way?"

She shook her head. "People were universally friendly; I had a good time. Honestly, the only person I wasn't getting along with was Douglas Fanshaw. Not communicating as I would have liked. But lately it's a tad better. I wouldn't say we're bosom pals, but our conversations are now on a decent business-like basis." She didn't mention his escorting her home after the barbecue. She wasn't exactly ashamed of herself, but she also felt no need to demean herself in front of William. She had a certain dignity to maintain, or so she convinced herself.

Their roast meals arrived and the next fifteen minutes or so were consumed with eating.

"A sweet?" William asked when the waiter cleared their plates.

Maddie shook her head. "I usually only snack in the middle of the day," she said. "But I have to say a meal like this has banished my blue mood. Thank you for suggesting it."

"Pure self-interest," William said.

• • • ● • ● • • •

That afternoon, Maddie worked off her recent excess eating by attacking the back garden of Briar Cottage. It was situated at the eastern edge of Woodley Bottom along Tick Lane which ran the length of the village and beyond, the opposite end from where Cherry Tree Manor was located. Not that the Manor was actually in the village, it was some way into the countryside on the far side.

The plot for Briar Cottage was long and narrow, perhaps about a third of an acre, with an overgrown front garden ringed in mature trees and the back garden was equally overgrown but in shrubs and bushes. The cottage boasted a ramshackle garage that had seen better days accessed by a small farm lane, not in such good nick as the one leading to George's barns, but the same idea. Here, the lane ended in a farm gate and open fields beyond her own plot.

She found some secateurs and started with the idea of trimming everything that obstructed the view from the little conservatory attached to the back of the cottage. First, she wanted to let the westerly sunshine in and, second, clear enough foliage so she could see the view now hidden behind lanky shrubs. She could imagine sitting with a good book, every now and again lifting her eyes to watch the sheep munching grass in the field next door. With a glass of wine. Or maybe not. A cup of tea was more to her way of thinking after her recent overindulgence.

She started with vigour. She vaguely recognised the bush was what her mother had called English Hibiscus. It seemed a shame to be cutting back a shrub so full of flower buds, but she wasn't exactly ripping it up. She snipped off several feet of the longest spindly branches then stood by the conservatory to see what was about to be revealed. Perfect – another foot lower and she'd be able to see the field next door.

Once the hibiscus was suitably shortened, she attacked a shrub with small yellow flowers, again stifling any anxieties she was doing it a permanent injury. By the time her hand was well on its way to developing a blister from the secateurs, she'd cleared a goodly patch. She went inside and collapsed on the old sun lounge inside the conservatory. Her plan had worked beautifully. She could not only see the sheep but the rooftop of the house on the far side of the field peeking up through the trees, and what were probably the Chiltern Hills beyond. She grabbed her phone, lay back on the sun lounger again and took a picture, immediately sending it to Caroline before closing her eyes. She drifted off wondering where on earth she could start looking for Beryl Fanshaw. Where she went. Or where she met her end.

She woke up with a text from Caroline pinging into her phone. "Can't believe we had that view all along," she wrote. "I remember it from years ago. How could I have forgotten? Thank you, dear tenant!"

That evening, she viewed the sunset in all its glory from the conservatory. But the garage ... bother. It should be locked up after dark. A bit like locking the barn after etc., but she would have to do something about it. And about her own safety as well. She checked that all the windows and doors on the ground floor were secure before going upstairs for an early night.

• • • • ● • ● • • •

William rang on Monday morning to say he'd talked to the car painters and she should drive the car there as soon as possible. Within the hour. "That suit you, Maddie?" he asked.

"Yes, of course," she said. She felt more muzzy-headed this morning than the previous one, which meant it had nothing to do with the consumption of wine. She'd suffered broken sleep with images of the message scratched in her car bouncing about her tired brain.

William was already at the car paint workshop when Maddie arrived.

"Greasing the wheels," he said when Maddie said he needn't have come. "This is young Bart," he said. "Mrs Brooks. With the problem I was telling you about."

Bart smiled at Maddie. "We almost met," he said. "At the Flores's house, remember?" So he was one of the black leather-clad motorcyclists. Had to be, as he was far too young to be a member of the Gardeners Club.

"You were in a hurry," Maddie said diplomatically.

"A mate bought himself a new machine. We wanted to see it before the light faded."

Maddie smiled back at him. A well-spoken young man. Most likely not someone who would have misspelled 'you're'.

They talked about what needed to be done to her car door. Bart estimated the repair and drying time for the new paint would require several days. They would sand and paint several times and it would need time for the paint to harden.

"We do have a loan car," Bart said with some hesitation. "I'm doing it up, though, and it's a bit of a mess."

"A mess I don't mind if it will get me from A to B," Maddie said. "And as long as it has no rude bits of graffiti on it."

"Clean as a whistle," Bart said. He took them behind the workshop where several cars were parked.

Maddie could tell straight away which one it would be – the car with the bright pink under-paint on all four doors. "This one?" she asked.

"'Fraid so," he said. "But it will only be for a few days."

William suggested a cup of tea back at his cottage.

"I have a heap of work to do," she said, "so it will have to be a quick one."

"I've had an idea," William said once back at his cottage.

"I use my car every now and again," he said. "You not only use your car for transport, but as an extension of your image as an estate agent."

"I suppose so," Maddie said, sipping her tea.

"So I'll have the loan car and you'll drive my big old boat," William said with a flourish. "It needs a good run anyway."

Maddie protested, William insisted and finally Maddie drove away in William's venerable Rover, feeling like a duchess. She headed for the ironmonger's in Goring to buy two padlocks, one for the side of the garage and one for the main door. She'd feel much better with William's car protected from whoever vandalised hers.

Vandalism. She had a thought. Douglas's dining room window was broken. Quite possibly it was vandalised too. How many vandals would a village, or even three small hamlets, support? She'd quickly eliminated young Bart from writing the message on her car door. But two other leather-clad lads were with him that Tuesday evening and, now she'd thought about it, possibly two acts of vandalism.

So, two other youths to investigate, however discreetly.

Chapter Fourteen

As soon as Maddie reached the office in Goring, she checked the other terrace house listings that boasted at least one more bedroom than the de Mille property. When she contacted the two families who indicated they were looking for something bigger, she wanted to have the information at her fingertips. Two houses had three bedrooms instead of two, and were commensurately larger in their living areas on the ground floor. They were more expensive than the customers had indicated they were willing to pay, but she'd have to cross that barrier now they knew what would be needed to buy a two-bed townhouse, and realising it would cost more for a three.

The first potential buyers she rang were the couple who had gone through the de Mille house first, those with one teenager at home.

"Just a quick call," Maddie said into the telephone after identifying herself, "to tell you I've found two more houses on our books, larger places, but very much like the de Mille property. Both are bigger, though. Both cost that bit more, as you would expect."

"The second bedroom is larger?" the woman asked. Maddie was pleased she was questioning the bedroom sizes rather than the increase in price. A good sign.

"Yes, another decent sized double," Maddie said. "Plus a third bedroom, or study or what ever. That also means a significantly larger living area below. One of these properties in particular might suit you well. It's close to the property you visited on Saturday. Sort of its bigger brother. It's only around the corner from the de Mille house."

"The price?" the woman asked.

"A bit up from the one you saw, but still sensibly priced."

"Hang on a minute, please," Mrs Reynolds said when told the asking price. She had excitement in her voice. "I'll check with my husband."

Maddie could hear the muffled conversation.

"You there, Mrs Brooks? Yes, we would like to see it."

"When would suit you?"

"After work. Say 5:30 or a bit later? Or on Saturday? As soon as possible."

Maddie well remembered the household chaos that reigned round about that 5:30 time slot – family coming home from work or after-school activities, the television often blaring, dinner preparation, and everyone a bit tired from the day and usually hungry. She sighed, imagining the vendors' disquiet. Yet it was important to capture the interest of the buyers while it was still high. She rang.

"Oh dear," the vendor said when Maddie told her the preferred viewing times of the potential buyer. "Between 5:30 and 6:30? Heavens."

"That's the time they've suggested. Not the greatest timing for most of us, but could you manage to bend your schedule to accommodate them?"

Maddie heard a sigh. She waited.

"We usually eat at six. If we eat at five, we can clean up before they get here at...say...six?"

Maddie felt a surge of relief. Organising timing that interrupted established routines was plain difficult. "Perfect," she said. "One more thing...would it be all right if I came over tonight or tomorrow to see your house?"

"Oh dearie me, that means having it ready for showing twice this week."

Maddie closed her eyes. She deliberately lightened her voice. "I'm sorry to be such a nuisance, but you understand, I can't really show a house I haven't seen."

"I do understand, Mrs Brooks. And we do want to sell." She paused. "How about you pop over tonight? Then the buyers have a choice of four evenings this week."

After Maddie put the phone down on the conversation, she felt her shoulders relax. A long day today but maybe, just maybe things might happen. Money was short, far too short for comfort. She crossed her fingers.

The phone rang and she had a sinking feeling something didn't suit someone and changes would have to be made, but no.

"Hello, Madeleine; it's George Higgins speaking."

"George. Before you say anything, I'd like to thank you for the most enjoyable barbecue on Saturday. Beautiful setting, interesting people and delicious steaks. Did you find the bottle of Aussie shiraz I left you on the garden feature?"

"Aha, it was you! Yes, we collected it the next morning, thank you."

"Talking of wines, you really have a mouth-watering selection in your cellar."

"It's nice to hear appreciation. I'm afraid many of our friends wouldn't know a supermarket cheapie from...well, you know," he said.

Maddie laughed. "One serves one's wines depending on the guests." She cringed at her words. Pretentiousness personified.

But George readily agreed. "What I've rung about is to persuade you to drop everything and have a cup of coffee with me. I'm sitting in my car at the station thinking I'd like another chat with you about the big house – and I could use a coffee. How about it?"

"The *Coffee Clique* in ten minutes?" she asked. Just what she needed.

They sat outside at one of the tiny tables on the pavement. George looked quite different dressed as the businessman he was. Maddie hadn't thought it through before, but all successful farmers must also be skilled in business practice nowadays. Again she reminded herself to forget his brooding face, a mere trick of configuration, not reflective of mood.

"Tina has noticed that Douglas is improving the big house," George said after they'd ordered their coffees. "She's tried to talk to him about it but he keeps referring her to you."

Maddie nodded, first at the waiter with their steaming mugs and then again at George. "That's how it works. I'm a protection for people like Douglas, slap dab in the middle between vendor and buyer. It means people like you have a buffer, too. Personal issues and relationships are kept away from the house sale."

George didn't look at her. "That's as may be but we're getting a little concerned Douglas is investing money into the house without asking us." He sounded as if he'd memorised what he was going to say. But the message was clear enough.

Maddie was flabbergasted. As if a vendor should consult a potential buyer. How ridiculous. But she hid her consternation. George had a little learning to do.

He was now looking at her. He said, "What's the form, Madeleine? Do we make an offer even though it's not officially on the market?"

Maddie put on her fluffy smile. "You can, of course," she said. "But where will you make the offer when Douglas hasn't yet put a price on it, or even a range of prices to act as a guide?"

"I take your point," George said.

Maddie sipped her coffee. Still a bit hot but very, very good. "Bear with me a moment and let me explain about offers in this sort of circumstance. What happens is this," she began, dredging up the information from her half-remembered internet course. "Perhaps a buyer wants a cheap property which needs work – a 'do-up' in the parlance of the trade – because he has the wherewithal to invest in it. Sometimes his idea is to create a finished product which is at the standard and taste he wants personally or, more likely, for selling at a profit. But the emphasis is on buying at a bargain."

"Yes, of course," George said, his face still passive.

"The vendor, on the other hand, only sells cheaply for a few reasons. First if he gets the same return as he'd get after investing money into the project – in other words, he sells at any time in the project with a net profit that is equal to what he'd get if the project is finished. Fair market value. You're with me?"

"You're making perfect sense. What you're saying is that for the buyer, it's at a much lower price because the labour and materials for the upgrade are now his responsibility. For the skilled handyman, it's a good deal."

"And for the vendor, a saving in time and effort." She smiled at him. Nice to talk to intelligent people who grasp things quickly. "Then there's the other situation: if the vendor desperately needs out of the project due to either time or money constraints – that's when, and only when, a canny buyer can pick up a bargain."

"Pretty big 'if,'" he said, not looking at her. Maddie was aware unspoken thoughts lurked beneath that gloomy exterior. She paused to see if he would explain, but he didn't.

She continued. "If a vendor has both time and enough money, unlike a prospective buyer, he won't see the project as a 'do-up'. His attitude will be only that the place needs a bit of care and attention before putting it on the market. All going smoothly, he'll renovate and ask a market price. What he hopes is that several buyers will be bidding for his property all at once."

"Yes," George said. "That's precisely the scenario we want to avoid." He was frowning, his eyes on the middle distance.

"You understand I'm not talking about the Fanshaw place, George. These are general principles." She didn't say they were, for her personally, purely theoretical.

"It always comes down to money," he said finishing the last drops from his mug. "Like most things." His words were tinged with bitterness.

"I know Douglas would welcome an offer at any time. There's nothing wrong with putting your toes in the water and seeing how he responds. Plus there's the 'bird in the hand' philosophy that can be quite compelling. Motivating, even."

"But you've spent quite a bit of time this morning telling me he has little motivation to sell now. We know he's organised an agreement at the bank for the renovations and he's not experiencing any pressures of time. At least as far as Tina knows."

Maddie was getting thoroughly bored with the way he kept bringing the conversation to his own situation. "Your interpretation only, George. Do remember I was speaking generally." She mentally slapped her hand; she was starting to preach.

"What's galling is that old Mrs Fanshaw had promised to sell us the house in exchange for the cottages plus cash."

That woke her up. "You were willing to sell the cottages? Where would you put your offices? The present arrangement is so perfect."

George flashed her a rueful smile. "That's why we didn't jump at the opportunity. I was dragging my feet. Trying to figure out what I could do – maybe re-open the track so my customers would drive up to the barns and a private road would lead them to my offices at the big house. But it's clumsy. The house is just too far away. And, of course, Tina now has her rose garden over part of the track."

"It could work, though. Where did you think of having your offices in the Manor? The study? The breakfast room plus dining room?" The more she thought about it, the more awkward the layout was for both business and living.

"Tina wouldn't hear of that. She wanted me to convert the outbuildings behind. But that's not nearly the sort of place I need."

Maddie nodded. Those tiny brick sheds? Totally impractical.

"I might as well build a fresh office block by the barns. Not got the readies for that." He sighed and Maddie was suspicious this was a significant family conflict. "Quite a problem balancing what we need for the business and for living. Buy the Manor in addition to the cottages? Most likely beyond where I can stretch. What we have right now suits me. Suits the business. Does not suit my dear wife." He smiled to take any sting out of his words.

Maddie nodded. She fully sympathised with Tina having to give up part of her lovely house. Poor George. Not a good place to find oneself. She decided now was the time to change the subject.

"Was Mrs Fanshaw senile, George?" Maddie asked.

"Annoyingly so," he said then shot her a look. "Oh, you're implying that nothing a senile old woman promised would hold up in court if there was a dispute. Like from her heir. Douglas."

That hadn't been what she was implying; she was merely asking another opinion about Beryl's senility. But sometimes information comes without seeking it.

"It could have been a tricky deal with two properties on the table seen through the obstructive gauze of senility," Maddie said. "Would you still contemplate an exchange? I hadn't heard about that idea before. Of course, the cottages are gorgeous ... and Tina knows Douglas."

"She didn't get to know him until after the old lady disappeared. Not that it will do her any good, at this point."

He pushed the flimsy chair back and stood, his eyes on the road winding its way through Goring.

Maddie stood as well.

He reached over the table to shake her hand. "Thank you for the time, Madeleine. I do see where you're coming from and I hope you understand my position, too." He smiled into her eyes. "And you think you're smack dab in the middle...."

Maddie walked back to the office knowing exactly what he meant by such a cryptic comment.

• • • ● • ● • • •

When Maddie arrived promptly at six that evening, the Anson's home was tidy, including the kitchen. But she was aware of cooking smells that persisted from their recent meal. She'd been afraid of that.

She dug into her handbag. "I've brought you a funny little gift for when potential buyers are expected." She produced a small vial. "Would you please turn on one of the rings on your cook-top for me, Mrs Anson? Only for half a minute or so, then turn it off again."

"I'm intrigued," she said as she followed the instructions.

Maddie placed a couple of drops onto the warmed surface. "Now smell. What does it remind you of?"

"My grandmother's kitchen. Delicious."

"It's a trick, of course." She grinned. "Vanilla. They won't smell your dinner nor anything else; they'll only smell the scent of recent home baking. You've heard of comfort food? A whiff of vanilla is a comfort scent, guaranteed to evoke lovely memories." Maddie put the little vial into Mrs Anson's hand. "Even if the smell is not identifiable, enough gets through to the brain subliminally to nudge the person's emotions into homely thoughts. And that's what we want when someone is looking through a house."

Mrs Anson tucked the vanilla into a cupboard. "Thank you," she said. "Now let me show you the rest of the place."

The house had the same kitchen as Louise's, the same exterior and the same orientation to the sun. The dining area was considerably longer and the living room was almost gracious in its proportions. Upstairs, the second bedroom was the same single as Louise's, the master the same but the extra bedroom stretched from front to back with windows at each end.

"It's quite an asset, this third bedroom," Maddie said. "Especially if potential buyers have already seen the two-bedroom version."

"We'd be staying if my husband hadn't the opportunity to head up his company's Birmingham office. We have to move; he won't consider such a huge commute."

They were coming down the stairs, again the same design found in the smaller version. Maddie regretted she hadn't time to borrow one of Kathleen Short's paintings.

• • • • • • • • • •

It had been a long day. Maddie was relaxing, glass of wine in hand, lounging in the dying sunshine that lit up the conservatory at the rear of Briar Cottage. She'd recently purchased an e-reader, and she found herself picking it up rather than a heavier book, especially when tired. A knock. The front door.

"Sorry to bother you," Douglas said, "but I hoped to catch you on my way home from Liverpool. Can I talk to you? Won't take a mo."

Glass of wine in hand, he told her what he'd been thinking when driving home. "I can't get away from the old picture I have of Aunt Beryl. Independent, wily, smart, totally unconcerned with what people thought of her ... that type. Somehow that woman I remember could so easily have grabbed her fortune and danced away from this old house. On her way for one last adventure."

"Fortune?" Maddie asked. "Not from the bank? We know she had little in her accounts."

He shrugged. "Jewellery? Hidden diamonds? Gold bars? I don't know. She may have hidden banknotes somewhere."

"The scenario is really enticing," Maddie said, meaning what she said. "I'd love to discover she was off having a good time."

"It's even more likely when you realise how alone she was. No relatives but me, no friends with the possible exception of Tina, other neighbours who didn't like her. Maybe she got sick of her life here."

"What should we do?"

"Talk seriously with Tina. Maybe Aunt Beryl swore her to secrecy. That's my first and only thought."

"Do you want to do it?" Maddie asked. "She likes you."

"I suppose. But ... I've a real problem with that. You see, Tina encouraged me to have her declared dead," he said. "Surely she wouldn't have done so if she'd known Aunt Beryl had merely run off."

"I could argue the opposite," Maddie said. "But let's follow it up. You or me?"

Douglas shrugged. "Me. I'll try anyway."

After seeing him out, Maddie washed the wine glasses. Staring out over the darkening back garden, she let herself imagine being in her eighties, no ties, wealthy most of her life and with a secret nest egg. What would she do? Stay in a village that openly disapproved of her? In a house needing thousands spent on it? Or take her money and live in luxury for her remaining days? No question. But where? Bermuda? Ibiza? The Greek Isles? The South of France?

The more she thought about it, the better she liked the idea. She rather fancied a hotel in the mountains of Switzerland with other retired folk, a choice of good food every night and a maid to make the bed.

As she drifted off to sleep, she changed the vision to a similar hotel on the southern coast of Italy. Or that best-exotic whatever hotel in India.

Chapter Fifteen

"Those are Beryl's," William blurted out. "My god. I'd never thought to see them again."

Maddie was showing him the long gowns and fur stole she'd found in Beryl Fanshaw's wardrobe, saying she'd planned on taking them to a retro shop in London next time she was there. They were sitting in the back garden of Briar Cottage watching the sheep chomp the grass in the field next door. William had popped in on his way back from grocery shopping in Goring.

Maddie looked at him curiously. "You recognise these dresses? I thought you said you didn't socialise with the Fanshaws."

He laughed but Maddie noticed he had flushed a little. "Complex story, my dear. And one I'm not all that happy about. I've only told you the start of it."

"I'm interested in anything that concerns Beryl, as you know," Maddie said. "I can't get hold of her character; I want to know if she's the type to wander off and get herself so lost she dies where nobody can find her old bones."

"She wasn't herself these past few years. All her redeeming characteristics seemed to fade. Then that old arrogance – I told you about that – came to the fore. Wandering off? Unlikely but maybe. Suicide? Never think that. Not Beryl. Murder, perhaps, but not suicide."

"People keep talking about murder—"

"Not her murder, my dear. What I meant was, she was a woman who was fully capable of knocking somebody off, doing someone in, if she felt it necessary. But not herself, not suicide. Never."

Maddie frowned. "It's a chaotic story. Confusing. First I thought she was this poor little old lady, a widow, living by herself in a mausoleum of a house." She paused at William's guffaw. "Okay. Not true. But then I heard she was a harridan, after that, senile and difficult. She only inhabited a few rooms, you know, in that huge house. Bedroom and bath upstairs, kitchen and sitting room downstairs. Maybe the breakfast room."

"I wouldn't know and, frankly, I don't care. She wasn't speaking to me. Not for many a year," William said. "Beryl doesn't do anything by halves. Didn't. I'm positive she's dead and gone; shouldn't speak of her as if she was going to return tomorrow. Hard to believe, actually." He sighed. "Damn woman was a big part of my life for many years. Too many years."

"Yes, your first love. You told me."

"First, yes, and last."

Maddie shot a glance at him. "Last? After your wife died?"

"I'm a divorcé, not a widower," he said shortly.

"Sorry, an assumption," she said, touching his shoulder.

"Long time ago now. Almost as long ago as when those dresses were last worn. Divorced in '76," he said. He turned to look out the window. His voice softened as he fingered the stole. "I do remember her wearing this mink wrap in '87. Unbelievable year for me. When my hopes were finally dashed. Or when I came to my senses. One of them, anyway." He grimaced.

"Thirty years and more since. Yes, a long time."

"Doesn't seem that long." He paused. "Did your husband ever indulge himself in an extra-marital affair?"

It was Maddie's turn to flush. "It ended our marriage."

"Yes, well, I can say the same. All my fault. Poor Viola. The only good thing is that she met and married her present husband only a year or so later. A good marriage, from all accounts."

"Ours is recent; we're still wrangling about who gets what," Maddie said. "To be truthful, I'd hate to see him marry that ... the other woman."

"It's easier when you're the injured party, my dear. You'll meet some dashing young man soon and forget all about that husband of yours."

"I wish."

• • • • ● • ● • • • •

After he left, she wondered about wishing she'd meet someone else. She reviewed all the single men she now knew. Both the boy Bart at the car repair place and William were outside of her interest because of age. Rupert was gay; Neil Black, whom she met once before he went to London for chemo was very ill, perhaps terminally. She was awkward with the attractive Douglas and he with her. Who else? George was married, as was the handsome Gabrio and Nathan, one of the other agents at work. Adrian the vet? Could she be at all attracted to him? He was interesting, intelligent, mildly good looking and presumably single. At least, he had no visible wife and never mentioned one. He was a good ten years older than she was, not really a problem. But could she imagine him naked? No way, because there was no spark there. Of all the men, if William was twenty-five years younger, maybe him. But she certainly didn't want to imagine him naked either. For sure. She dismissed the topic.

But the problem was Wayne. Wayne who stubbornly inhabited her mind. She hated this stupid obsession she'd developed over Chrystal claiming they'd known each other for five years. It was lurking there, day in day out, just under the surface. She couldn't help but recall some of the more tender moments she'd shared with Wayne over those very same five years, like when she'd wrenched her back so badly. She'd been bed-ridden for a week, totally dependent on his nursing. He'd stayed home, tenderly caring for her, overseeing her medications, helping her to the loo, washing the clothes, cooking all her favourites to tempt her appetite. That was four years ago. Within the five. She wrenched her mind away from the topic. It was driving her mad.

Maddie used the false energy generated by the thoughts of Chrystal and Wayne to attack the shrubs around the garage at the back. They did serve a purpose in hiding its peeling paintwork but also could provide cover for an intruder trying to get at the car inside. She owed it to William to protect his car.

She started with the foliage that actually touched the garage itself. Maybe she could give the external walls a coat of paint once she hacked back the jungle.

As she snipped, she contemplated William's relationship with Beryl. Obviously it was far more serious than he'd led her to believe. It seemed to have started ordinarily enough when two young people meet and fall in love. William certainly fell in love; who knows about the lovely Beryl? Then they broke up, as happens, and both moved on to marry other people: William to the pleasant sounding Viola and Beryl to the thoroughly unpleasant but presumably wealthy Freddy. What happened next? William remembered the long evening gowns from the mid-seventies (at a guess William would have been 40? 45?) and it was about that time he divorced Viola – or most likely, the other way around; Viola divorced the philandering William because he was having an affair with his first love. It's always a risk, that initial emotional involvement. Or, she thought with some bitterness, when a man meets a new young woman who reminds him of the first love.

Maddie trimmed the shrubs, clearing a shoulder's width passage between the garage wall and the bushes. Were they lilacs? The remains of flowers formed brown cones on the branches and she delighted in snipping them off leaving a tidy green bush. Once she'd finished the side facing the conservatory, she intended continuing the procedure along the back of the garage which faced the field, not that the view was visible through the tall shrubs along the fence line. Those particular shrubs were, she was almost sure, hydrangeas and they were flowering. She wanted to leave them to finish. Their massive heads of bright blue were a marvellous addition to the basic green of the back garden. She walked over to the field side and looked back to the bank of blue. What should she do? This gardening lark was full of complexities. Maybe she'd snip off some of the flowers to put in vases throughout her little cottage, taking each stalk back to where it came from a major branch, thus shortening the plant naturally. She could just picture these showy heads of blue in the sitting room, her bedroom, even the conservatory. And take a big bunch to William. Maybe some to Jenny's shop? And Rupert. Brighten the Goring office. And in doing so, she would be cutting back the tallest of the branches.

She thought back to William and what he'd told her. Significantly, his divorce in 1976 was not part of his worst year. That occurred eleven years later in 1987 when he was somewhere between 51, say, and 56. What happened that year? William said the last time he saw the stole was then and the subject they'd been talking about had been extra-marital affairs. Was he saying he had an on-going liaison with Beryl Fanshaw that spanned decades? Spanned his marriage, his divorce and well beyond? She smiled at the thought. If so, the younger William had been quite the lad.

Her smile faded as she thought of her promise to Douglas. She shouldn't have taken it on. He deserved better than a nosy Parker who was merely motivated by some latent curiosity. She put all her strength into cutting off a particularly big branch. It came away suddenly and fell with a crash with far more foliage than she'd expected.

What happened to you, Beryl? What did you do? Where did you go?

Maddie gathered all the trimmings and piled them behind the garage. They'd produce good kindling for the fire in the coming winter, given she was still living in Caroline's cottage then. She then took her secateurs to the hydrangea bush, gathering long stemmed huge flowers to distribute according to her grand plan.

She found several large vases that she suspected were bought for the purpose and loaded them with the profusion of blooms and put the rest into the laundry tub with their stems in water.

She changed from gardening clothes to jeans and a soft blue t-shirt. How on earth could she clear up the mystery of Beryl's disappearance? She'd like to discuss it all with Douglas. He was undoubtedly up in Liverpool yet again. If anybody knew how William despised Beryl – and the old men at the Catherine Wheel obviously did – William could easily be considered a suspect in Beryl's disappearance. Or murder. No matter how uncomfortable, it was food for thought.

She didn't want to irritate William about his relationship with Beryl but clearing up the mystery may do him good, if only in the eyes of his drinking mates. And, she reminded herself, it could only help pave the way towards a sale of the Manor. But she was mainly involved in the mystery because Douglas asked for her help. For his peace of mind. Except – another uncomfortable thought – he remained the only person to benefit from her death.

• • • • • • • • •

Although she had an appointment at six to show the Reynolds over the Anson's house, she wanted to distribute the hydrangeas while they were still in pristine condition. First stop was *Jenny's Kitchen*. The only person there was a young man, tall, with curly dark hair and, she felt, reminiscent of somebody she should know.

"Hello, Mrs Brooks," he said cheerfully as she pushed her way inside.

She smiled back. "Did we meet at the Gardeners Club?"

He grinned. "Sort of. I almost bowled you over at our front door. I'm Miguel Flores, usually called Mel." Yes, of course. A younger, taller Gabrio Flores, equally handsome. Mel held out his hand. So, another of the motorcycle gang. Even more clean-cut than the young Bart, the car painter, if that were possible.

Maddie gave him the large bunch of hydrangeas. "From my garden. I have tons and I thought Jenny might be able to use them here. Have you a vase for the counter top?"

"I do. Mum will love them," he said, taking the flowers from her.

"Are you minding the shop?" Maddie asked.

"Always on a Wednesday morning," Mel said. "I have a regular seminar Wednesday afternoons so I work for Mum in the mornings."

"Seminar? Are you studying?"

"Balliol up in Oxford. Classics," the young man said. "In my second year."

Maddie hid her astonishment. She'd have to rethink who dressed in black leathers and roared away on motorbikes.

"Good on you," Maddie said quickly. "I was at University College, part of the University of London. I loved my student years."

Mel fetched a vase and plunked the flowers in with no attempt at artistry. Maddie hid her amusement.

"And I'll have a couple of your mum's cream buns," Maddie said.

Her next stop was William's, laden with gifts. He greeted her with enthusiasm, although she got the distinct impression he was mostly responding to the prospect of cream buns and a hot cup of tea, not the hydrangeas.

Once settled in his sitting room and she saw that William had taken a big bite of cream bun, Maddie said, "I was trying to figure out what you were telling me on Sunday, about you and Beryl. Did you mean to say you'd had a long relationship with her? It broke up your marriage but it didn't break up hers? Is that what you were saying?" She was acutely aware she was pushing the boundaries of their friendship and unconsciously she was holding her breath.

William sat back in his chair looking at her. Was he wrestling with what he would tell her and what he'd leave out? His scrutiny seemed to last forever. Then he leaned forward. He stopped chewing and swallowed his mouthful.

"Yes," he said simply. He sighed. "We told each other we wanted to be together; we'd married the wrong people, all those lies. I sort of let Viola find out about Beryl and me and, as I'd known she would, she did the predictable thing. Not long afterwards, I was divorced but Beryl wasn't." He took another bite and slowly chewed it. Maddie suspected he didn't taste anything. She stayed quiet, somewhat embarrassed she'd pushed him into this sort of detail but she certainly didn't want to stop him now.

"And she stayed married?" she asked. "Not only then but for the next ten years or so of your relationship?" She was only stating what she understood.

"The most exciting yet frustrating decade of my life," William said. "The thrill of meeting on the sly, the constant desire that was only ever partially extinguished ... heady stuff. On the other hand, there was always one reason or another why she couldn't leave Freddy. The timing was always wrong. Of course with twenty-twenty hindsight, she was never going to leave Freddy and the lifestyle she had with him. Then, by the time he'd lost his money and things became tough, she wanted me. Trouble was, it was too late." His voice was glacial. "Emotionally, I was spent."

"So not the Charles and Camilla happy ending," Maddie said.

"I watched them with considerable interest," he said. "They had the disadvantage of negative publicity but the advantage of money."

"And, in spite of Diana's popularity, the support of family," she said. "Surely that was an enormous help."

William's shoulders drooped. "You know, it's difficult to talk about Beryl. She was complex and she twisted my guts; I went from ecstasy to despair, dependent upon her mood. To be truthful, it's a relief she's gone," he said. "I've lived a very long time avoiding her whenever I could yet I certainly have felt a freedom this past year or so I hadn't felt before. At least not since the day I met her the second time. I rue that day."

Knowing this story depressed Maddie. It only put him more squarely in the running as a suspect in Beryl's murder. If she was murdered. If William was capable of such a thing.

That was his saving grace.

• • • • ● • ● • • •

The Reynolds arrived at the office in good time for Maddie to drive them all in William's large and comfortable car to the Anson property. She had her mental fingers crossed the place would be as neat and tidy as the inspection, with the addition of smelling like freshly baked biscuits. As they walked up the front path, Mrs Reynolds pointed out to her husband the front façade was identical to the de Mille house. That seemed to be a positive.

"But a bit wider," Mr Reynolds said. "I can see an extra set of windows top and bottom." Maddie noticed his voice held warmth. Her heart beat a fraction faster.

"We really liked the place you showed us on Saturday," Mrs Reynolds said. "We thought it such a pity about its size."

Maddie unlocked the front door and pushed it open, standing so the couple could see the identical staircase and the longer sitting room. She sniffed the air surreptitiously. Did she smell a faint whiff of vanilla? At least no cooking odours.

"This is where the flower painting was," Mrs Reynolds noted, "but even without it, this place has the same homely atmosphere."

"The painting in the other house is from a gallery out from Henley," Maddie said. "The de Milles borrowed it because it set off their sitting room so beautifully. It's for sale, along with masses of exceptional paintings done by Kathleen Short." She reproved herself; she needed to concentrate on selling the house, not the paintings. Yet she'd love someone to buy a painting because of their arrangement. "You'll notice much of this house is similar to the other house, with some considerable improvements," she told them. "Please have a look around and you can tell me what you think."

From her position at the base of the stairs, she could catch scraps of conversation between husband and wife as they explored upstairs. Mrs Reynolds tended to point out the features she liked in both houses; Mr Reynolds was exclaiming over the differences, most of which sounded positive. Probably, Maddie thought, *she* had wanted the other place and *he* had made the objections.

"We're interested," Mr Reynolds said as they came down the stairs, "but I want to check out the garden first."

Maddie opened the back door onto a wooden deck. "The family has a vegetable plot at the back," Maddie pointed out. "If veggie gardening is not your thing, you can eat up the produce this year then turn it into a flower garden next year, or return the area to lawn." She felt pleased she was thinking of off-the-cuff possibilities and putting a positive slant on it all.

"I love fresh vegetables," Mrs Reynolds said as her husband explored the small garden.

"If you're interested, a Gardeners Club provides free advice here in the village," Maddie said. She went on to tell her about how friendly it was and how people shared their extra produce. "I know you'd be inundated with people wanting to shepherd you along. I joined mainly to meet others in the area and it was excellent for that. And now I'm out in the garden whenever I can."

"Meeting others in the village? I'd love that part of it."

Maddie mentally thanked Rupert for pushing her into joining local activities. Payoff already if it tipped the balance on a house sale.

Mr Reynolds asked Maddie if the vendors would be amenable to an offer lower than their asking price. Her heart rate took another leap up. This was the first time anybody had sounded serious about buying in her whole, albeit short, estate agent career. She told herself to dampen down her enthusiasm and pretend it was all merely routine.

"So far, I've found the vendors to be reasonable people," Maddie said. "I know they'd welcome an offer."

By the time she'd written down all the ins and outs of the Reynolds' offer back at the office, she was very glad she'd taken the time to snack on some cheese and crackers before meeting them.

After ushering them out, she searched for and found the agent who had originally listed the Anson townhouse – he was still at the office.

"They must have liked it," Nathan Levi said with a wide smile. It was already after eight but the summertime sun was still high in the sky.

"They did indeed," Maddie said. "And here's the proof." She waved her notebook in front of her. They had agreed, given Maddie's inexperience, that Nathan would do the negotiations for the Ansons and Maddie for the Reynolds.

Maddie described the offer, not perhaps the best one could hope for, but not ridiculously far off. Nathan immediately rang Mr Anson who suggested he hang on while he did fresh calculations. Eventually, he suggested a counter-offer which Nathan thought was appropriate. He came off the phone with a smile.

"Most of the time I was listening to Mrs Anson wittering on about how they loved it here, how the house had suited them and her fears they wouldn't be able to replace it with another they loved so much." He laughed. "Getting the jitters now the end might be in sight. Mr Anson is seeing it as a straight business deal. Easier to deal with, but she might push up the selling price."

Maddie looked at her watch. "It's too late to present the counter-offer to the buyers tonight, but I'll ring them first thing and arrange to discuss it with them further."

By the time she flopped into bed, she was beat. It had been a very long day. But she didn't drop off immediately – too much excitement. She was on the verge of making her very first commission as an estate agent. Actually earning money at what still felt like a game.

Chapter Sixteen

M R REYNOLDS LOOKED AT the counter offer and nodded. "It's fairly close, don't you think, Mrs Brooks?"

She nodded. "I think so. If you make what we could describe as a final offer midway between the two, you just might get it."

Mrs Reynolds nodded at her husband's figures. Her eyes shone. "Fingers crossed," she said.

Maddie rang Nathan with the offer. He said he'd get back to her. A terribly long anxiety-filled ten minutes later, he rang to say they had a deal.

"Congratulations," Maddie said to the waiting Reynolds. "You're about to be the proud new owners of the house you want."

Mrs Reynolds screeched and turned to her husband to give him a kiss. She whirled towards Maddie and hugged her. "Thank you so very much," she said. "I can't believe it! We have it!"

Maddie left on a high. She was probably as excited as Mrs Reynolds. The first money she'd earned as an estate agent. What a relief!

She rang William with the news. "How about we celebrate with cream buns? I want to show you the next bits of what I've been doing in the back garden, as well. Half an hour at my place?"

• • • • • • • • •

William parked the garage's garishly painted loan-car in the short drive outside of the garage at Briar Cottage.

Maddie opened the back door for him. "In here, so you can see properly what I've done to open up the view from the conservatory," she said. She sat him in the chair with the best outlook of the field and its woolly inhabitants, framed by far trees and hills beyond.

"Very nice. Good job realising you had a view behind all that foliage," he said as he reached for one of Jenny's cream buns. Although the sun wasn't shining, the woolly coats of the sheep pleasantly contrasted with the summertime green of the grass they were chomping. "But we're both going to put on weight with all these treats."

"I have something to celebrate, my first sale," Maddie said, pouring his tea. She liked using the old teapot she'd found in one of the kitchen cupboards. It was white with bright red, blue and yellow embossed fruit on the side, with a red lid. Very fifties.

"To your continued success," he said, raising his teacup.

As soon as they'd demolished most of their respective buns, Maddie took a deep breath. "Beryl," she said.

William rolled his eyes. "You have a bee in your bonnet, Madeleine Brooks."

"I know," she said, "but I have good commercial reasons for finding out what happened. If I can do that, I can put the subject to bed and it won't rear its ugly head during any sale negotiations and that will help Douglas." True enough but also she was feeling an unspoken spur she couldn't put her finger on, an intuition that something was very wrong. She'd experienced this sort of gut reaction in her previous career.

William sighed. "Douglas? It was probably him wot done 'er in."

Maddie stifled an impulse to giggle. "Her character ... were you implying she was two-faced?"

"More than two," he said as he fiddled with his teacup, turning it this way and that in the saucer. "She was one of those people whose face was always put on, manufactured, if you will, for either the circumstances or the people she was with."

Maddie nodded. She'd long been familiar with that type of disordered personality. 'Slippery' is how she designated them. And never, ever, to be trusted.

Poor, poor William having been entangled emotionally with a character like Beryl.

"It took me many years to figure it out. Once I did, it was so obvious, I kicked myself," he said. "With me, she was charming, seductive, giving ... but, in retrospect she always managed to get her own way. If I wanted the relationship to continue – in the latter years she used the threat of breaking up as a weapon – I complied with whatever she wanted. With someone she didn't like, for instance Jenny from the bakery, she was cold and downright rude."

"How did you extricate yourself, William?" Maddie busied herself putting the empty plates in a pile so she didn't have to look at him.

"Partly it was because I met another woman. A good woman."

"You devil." Maddie glanced at him and grinned.

He shrugged. "Mary Beth was American and my nickname for her was 'Witchy'. She was a herbalist. You wouldn't believe the concoctions she'd make from the garden and local hedgerows – potions, creams, vials of this and that. Tinctures and herbal teas. She was a large woman, full of life and enthusiasms." William's face was soft as he described her. "She wore gypsy-like clothes, layers of vibrant colours. She couldn't have been further from Beryl if she tried. Beryl hated her, of course. But she would have hated her even if I wasn't involved, simply because Mary Beth flouted society's values."

"What happened?" Maddie asked.

"She died. When they autopsied her – sudden death of a supposedly healthy woman, I gather it's routine to do an autopsy – she was riddled with cancer. The coroner decided she'd been taking her own medicines and took too much of something toxic. Accidental death."

"Accidentally took an overdose? Not suicide?"

"Supposedly for the cancer", he said. "She'd beaten it years before but it came back with a vengeance. We only had four years."

"But you weren't married?"

"She had a husband somewhere. We didn't care. It suited us. I was distraught at her passing. I missed her terribly."

Maddie narrowed her eyes. "But she wasn't your first and last love."

He shot her a look. "Too sharp for your own good, young lady. Yes, I said that about Beryl. Mary Beth was not my ultimate love. I loved her for herself and her good nature and all the things she was that Beryl wasn't. But my heart? A chunk was still fascinated with Beryl even though I no longer held any illusions. I knew I couldn't be anywhere near her. I'm afraid I was using Mary Beth in some ways. Using her to get over Beryl."

"Tsk tsk," Maddie said lightly. William had experienced far too much tragedy in his life.

"We didn't speak of love. But we did speak of how much we enjoyed each other's company," he said. "She was a great gal, as her fellow Americans would say."

"She knew Beryl?"

"Everybody knew Beryl. Yes, Mary Beth knew her and was made fully aware that she was *persona non grata*."

"I suppose Beryl's unpleasant characteristics became even more exaggerated as she became more senile."

He looked at her again with a frown on his forehead. "She wasn't."

"Not senile? But I thought you said—"

"Just one of her roles. She had dozens. Senility served a purpose. It worked. In the last few years, she would go into the bakery and help herself to some delicious concoction or other and, laughing, waltz right back outside again without paying. If Jenny ran after her, Beryl would place whatever she hadn't eaten into Jenny's hands, sticky side down if she could, laugh some more and walk away, saying she'd 'forgotten her purse' as if she had memory problems. After a while, Jenny stopped running after her. Her son did, though, every time." He rolled his eyes and shook his head. "People started making excuses for Beryl, even those who disliked her. Jenny was positive Beryl wasn't senile. But since everybody else thought she was, Beryl got away with it. Just part of her persecution of Jenny."

"Why, for heaven's sake? Jenny is well respected in the village. I can imagine Beryl disliking your new lady friend – after all, Mary Beth was her replacement, but Jenny?"

"I really don't know but I can guess why she took so strongly against Jenny. Pure prejudice. Beryl's thinking was simplistic. A foreigner can't help being foreign but for a nice young lady to marry a foreigner and not only that, move him into the village as if he belonged here? She hated foreigners; blamed them for all the social ills in the country."

"Do you think she maybe just skedaddled off with a hidden fortune and is now ensconced in some hotel for genteel old ladies? Living the life of Riley?"

William snorted.

• • • • • • • • • • •

Later, as Maddie headed into Goring, she went over and over their conversation. Beryl, according to William, would have shown a different face to every person she met. But it was worth a telephone call to Jenny, at least, to see what her take on Beryl was.

"Could I tell you about Beryl Fanshaw? Have you hours to spare?" Jenny's voice was light. "If you really want to know what I think, how about you swing by the bakery about four or so one afternoon? We're usually quite quiet by then."

"Today?"

"See you then."

• • • • ● • ● • • •

Jenny served her coffee and a cream bun ("I know you love them.") and refused payment. "I invited you, remember? Besides you're the best free advertiser I've had in a long time. The village has re-discovered my cream buns since you raved about them at the Gardeners Club. There's nothing better than word of mouth."

"Simply telling the truth," Maddie said, after she finished her first delicious bite of bun.

"You're curious about Beryl?" Jenny said as she settled in the other seat at the little table.

"I figure we need to know what happened," Maddie explained. "It's the sort of thing that can rise like a crocodile from a swamp right in the middle of negotiations. If this sort of thing is not settled well beforehand, Douglas Fanshaw could lose money on the sale. Besides, I'm plain curious about her."

"Ask away," Jenny said. "I'll give you a thoroughly personal take on the woman."

"I'm trying to get my head around who Beryl Fanshaw was," Maddie said. "I've been talking to William. He knew her well."

Jenny looked up and grinned. "Very well, I gather," she said. "But to most of us, she was a thoroughly nasty woman who only got nastier as she aged. She did what she wanted, when she wanted to whoever was currently in her sights."

"You, I gather, in the latter part of her life."

"Me in particular. I was her secretary for a while and she knew my hot buttons. She pushed them whenever she could."

"Secretary?" Maddie asked. "Why would a woman like Beryl Fanshaw need a secretary?"

"She was writing a modern day manners-for-young-women. Pretty awful stuff. Preachy. Never published, of course. That was about the time old Freddy started going off the rails. In retrospect, maybe she thought she could make some cash in a genteel way."

"Did you have a grand falling out?" Maddie didn't want to mention William's theory about the significance of Gabrio's immigrant status.

"Not particularly. She developed writer's block, or so she claimed. I think she merely ran out of things to say. About then I had the opportunity to go on a European camping holiday with some girlfriends. Met Gabrio in Italy, not Spain. I worked for her ladyship for about a month after I got back tidying up what we'd originally produced and sending the manuscript off to publisher after publisher. Then for the next six months or so, I cut my hours down to one day a week for publishers' letters, that sort of thing. I hadn't wanted to leave her in the lurch but I was already working at the bakery in Wallingford, loving it and learning heaps. That's where I first made cream buns." She smiled at Maddie.

Maddie grinned back. "I bet you've twiddled the recipe since then."

"I still use the same amount of flour," Jenny retorted. "They're a good bunch over there. A bit of an antidote to crabby old Beryl."

"No book contract, I gather."

"The closest was a kind editor who treated what Beryl had sent her almost as if it was a long synopsis. She made some helpful and salient points about the next re-write. To no avail, of course, so eventually I quit." Jenny gave a deep sigh. "Beryl blamed her lack of success on me. I should have anticipated it. She was never wrong; someone else was always responsible; she thought of herself as the ultimate victim."

"Boring," Maddie said.

"Totally," Jenny replied.

They sipped their teas in easy silence.

"Were you around when William had his American girlfriend?" Maddie asked.

"Of course. I've always lived in this village. He told you about her, did he?"

"Mary Beth. A bit of a tragedy for him, poor William. Finally meets an interesting woman and she ups and dies on him. An overdose of one of her concoctions, I gather," Maddie said.

"So the coroner said," Jenny added. "The underlying problem was the cancer. Metastases throughout her innards, poor thing."

"William wasn't going to have her around for long."

"I suppose not," Jenny said. "But you know villagers. They had it that Beryl murdered her by poison." She finished her cup of tea. "Flummoxed the coroner because Mary Beth was such a bohemian. And always fiddling about with dangerous substances. William said she knew what she was doing, would never have taken a wrong dose; so the accidental overdose was all hogwash. The village believed him over the coroner. As far as the village is concerned, Mary Beth's death is an unsolved murder. Long time ago now, of course."

"Could Beryl have taken off with some secret funds? Living on a beach somewhere?"

Maddie was half expecting the same sort of snort she got from William but Jenny considered the idea carefully.

"Not beyond her," she said. "But I think it would have taken too much work. She was lazy, that woman. She always manipulated others to do her will. She'd have inveigled someone else to do all the arrangements, then thumbed her nose at us all as she left."

• • • • • • • • •

The next morning Maddie dropped into the Manor. The day was cloudy bright, a day that promised heat later. The fields were browning off from lack of water. What they needed was a good storm.

As soon as she stopped the motor of William's big Rover on the now weed-free pea gravel in front of the Manor, she heard construction sounds. She followed the noises around the house to the utility room and found Gabrio and Douglas ripping up the floorboards with gay abandon and great good humour.

"Hi there," called Gabrio when she came into view.

"This was obviously an add-on, probably eighty or ninety years ago," Douglas said when he saw who it was. "We'll probably have the new floor in and ready for the vinyl tomorrow."

"Vinyl's certainly practical," Maddie said. "but hardly in period." She kicked herself. Here Douglas was being friendly and appropriate and she was being a damp squib. Then it hit her. They're doing work on the Manor.

"Er...has something changed since we last talked?" she asked Douglas.

"The will's been ratified," he said, beaming. "Heard last night when I picked up my mail. And the bank has okayed the first part of the funding I asked for."

"Congratulations," Maddie said with genuine enthusiasm and held out her hand.

He grabbed it, shook it vigorously then hugged her.

A hug? So un-Douglas. She hoped her blush wouldn't show.

"You think period features are important in a utility room?" Douglas asked. "What do you think, Gabe?"

"Me? Easy to clean is best, no matter which house, no matter which era it was first built in. Certainly no floorboards without a damp-proof course again. That's why the wood became rotten in the first place. Tile it? That would work."

Douglas shook his head. "Twice the price at least. I'll get a vinyl that looks good. Trust me, okay?"

Gabrio grinned and Maddie inwardly shrugged. His money.

The old storage cupboards and bench top lay strewn in pieces around the yard, obviously discarded.

"Are you replacing the storage space?" Maddie asked, adjusting her hair and regaining her cool.

"Flat pack cupboards with a modern melamine bench top," Douglas said. "New paint and it will look totally utilitarian, clean and easy to maintain." He was obviously in his element, using his muscles, working in easy companionship with Gabrio. What a difference to his demeanour with his money worries resolved, at least temporarily.

But why wasn't Douglas at work? Maybe he had some sort of odd schedule? When the time was right, she'd ask him. Also tell him more about Aunt Beryl in light of the new information she'd been gathering lately. Maybe their little investigation would now be redundant. She did need to talk to him and she did want to tell him the latest, anyway. But there was no opportunity with the two men so involved in the utility room floor. It could wait.

She drove into Goring with her mind full of her own work. She had telephone calls to make to follow up on the de Mille Open Day. She needed to talk to Nathan Levi about the Anson sale and to ask him what she needed to do next.

Plenty to keep life interesting.

Chapter Seventeen

MADDIE METHODICALLY CONTACTED THE list of potential clients she'd created at the de Mille Open Day. One by one, they eliminated themselves as potential buyers until two were left. One couple requested a second viewing and the other said they were comparison viewing other two-bedroom homes but they were still interested in the de Mille property.

She was hot and cranky. When she stopped for lunch, she felt as if she'd been working every minute of an eight hour day already. She thought back to her Probation Service days. It was always the office work she hated; when she left both her job and her career, she cheered the freedom from paperwork. Of course that wasn't the whole story.

Not long before she left, Maddie had applied for the supervisor's job but, to her intense disappointment, she did not make the short list and someone young and ambitious was appointed. The new appointee, Maddie's direct boss, put more and more paperwork Maddie's way. Her excuse was that Maddie was far more experienced in coping with paperwork than the younger staff. Maddie figured the new woman saw her as a threat. She was making life difficult so Maddie would quit, thus providing a vacancy she could fill with a younger and cheaper version, ready to be moulded to her requirements.

Maddie had been embittered by it, given her sensitivity after Wayne had replaced her with a younger woman. But not cheaper, apparently. She'd heard from daughter Jade that Wayne complained about Chrystal's spendthrift habits. Serves him right.

In the afternoon, Maddie the estate agent was definitely going stir-crazy in her cramped and hot little office space. She headed out, ostensibly to check on her car.

Bart met her with good news.

"The lettering wasn't through to bare metal," he said, "allowing us to fill in the scratches and repaint. Quite a saving there."

"Excellent," Maddie said brightly to match his enthusiasm. "When will it be ready?" It was hard to maintain such gusto in this heat.

"The final coat is drying now. Say, late tomorrow? Five-ish?"

In spite of herself, Maddie was buoyed up with the good news about the car. And again young Bart seemed fine; she couldn't see him capable of the vandalism. Still, she was not buoyed up enough to handle more paperwork. She decided to see how Douglas and Gabrio were doing, guiltily aware she was merely skiving off. Maybe she could have a word with Douglas about the Beryl investigation. But first, she needed to tell him the charity shop people were coming around. Good excuse to drop in at the Manor.

• • • • • • • • • •

The utility room's new flooring was ready to be fitted. Maddie squeezed herself past a tall roll of light coloured vinyl leaning in the doorway. It was patterned to look like a stone-paved floor; fairly innocuous all in all. From rotten floorboards to the definitely modern under-flooring had been a quick operation.

"Impressive looking so far," Maddie said. "What's next, this vinyl?" So she hadn't convinced him to use tiles. His house, she reminded herself, and losing a battle for the utility room flooring was not going to be significant. Hopefully.

"We'll fit the cupboards first," Gabrio said, pointing to a stack of shallow boxes.

"Do you fancy me giving you a hand with anything non-technical?" Maddie thought of the awaiting paperwork for a millisecond and dismissed the thought.

"Boxes, Gabe?" Douglas asked.

"Good idea."

"Point me in the right direction," Maddie said.

"Open up each of those boxes," Gabrio said, indicating a stack off to one side. "You'll need my knife. If you do that for us, we can get right into assembling the flat pack cupboards without forever stopping."

Having a paperwork day meant Maddie had worn summer slacks and casual shoes. She started on the job with enthusiasm. She chatted about the horrors of paperwork and how she was avoiding it.

Douglas agreed. "One of the least fulfilling aspects of my job, too," he said. He had fetched the next piece of pre-cut flooring and was laying it flat.

"What do you do?" Maddie asked as she concentrated on removing the copious tape that bound the flat pack boxes shut. She was glad Douglas couldn't see the curiosity that must show in her eyes.

"Civil engineering," Douglas said. "General consulting now. I worked for the city of Liverpool for years, made redundant there which sparked off ... well ... long story short, my marriage hit the skids, then this whole situation here happened. So I left and here I am."

Aha. Question answered. Sort of.

"You're up there a lot. Liverpool, I mean."

He sighed. "Did you leave your husband?"

She shot a glance at his face. "Yes. For good reasons."

"Well, maybe you know then. I left Sonia and she didn't want me to go. But I had to do it. I was smothered, the kids too. They escaped to university and I ... I escaped by calling quits on the marriage. The double blow of kids leaving then me too." He took a deep breath. "It crushed Sonia. She's not a competent person. She's, well, a dependent person, needs taking care of, that sort of thing. So when things get on top of her in the house or the garden, I'm asked. Still. Definitely playing on my guilts."

"I did leave Wayne, but it was his infidelity that drove me away," Maddie confessed. She didn't want Douglas to misunderstand. His situation was nothing like hers. Wayne coming miles and miles to help with a household problem? Ha bloody ha.

"Oh, I see," Douglas said. "Of course, you're the opposite of incompetent. Or dependent." He slowly smiled at her and she felt once more that whisper of interest on his part.

"You're having fun with Gabrio instead of looking for a new job, is that it?" Maddie said with a quick change of subject.

Douglas widened his grin. "If Gabrio needed a mature apprentice, I'd be first in the queue."

"But then I'd have to pay you," Gabrio said. "Not much, mind you, but still something."

Maddie popped the last of the tape on the first box so the lid could be raised easily; she tackled the second box. Working with this more relaxed Douglas was almost enjoyable.

"I've been hearing all sorts of gossip about your Aunt Beryl," she said to him to let him know she was making good on her promise. And letting him decide whether or not to talk to her about his aunt in front of Gabrio. "Sounds as if she was quite a complex character."

"I hardly knew her," he said, glancing at Gabrio as he manoeuvred the edge of the large board into place. "As I told you, my mother couldn't stand her. But Aunt Beryl liked small boys so she'd bring me little presents – like a nifty jack knife Mum immediately confiscated. Fuel on my mother's fire, of course."

"Not senile back then, but at the end?" Maddie asked.

Gabrio snorted. "As senile as you or me," he muttered.

Douglas looked at him. "But people around here say she was," he said.

"Cunning as a gambler with an ace up his sleeve, if you ask me," Gabrio said as he screwed in the edge of the board. "Not that you are asking me."

Douglas met Maddie's eyes.

"Of course we're asking you," Douglas said. "Maddie and I are newcomers here and you're a local. As I've told Maddie, I'd love to discover what happened to her."

"Can't help you with that," Gabrio said coldly, "except to say I wouldn't be surprised if someone did her in, she was that irritating to everyone. Hell, if she'd bothered Jenny one more time I'd have cheerfully murdered her myself. Do you know she once started a rumour ... oh, god, I could tell such stories about that ... that cow. Sorry, Douglas."

"I had nothing against her, ever. But I bet loads of people think I still have the biggest motive to do her in," Douglas said easily, "except for the fact that I had no idea I would inherit. Masses of nerve-racking things were happening at the time of her disappearance. I was in the middle of a divorce with all the stress that brings; I was living in a horrid little flat in Liverpool; suffering as friends took sides, especially when they sided with my ex; riddled with guilt that I was unfair to my wife; I was busy handing my job to consultants who were about to make much more money than I ever did, and, frankly, my life was upside down and going nowhere."

Maddie was amazed at this more relaxed version of her client. She wanted to encourage it, and, frankly, would like to know him better.

"Still working full time?" she asked. With another pop, she freed the second box of the thick tape binding it shut.

"Working crazy hours, actually. Two kids at university who took the marriage break up hard. Needing to find somewhere else to live. Frankly, I didn't give dear Aunt Beryl a thought. Hadn't for years."

• • • ● • ● • • •

Maddie couldn't avoid the mounting paperwork forever, so reluctantly took her leave.

As Douglas opened the massive front door for her, she asked, "Our investigation ... are you okay with Aunt Beryl's disappearance now?"

"Hell, no," he said. "You're actually finding out things I need to know. I've got to be able to sleep nights as I get stuck into making changes to the Manor. For heaven's sake, I'm setting up to sell her place. It might be different if I was merely moving in, then I'd have all the time in the world to find out what happened to her. But I must sell. And how can I sell with this big question mark in my head?" He patted the solid stone surround of the front door.

"Okay. We forge ahead, then." She smiled at him. "We'll figure it out. I've got the nosiness and you've got the drive. Right?"

"Pardners," he said in a fake American accent. He held his hand out for a 'high five' and walked her towards William's car.

"What's this? New wheels?"

"Hardly new," she said and found herself explaining about the scratched message and borrowing William's car. He frowned. "I can't imagine anyone giving you that message," he said. "Maybe it was meant for someone else."

"I'm a newcomer here. It was obviously aimed only at a newcomer," Maddie said. "I would love to think it was all a horrible mistake, but who else could it be meant for? My car and my circumstances fit." She shrugged her shoulders, but inside she was nowhere near so nonchalant about it.

"Gosh, I almost forgot. I've something to tell you. I might have a clue. I think it's important, or could be. I've told the police, but they're dismissive. Still, it might change our ideas about Aunt Beryl."

"What clue?" Maddie was interested. Very interested.

"I found a shoe yesterday. It has to be hers. In the drain by the old potting shed. It had been there for some time, covered in leaves and debris. But I couldn't find its mate. Come with me and I'll show you where I found it," he said, striding towards the corner of the house. Maddie followed.

The drain was a simple trap to take water from the courtyard into some sort of hidden culvert. It had been cleaned recently.

"One shoe," she said. "You're thinking Beryl didn't lose it voluntarily."

"Unlikely."

Douglas opened the door to the former potting shed.

"Here," he said taking a shoe off one of the dust-covered shelves. "I don't have any reason to keep it, but can't throw it out in case it's significant. Look, it's not overly worn and it still has polish on it." He turned it over, handing it to Maddie.

"So I see," she said. "Did the police test it for fingerprints?"

"I think they did. I certainly gave them the shoe as soon as I found it, but I'd wiped the leather clean of the dirt and leaves without giving it a thought. Until afterwards."

"Let's compare it with the others." She took him to the bag of shoes she'd readied for the charity shop people. "We're lucky they haven't collected them yet."

The shoe was obviously distorted by the same elderly foot that deformed the other left shoes.

"It's hers all right," Maddie said. "And I agree, we can take it as a given she did not wander off wearing one shoe."

"The police argued that it was old and decrepit and thus discarded. But just look at this lot. Plenty far more worn and not thrown out."

She fingered the soft leather. "Good quality, once upon a time."

"See, you notice things. You're sure to find out about Beryl."

She smiled up at him. Nice to get a compliment.

After reminding Douglas about the charity shop people coming that morning, she took the shoe and walked back to her car. She'd look after it. For some reason, she felt she wanted to keep it at Briar Cottage. Just in case someone ... she dismissed the thought. Even if someone had kidnapped Beryl and noticed one shoe was missing, surely they would have come straight back to collect it, not wait a couple of years later. No, whoever kidnapped Beryl – and she was reluctantly having to reconsider Beryl had not left on her own accord – hadn't noticed the missing shoe. That bode ill. Kidnapped and killed? She shook her head. Enough of this. She had money to earn.

But the conversation at the Manor bounced around her brain.

The will was going to be straight-forward; what a weight off his shoulders. And Douglas was also recently out of a marriage. Interesting. Two kids at university and losing his home, half his savings and his job at the same time? Food for thought. Including the plain fact that Aunt Beryl's inheritance was mightily convenient.

At the office, Maddie found a message from George Higgins. Could she please help them formulate an offer she could present to Douglas?

She called him back immediately. "Would you like me to pop over?" she asked. "Best if both of you are there so we, the three of us, can discuss it."

"I'm free about five or so this afternoon," George said, "and Tina is here."

• • • ● • ● • • • •

Maddie left the car in front of the Manor and walked down the shady lane to the cottages. Fresh air to clear her thoughts. Right on five o'clock, she rang the bell for the private part of the house.

"Come right in," Tina said with a welcoming smile. "George will be along shortly."

She ushered Maddie into the sitting room which still betrayed the fact it had started life as two rooms. The floor was hardwood rather than the original brick but the inglenook fireplace dated back to the cottages' origins, no doubt. The place was furnished in white, which contrasted beautifully with the terra cotta coloured wattle and daub walls interspersed with twisted dark wood beams. Cream and the palest yellow roses, certainly from the bank in the back garden, spilled out from a bowl on the coffee table. What a house to sell. The presentation was perfect.

Maddie made all the right noises about the décor, the walls, fireplace and roses. Tina told her about the local tennis club, their tournaments, their trials with grass and hard surfacing. How wonderful the 'girls' were. Changes to racquets. Whether it's best to breakfast before or after exercise. Maddie, never a sportswoman, stifled her yawns.

"I can guess interior design is a particular interest of yours," Maddie said in an attempt to steer the conversation into some topic they both had some interest.

"It is," she said. "I've done what you see here." The room they were in was sensitively presented to enhance the old yet portray modern elegance and warmth. "It didn't start like this, I can tell you. I even did the painting in this room myself." She twinkled at Maddie. "When you're young and penniless...." She pointed out the curtains. "The first lot of these came from my own sewing machine. Those days are well past, aren't they?"

Maddie nodded, although she'd never owned a sewing machine. "Of course," she said with sudden insight, "you've such a flair for interior decorating, no wonder you're interested in the Manor. You'd love to do it up yourself."

Tina nodded with a broad smile. "You understand. I knew you would. I did offer my services or at least my advice to Douglas," she said with a charming shrug, "but I think he needs to know we're serious buyers before he'll listen."

"I gather you've wanted to buy the Manor for ages," Maddie said, consciously imitating the casually elegant way Tina was sitting. Too bad her legs weren't as long.

"I've always known it would be mine one day." Tina said it as a flat statement even though softened by another genial smile.

Still, Maddie was a little taken aback at such an assertion, but maybe, just maybe, it meant the Higgins would be willing to pay a decent price if they bought it straight away. "George said you were promised first refusal from old Mrs Fanshaw," she said. "That was a long time ago?"

Tina looked over Maddie's shoulder, perhaps anxious that George wasn't here for the discussion. Maddie decided it was only fair to keep the topic neutral until he arrived. She hoped he was coming soon. She and Tina had not many conversational areas in common.

"Well before she left, yes," Tina said. She glanced at her watch and sighed, her mouth a pout. "That dear husband of mine. No sense of time." She smiled woman-to-woman.

"Did you talk price with her back then?" Maddie asked, loath to suffering more talk about tennis.

"Not specific numbers, no," Tina said, again with that glance towards the end cottage where George had his office. "But we'd bought land and other buildings from the Fanshaws over the years. Buying the Manor is nothing extraordinary. Simply us gaining the last bit of Cherry Tree Farm."

"I understand," Maddie said. "But it's a shame no numbers were mentioned. It would have given you an indication where to start."

"Start?" Tina looked disconcerted. She flicked her eyes again to her watch, to the other part of the house. She became restless. Where was George?

"Negotiations," Maddie said with an inward sigh. This topic was still uncomfortably close to where she wanted to be after George arrived. She needed both Tina and George to be present. Where was the cursed man? Tina glanced at her watch, something Maddie kept herself from doing. No use two of them showing anxiety. Or anger. Tina had developed bright spots of colour in her cheeks. Probably annoyance.

"Sherry?" Tina asked. "Or I have some cold white wine in the fridge...."

"The wine sounds wonderful, knowing your wine cellar from the barbecue," Maddie said, as much to get away from Tina's distress as wanting a glass of wine.

As it turned out, the wine was both fruity and crisp, perfectly suited to a late afternoon.

"I'm curious, Tina," Maddie said after enthusing about the wine, "were you friends with Beryl Fanshaw?"

"Oh yes, great friends," she said, having achieved a bit of control with the downing of her glass of sherry. "She didn't have many, you see. Friends, I mean. I was important to her."

"Was she senile at the end? I've heard it from several people. Others disagree. But you obviously knew her best."

"Sadly, yes, she was in decline. That's why she wandered off. If only she had wandered along here." Tina sighed and Maddie shifted in her chair. Tina acting as if this topic was awkward for her. Was it such an awkward topic?

Noises behind her signalled George's apologetic arrival. He came in like a benevolent whirlwind and immediately pushed aside the rose bowl so he could spread out several papers on the coffee table.

"We've done some homework." He was all business. He produced a dossier of large country houses, listing the particulars such as size, distance from railway or motorway access and shopping areas, condition, upkeep and modernisation. Plus prices.

"I figure we can knock down any price shown here by a decent percentage because of the work needing to be done," he said.

"You're showing good thinking, George," Maddie said, wanting to start with something positive. "This is what estate agents do when they're pricing a property. But you must remember that usually a gap exists between the asking prices and final prices paid. Estate agents use *actual* selling prices for a valuation."

"I was aware of that, of course, but here I intend on covering that sort of variation." He glanced at Tina who was sitting biting a lock of her hair, staring at him. "At least my estimates are probably high rather than too low."

"All a bit dry for you, Tina?" Maddie asked in an attempt to bring her into the discussion. She smiled at the other woman.

"Not really," Tina said, playing with her glass. "I merely want everything to be done and dusted. I want in there so I can do what I'm good at – I will transform dreary old Cherry Tree Manor into Cherry Tree House, a modern version of its former glory."

Maddie dutifully laughed at what sounded suspiciously like estate agency-speak although she could see Tina meant every word.

George had several suggestions ('sweeteners', he called them): an early settlement date, no need to carry on with the repairs although he'd welcome the list they were undoubtedly working from. And willingness to negotiate. He also wanted to acknowledge the newish roof, the modern wiring and the new plumbing put in over the past twenty years or so.

"Douglas told you about those things?" Maddie asked.

"Told *me*, not him," Tina said, spreading one hand over the skin of her décolletage. "We're great friends." Woman-to-woman again and Maddie got the message. She noted Tina was 'great friends' with owners past and present of the house she knew she'd own one day.

Maddie mentally slapped her hand and told herself to stop being cynical. But she had noticed George had clenched his jaw. So all wasn't well there.

Maddie walked to her car with a carefully constructed range of prices. She should have already done her own research. Now she'd need advice from Rupert, Nathan and anybody else at *Green Acres* with expertise, compare real prices with George's spreadsheet, then get back to George and Tina with either good or bad news about their expectations. Apart from that, she would have to consult with Douglas first before conveying any indication of a price range.

• • • • ● • ● • • •

Friday. She could pick up her car at five. She rang William with the news.

"Would you like to come to dinner tonight?" she asked him. "Chauffeured, of course."

"What are you cooking?"

"Don't trust me, do you?"

"You're not going to serve up Beryl, are you?"

"William. As if I'd ruin a home-cooked roast meal with boring Beryl."

"Roast? Beryl or no Beryl, I'll be there. Which roast – pork? – lamb? – beef?"

"Pick one. I'm off to Goring today and I'll pop into the butchers when I'm there."

"Pork, please. With crackling."

Maddie arranged to return William's Rover, and drive them both in the loan-car to the car painters to return it and pick up her own. They'd then head back to Briar Cottage where their roast meal would be cooking in a slow oven.

"And I'll deliver you home afterwards," she promised.

Friday was a busy day at the Goring office. Rupert was out of the office all day; Nathan was closing a deal and couldn't spare any time. Little Samantha on the front desk (aged twenty but looked fifteen) was the only one there and she was never any use, unless the topic involved fingernails or hair colour.

Maddie started the job by downloading the details of as many large country home sales as she could find and entering the details into her own spreadsheet. Eventually twenty-seven large houses were in her new database. And it was complete with sale prices and other little details.

By the time she shut the computer down, she felt cross-eyed with fatigue. She had to get home to start cooking the roast. The roast! She'd not bought the silly thing yet. She flew to the butcher down the road, picked out a decent sized pork shoulder covered with loads of fatty skin to be turned into crackling and headed home. As soon as the joint was in the oven, she stepped into a reviving shower.

After seeing her car was back to new as if the rude message had never been scratched into the paintwork, then swapping the cars, Maddie and William were back at Briar Cottage.

The roast was tender and juicy; the crackling crunchy and melt-in-the-mouth; the potatoes crisp and the broccoli and carrots provided needed colour and fresh taste. The bottle of Aussie Shiraz was perfect with the pork. As an aficionado, she tended to serve it with everything.

"I've been thinking about your car, Maddie," William said as he dabbed at his lips with the paper napkin. "I know you thought those boys might be responsible, but—"

"No longer," Maddie said. "Bart simply doesn't have the temperament and the Flores boy is reading classics at Oxford and wouldn't make that silly spelling mistake. Besides, he doesn't seem the type either. I haven't tracked the third boy down yet, but with friends like Bart and Mel, he, also, is unlikely to be the culprit."

"I totally agree with you," William said. "They're good lads." He paused. "You've annoyed someone, Maddie, and it's not one of these young men."

"I know," she said. The obsessing about Beryl had taken her mind away from the unanswered question of who would be motivated enough to scratch that rude message into her car's paintwork. A bit of denial, perhaps? She concentrated on what William was suggesting. "My life can be divided neatly into two broad categories. Life in Briar Cottage and life beforehand," she said, thinking of Wayne and Chrystal.

"Much too broad, my dear. We can eliminate the before. Nobody from your former life would bother finding your car parked in an out-of-the-way spot to deface it. We need to think about who might have been there that evening and seen your car in the Cherry Tree Farm carpark then exacted revenge."

Maddie winced. Revenge? For what, for heaven's sake? "Wait." She held up a forefinger. "Someone could have seen me come along the farm track from one direction and leave in the opposite direction. I was abandoning my car or I'd have gone back the same way."

"That just tells someone you've left your car there." He tipped his glass to have the last of his wine. "How many people were still at the party when you left?"

Maddie shrugged. "A dozen or so – the people I'd been talking to earlier were leaving about the same time as I was."

"Who were they again?"

"The judge and his wife, Adrian the vet, Jenny and Gabrio, a couple called Wendy and—"

"Roger Simpson," William said at her pause. "Good man. Honey producer north of here. I know them from the Gardeners Club."

"That's part of the problem, William," she said not checking the strain in her voice. "We met so many at the Gardeners Club last Tuesday. They'd know me but I wouldn't know them."

"Not relevant," William said. "You can't annoy people you've merely been introduced to. It's only people you've interacted with – exchanged views with or, I don't know, stumbled over somehow."

"Trod on some toes without knowing I'd done so?" she asked. It made sense even though it irritated her to think she'd done something inadvertently.

William nodded. "But it has to have been something a little more serious than forgetting to compliment the newly picked lettuces."

"I still can't think of anything negative that happened either at the Gardeners Club or the barbecue. That only leaves work and I think things are reasonably sweet there." She closed her eyes to think. "I haven't mentioned politics, religion or even the weather in casual conversation."

William smiled and rose to his feet. "Home, James. My old bones like to get into bed early these days."

· · · · • · • · • · ·

After dropping William back, Maddie carefully locked up her car in the garage. She was in the habit of so-doing when she had the responsibility of William's Rover and she decided to continue the precautions now her own car was back. As she entered the back door of the cottage, she thought about what William had said. What toes could she possibly have trampled on?

Her hunt for the real Beryl hadn't started by the day of the barbecue, had it? No, definitely not. So eliminate her nosiness about Beryl. Adrian? But their conversation was wide ranging and she knew he merely saw her as an attractive female and she'd been flattered. An idea popped into her head. Jealousy. Was there a woman at the barbecue who fancied Adrian? The more she thought about it, the more enthusiastic she became. Jealousy. It would explain a lot. She and Adrian had spent at least half the evening talking together, more if you counted the time they were both in the same conversational group before dinner. And besides, they were mildly flirtatious with each other.

Maddie went to bed that night determined to discover if she was right. Jealousy. It must be.

Chapter Eighteen

As soon as Maddie reached the office, she rang Douglas about sorting through the wide range of prices of similar properties to the Manor spread across their part of England. "I can give you a broad – very broad – band of prices that may be applicable. Maybe it's better to see my spreadsheet?"

On the other end of the line Douglas sighed. "This is coming up now because of the Higgins?"

"You've guessed it," she said.

"Look, I'm deep into something I've got to clear up in Liverpool. Just let me know if they're willing to put their money where their ... you've got the picture. Then and only then we can go into it. Okay?"

"I hear you," she said. She also heard his impatience. Of course he was right. Too many decisions to make about what to do about the Manor, unless the Higgins made a don't-look-a-gift-horse-in-the-mouth type of offer. Fat chance of that.

She was pleased she'd made her call to Douglas straight away because Tina rang to ask if she could meet to discuss the offer they wanted her to present to him.

"I've been knocked out of the tennis round robin and I'm free. I'm hoping you work weekends," she said.

"I do, Tina," Maddie said. "Weekends are when things happen for estate agents. Can you come in straight away?" She was starting to get used to working weekends, probably the most likely time to make a sale. She reminded herself to mix pleasure with work during the week. She did not make the move away from London and her friends to become stressed.

Tina arrived without George (off to meet a client in Bristol) and the two women discussed both the database George had assembled and Maddie's new one, and Tina's thoughts about how much Douglas would be willing to accept and what Maddie thought reasonable. Tina and George would have to sell Cherry Tree Cottages, ("George is doing well but not *that* well"), which would mean a fresh listing for *Green Acres*, a possibility Tina dangled with a smile. Maddie still wondered where the business offices would go but she kept those thoughts to herself. Their problem.

Tina thought the bank would provide a bridging loan in the meantime. But she made one thing clear. George was only interested if he could pick up the Manor at a bargain. Nothing would change his mind on that. "I'll do my best to influence him in the right direction," she promised, rolling her eyes.

Using the two spreadsheets, they came to a figure Maddie hoped Douglas would, at least, consider, even though very much on the low side. She would have to sit down with Douglas to figure out potential profits to know if selling 'as is' could be acceptable. At the offer price, she doubted it.

Tina went off to confirm with George – she'd ring Maddie after she'd contacted him. In spite of Tina's ladies-who-play-tennis appearance, Maddie was impressed. Tina had a head on her shoulders. She was proving to be a business-like person with whom to work, affable, intelligent and calm.

Meanwhile Maddie had made an appointment with the de Milles to show their property again to the couple who wanted a second viewing. She met them at the Goring office at eleven that Saturday morning.

The Campbells, Fiona and Clive, were a professional-looking couple of about thirty who chatted easily on the drive to the de Mille house. Fiona worked in Hammersmith at a big publishing house and she thought the commute by train was do-able. Clive was in IT, working often in London where he'd also commute by train, but at times business took him to Manchester, Birmingham, Glasgow and other places further north. They wanted to live in a village; they liked that the train station was handy with good parking in Goring and the M40 was easily reachable for when Clive drove north.

Maddie mentally put a check by 'location'. The de Mille place met their size criteria. They had sold a cramped little one-bed flat in London for a sizable sum, a flat without a balcony to snatch a breath of fresh air (if London air could ever be called 'fresh'). They loved the green fields they were seeing out the windows of the car and the fleeting glimpses of local sights like a thatched roof here or a grand set of gates to an estate there. Once they were in the de Mille house, Maddie left them to it. She heard happy sounds from various rooms. Today, she could distinctly smell vanilla so she opened the kitchen window to help dissipate it. Louise had been a little heavy-handed.

The most interesting part of the viewing – and this was when Maddie really started to hope she was reading the signals correctly – was when Clive stood at the back door and painted a picture with words and wild gesticulations of a professional couple's ideal back garden. He'd put in a two-level deck near the house with a covered spot for the gas barbecue on the upper level and a solar heated spa pool on the lower, an easy-care stone covered garden with hardy shrubs for privacy, an awning for sunshade in the summer, a big round wooden table and chairs, sun lounges and various other bits and pieces. His eyes were shining as he spoke and Maddie could see that Fiona was right there with him in this after-work fantasy. What the de Mille's had in the space was a piece of scrappy lawn complete with sandpit and a little swing set suitable for very young children.

Maddie closed her eyes and crossed her fingers.

The three of them sat in the *Coffee Clique* with pencils and notebooks. Clive and Fiona had a pretty good idea of the market value of other similar houses.

"I'd like to make a fairly low offer," Clive said. "Gives us room to negotiate."

An offer! Maddie kept her voice steady. "Too low and the vendors get cranky," she said. "I'd suggest you figure out between yourselves what you would willingly spend, given there was, say, another buyer who was trying to push you up. Pretend you were going to lose this house. Would you regret losing it because you hadn't been prepared to spend that little bit more? Discuss it and I'll go back to the office and do some paperwork for, say, fifteen minutes? Then I'll pop out and see how you're doing. If it's earlier, come and find me."

Once back at her desk Maddie was far too keyed up to be effective and she was quite relieved when fourteen minutes had gone by and she could return to the Campbells.

"Okay, this is what we think," Clive said. "We've decided on our maximum but that's not where we want to be. We have some work to do on this house and we'd prefer doing it now rather than waiting to put more money aside."

"Fair enough," Maddie said.

"Okay, we have a figure. With a bit of luck they'll take it." He passed his notebook to Maddie.

"We're acutely aware of keeping it all civilised," Fiona added while Maddie copied the offer into her own notebook. "The last thing we want is for them to harden their bargaining because we've pissed them off." She smiled. "I was going to say 'annoyed', but 'pissed off' is more evocative," she said with a grin.

Maddie smiled her agreement. She'd smile at any comment at this point. "Don't worry. I would never allow that to happen." She tidied away her notebook. "I'll let you know as soon as possible. Keep your mobiles on and I'll either ring or text you the reaction," she said. "But be prepared for a counter offer. They'll most likely want something more than this."

As soon as she bade goodbye to the Campbells, her phone rang. Tina. George had berated her for thinking she could negotiate without him ('Damn misogynist' and Maddie knew it would be accompanied with a roll of her eyes). He refused to agree to the figure they had discussed. Tina was full of apologies for causing Maddie unnecessary work, but the offer was to be reduced.

"I'll present the new figure," Maddie said. "But it's almost insulting, as you know. Your friendship with him would have to be so incredibly strong that his business sense deserts him completely. I'm afraid the reality is, he'll only crumple it up and toss it into the fire."

"I'm confident our friendship is quite strong. Fingers crossed his reaction is more positive than the picture you're drawing," she said with her characteristic tinkle that stood for her laugh. "Do present it, please, Madeleine. I'd appreciate it."

Maddie came off the phone certain that that couple were arguing about more than the price on a house, grand though it was. She would present the new figures to Douglas, but she had no illusions. And neither, she was sure, did Tina.

Maddie rang the de Milles to tell them she was bringing an offer for their contemplation. Could she see them as soon as possible? "It's always best catching a potential buyer while they're really hot about your property."

"We're off to my mother's for dinner," Louise de Mille said in some despair. "Can you please tell us what they've said and we can meet first thing tomorrow? The two of us can talk it over in the car, maybe even discuss it with my parents. Damn, tomorrow is Sunday..."

"Of course I can meet you tomorrow. When?"

"Nine am? The baby will be down for his morning nap then and I can have Mum look after Melissa for a couple of hours."

Maddie relayed the offer and rang off. Life interferes at times.

She then rang the Campbells to say nothing had happened yet, and wouldn't until sometime tomorrow. They sounded relieved and set off for a dinner out with friends they'd almost had to cancel.

As she put the phone down, it rang immediately. Jade.

"Hello, darling, how are you?" Maddie said delighted her daughter had rung.

"Not got much time, Mum. Just wanted to tell you I have the gen on why Chrystal was telling everybody she'd known Dad for five years."

Maddie clutched the phone tightly. Such a stupid thing, but it was worrying her. Eating away at her peace of mind. "And?" she asked.

"Stupid woman was talking about the first time she met you guys," Jade said. "You remember the time when Olivia was seeing the Creep?" Maddie remembered. The Creep was covered in tattoos and reeked of beer and who-knows what else. It didn't last long but worried both Wayne and Maddie considerably. "She held a party when he was offered that job in Siberia, remember? She spent half of it crying because she couldn't go with him. Chrystal was at that party. She met both of you but I don't expect you to remember. Dad doesn't because I asked him."

"Oh," Maddie said. So trivial. A silly young woman making something out of nothing.

"By the way, Dad says 'hi'," Jade said.

"Next time you see him say 'hi' back, okay, darling? And tell him things are going swimmingly out here." She knew he thought she'd buried herself in the countryside away from real life.

Maddie rang off stupidly relieved. How had she allowed such a silly little thing to affect her?

She took a deep breath and renewed her juggling act by throwing yet another ball into the air. She rang

Douglas to say she'd had a preliminary offer from the Higgins.

"I'm on my way out," he said. "How about joining me for a drink and you can formally present their offer in congenial circumstances? The *Catherine Wheel* in Goring? You know it? In an hour?"

Tired as she was, the prospect of a civilised drink in the old pub was enticing. Saturday evening drinkies? The more she thought about it, the more she felt a pleasurable anticipation.

At home she changed from her work-uniform of summer frock and matching jacket to her white trouser suit with the pink and orange top. She renewed her makeup and headed out to meet Douglas, the offer in her handbag.

Douglas was seated in a corner nook. As she came in he stood to fetch her a drink.

"White wine," she said automatically, thinking she'd been enjoying whites lately. "Thanks."

She settled herself on the bench behind the small table and got out the Higgins' offer. She placed it so he could read it when he returned.

Douglas gave Maddie her drink and glanced down at the paperwork without speaking. He pushed it to one side and raised his pint for a toast. "To selling the old pile."

"Amen," she said as they clinked glasses. She sipped at the wine; she'd made a mistake. After that white at the Higgins', anything else tasted second rate. George and Tina knew their wines and were not afraid to spend a bob or two on them.

"I'm so glad we're getting on better," she said candidly. She hoped this was an appropriate time to bring up their rocky start.

He smiled and clinked glasses again. "Tina – before she got to know you, of course – thought you were too new at the game and ready to persuade me to do inappropriate things for a quick sale. She's been a good friend so when she warned me to keep my distance, I did so for quite a while. She didn't know you then, of course. She thinks you're cool now, I should add."

"Her facts were quite correct," Maddie said, suddenly awkward. "I was new – still am – and I would like you to have as quick a sale as possible, which is why I'm doing my best to help it along, but that doesn't mean it's not to the benefit of the vendor. You. That's my primary aim – to get the best possible price for you."

"Like this one?" Douglas tapped the paper in front of him. "Come on, Maddie. This is rubbish. I can't believe Tina had anything to do with it. Must be ol' Georgie-baby," he said with a crooked smile. "Is he serious?"

"I thought you might react like this," she said, meeting his eyes and avoiding any discussion about who was responsible. "But I'm learning that an offer on the table is a huge step forward from no offer, no matter how inappropriate it appears." Maddie couldn't help being disappointed he didn't want to discuss it, no matter his initial reaction, but she couldn't blame him. It was a ridiculously low offer.

"I suppose," he said. "I'll give it some thought sometime, but not now." He took a deep draught of his beer. "This is nice, isn't it?" He looked around the pub. "I had meant to spend some time with you at the Higgins' barbecue but you were busy with someone else."

"Adrian, the vet," Maddie said cheerfully. "An interesting man. Well read. I kept an eye out for you, too, but didn't see you until the end of the party, of course."

"Too many people there."

"Think of how many steaks George provided." And so the conversation went. This way and that, his questioning her about her children; her interest in his two; mutual problems when dividing up property with ex-spouses.

Someone waved from the bar. Maddie half raised her hand in reply, just in case it was for her or Douglas. Two people approached. Sebastian the judge and Simone.

"Join you?"

"Of course," Douglas said, shuffling along the bench seat.

Maddie, realising they hadn't met, made the introductions.

"You're Beryl Fanshaw's relative," Simone said to Douglas as she sat beside him.

"Grandnephew, technically, of her husband Freddy. Always called her 'Aunt Beryl' though."

"We were discussing her disappearance just the other day, weren't we, dear," Simone said to Maddie. "So sad," she said turning to Douglas. "Do you know anything we don't?"

"Wish I did."

Maddie seized the opportunity to change the slant of the discussion. "Did either of you notice a change in her behaviour in the last year or so of her life?"

"Oh, you mean the senility," Simone said. She turned to Douglas. "You don't mind us talking about it?"

"I'd rather hear it all, actually. I've been able to glean very little so far," he said.

As if given permission, Simone spoke to Maddie. "Yes, her behaviour definitely changed after Freddy died. She was out and about more, interacting more with village people and less socially. I don't think we've actually been in the house since Freddy died."

Maddie leaned forward so as not to miss a word. So, Sebastian and Simone had been in the Fanshaw's social set.

"But she seemed to irritate all and sundry," Simone continued. "I suppose it was early Alzheimer's. Maybe. But I actually think it had more to do with losing Freddy and the downturn in her financial situation. And, of course, Jenny's success was like a knife in her heart."

"Jenny?" Maddie asked. "Jenny Flores?"

"She was like an adopted daughter to her. She never had children of her own. Sort of half adopted Jenny from a young age. Sent her to a good school. Employed her afterwards when she was writing that book."

"Jenny mentioned it," Maddie said.

Douglas stared at her. Had she forgotten to tell him that part?

"She felt Jenny was ungrateful," Simone said. "Felt she should be treated better after all she'd done for her."

"Water under the bridge," the judge said, gathering up his empty glass and his wife's. "Thanks for letting us join you, but we'll be getting on now."

Maddie noticed Simone was about to protest, but she stood up with a smile and made her goodbyes.

"Senility or a bit of retribution?" Maddie asked after waving them off. She told Douglas about the cream bun episodes and the history of Jenny's career as a secretary as had been told to her. "But she didn't mention that Beryl had mothered her in some way. Or that Beryl had paid for her schooling."

"Yes, but nobody owns their children, whether adopted or biological."

Suddenly it was after eight and Maddie was hungry. "I'd better be off," she said. "Thank you for inviting me. I haven't had a drink out in ages."

"I'm going to grab their Saturday night special. A pub meal to end all pub meals," he said. "Join me?"

Maddie was vaguely aware that a drink out was one thing but a meal out was another. "I'd love to, but...," she said, "I'm in the middle of negotiations and have to be up and at 'em early tomorrow."

She drove home for a frustrating evening where she could think of nothing else but whether she'd made the right decision to end the evening when she did. Damn. She was out of practice at this sort of thing. Besides, he was probably only being polite. And, she reminded herself, he was a client. Better to keep things professional.

She also worried about whether she'd advised the Campbells correctly and how she would handle the de Mille's expectations. She figured she was more anxious about the deal than either of the couples. She was having an attack of confidence. Pure collywobbles. Still, she was very glad she'd taken time out for a social drink with Douglas. A social drink not a work drink.

Chapter Nineteen

MADDIE ARRIVED AT THE de Mille house in good time but with some trepidation. The night before, Louise had not been excited about the offer.

Maddie knocked on the door and was ushered to the dining room table, passing through the sitting room which was again festooned with baby gear. Louise would be caught on the hop if someone wanted to view their house without much warning. But, mercifully, the little reigning lord and master was safely asleep upstairs. Maddie's heartbeat had risen in anticipation of the difficulties of shepherding these two couples into a mutually acceptable agreement. She told herself that estate deals were made every minute of the day in the UK, and this was only one of them. But she couldn't get away from the fact that she felt very much on her own.

"We think it's a bit too low," Louisa said once the three of them were seated around the table. It was stuffy in the little house and Maddie felt she could hardly breathe. "We've looked at other houses like ours – two bedrooms on a nice estate – and ours is in the middle range."

"I do agree," Maddie said. "It's being marketed at the right point to elicit a sale. The asking price is where it should be."

"You agree, then? This offer is at the lower end of things?" Antoine de Mille asked.

"There is an important factor we haven't discussed," Maddie said. She was pleased her voice was as steady as she wished it to be. "Most vendors don't get their asking price unless something unusual happens like a bidding war between two determined buyers. A vendor's dream, of course, but very rare."

"Do you think it's low?" Louise wasn't going to be diverted.

Put on the spot, Maddie bent to the circumstances. "I think the buyers are putting a shivering little toe in the water. This is their opening bid. It will be up to us to find a level they can afford and you can live with."

She hauled out of her case a list of two-bed houses and what they were sold for. "If we all agree your house is priced in the middle bracket, let's see what the middle bracket of two-bed houses actually sold for over the past few months." She gave them the figures and Antoine immediately calculated an average price.

He turned to Louise. "If we ended up getting this mid-point, it would be okay, wouldn't it?"

Louise stared at the figure. "I was hoping for a bit more," she said so softly Maddie had to strain to hear. But her mouth was firm and she wasn't talking to Maddie but to Antoine. "I told you, Antoine. I need more. And that's that."

Maddie glanced at the figure Antoine had produced. "Let's work backwards. We'll put a couple of thousand onto this figure..." She looked at Louise who had eyes only for her husband.

"I need to talk to you," she said. "Excuse us, Madeleine, won't you?"

The two went upstairs and Maddie was left trying not to listen. Louise wanted more; Antoine wanted a sale. Never able to be completely out of earshot in such a small place, Maddie was uncomfortably aware of their arguing. It was a long ten minutes before they came back downstairs.

Louise named a figure, considerably higher than Antoine's suggestion. Maddie looked at Antoine for confirmation. He nodded glumly.

"Well," Maddie continued, "we'll say this is the aim, not that it's in any way guaranteed, you understand." She watched Louise without staring at her.

"Then what?" Antoine asked.

"Then we calculate the last bargaining flourish which could well be 'let's split the difference'."

They set to devising a plan.

• • • • ● • ● • • •

"They're still way high," Clive Campbell said when Maddie presented the de Mille's new price.

"You remain keen on this house?" Maddie asked. "You're willing to take another step up?"

"Maybe a couple of thousand," Fiona said. "We don't want to look too eager."

Maddie sat back. They were in the little conference room set aside for the estate agents' use in the Goring offices. "You're definitely not looking too eager with that first offer. It was on the edge of being too low. Now you have to make an offer that says you are serious buyers. A good offer means all it will take is some final tweaking." She leaned forward again. "Are you with me here? They have to know the negotiations are in the stage of fine tuning now."

"So a chunk that takes us close to the price we're willing to pay but not quite there," Clive said.

Maddie had to remind herself to breathe. "That would be my advice." She hoped her memory of this type of negotiation was accurate. She really wished she'd retained more of her course.

In the midst of her musings, her telephone rang. Douglas. Maddie excused herself to answer it, leaving the couple to sort out what that offer should be.

"Hi there," Maddie said. "What's up?"

"Any chance you could come by the Manor? I have something to show you."

"I'm in Goring in a meeting right now. Later? Or is it urgent?"

"Not urgent. But I've found something that's curious, something you'll want to see."

She looked through the glass walls of the office to see Clive and Fiona in earnest discussion. Probably best to leave them at it for a bit. She waved and pointed to her own desk. They nodded and smiled and turned to each other again. Yes, all going well. She crossed her fingers.

"I'll come as soon as I can," she said to Douglas.

While waiting for the Campbells, she was too keyed up to work. But she pretended to do so by bringing up her database of large country houses. She needed to absorb the implications of price variation but this was definitely not the time.

The Higgins' offer; it was a beginning. Significantly advanced from no offer at all.

Douglas's call; what did he want to show her? Had Tina taken the offer directly to him? She wouldn't be surprised. Tina Higgins was an unknown quantity. Maddie felt she still couldn't predict her behaviour. Nor George's, for that matter.

Maddie sensed rather than saw the Campbells waving through the glass walls of the conference room and she hastened over.

"I wish we knew what we were doing," Fiona said with a wry smile. "But we've chosen a new offer using what knowledge we have."

"What little knowledge we have," Clive said. He passed his notebook to Maddie. It was higher than she'd dared hope.

"Sensible offer," she said. "Yes, I'll get this to the de Milles straight away."

She didn't trust the de Milles, Louise in particular, to see how good this offer was. That meant she needed to be there in person. She thought she'd go to the Manor to see what Douglas wanted to show her, then ring the de

Milles Sunday afternoon. She had to take into account parental reluctance to shift their kids' schedules.

No. Better not wait. She would ring immediately.

The de Mille's phone rang and rang necessitating a voice-mail request to return the call.

"I'll get back to you once I've heard something," she promised the Campbells. She headed towards the Manor to discover what Douglas was so anxious to show her.

• • • • ● • ● • • •

The weather was closing in. Dark clouds had moved across the sky while she'd been with the Campbells, and the temperature had dropped several degrees. They were in for a storm, she hoped, a break in the drought-like conditions they'd been experiencing. Never in her life had she been so aware of weather. Since leaving London she'd felt closer to the earth, more mindful of the unpredictable elements that make up the British climate.

She parked in front of the Manor, the drive and front gardens looking well kept. The wind had picked up so she ran to the front door, opened by Douglas before she could knock.

"That was quicker than I expected," Douglas said. Maddie was still surprised at this new friendliness of his. Had he been holding back because Tina had suggested she wasn't ideal for the job? She had another thought. Maybe he'd only been feeling uncomfortable in working with a woman on a one-to-one basis in his newly divorced state. She followed him through the hallway into the kitchen to the window that looked out over the yard at the back. The sink had been removed; in fact, the kitchen was a bare space with the terrazzo bench propped on one side.

"I don't know if you can see it now," Douglas said. "It's difficult enough in bright sunshine, but this morning I spotted it immediately."

"What am I looking for?" Maddie asked.

"I'd like you to describe what you see. I mean in detail. I don't want to put ideas into your head."

Maddie gave him a swift glance then concentrated on the view from the window. "Erm...the courtyard, two outbuildings, one probably older than the other. The newer one used to be a hen house and the old one a potting shed." She glanced at Douglas to see how she was doing.

"That's right," he said. "Go on."

"Okay, I see both are made of brick and the yard is cobbled in old brick as well. You've sprayed out the weeds and you've put a fresh coat of paint on the hen house trim."

"Well done. You're getting warmer."

She peered at the old potting shed. "Is there something odd about the white trim on the other shed? I can't quite see...."

"Bingo!" he said. "Someone has painted it relatively recently, but with poor preparation. I'd already painted the hen house and it looked so good, I decided to sand back the potting shed trim too and paint it to match."

Maddie peered at the trim. "Something pink? Is that what you want me to see?"

He nodded. "Straight away I came across some pinkish blotches. Then I collected my paint and brush from the utility room – from a distance I could see...what do you see?

Maddie squinted. "The pink? They're not random blotches, are they? Letters. Not graffiti? Another rude message?"

Another one.

"'Fraid so."

"Beryl too. What is going on?" She squinted again out the window. "What does this one say?"

"You can see it best from the utility room door." They braved the wind to stand outside it.

"Offensive, as you see," Douglas said, "but the message brings to mind yours, don't you think?"

The message, now able to be discerned, read, 'Freddy drank himself to death cuz your a bitch wife.'

In spite of herself, she was excited about his discovery. "You're right. It has the same misspelling as mine. 'Your' instead of 'you're' and this one has 'cuz' instead of 'because'. This could be the third instance; first was probably the amateurish job of repairing a broken window which I think could have been due to vandalism. Old ladies don't break windows and they don't repair them either except by getting somebody in. Not Gabrio. The repair was amateurish. Then my car. Obvious vandalism. Now this. Three."

"Wrong chronological order, but yes," Douglas said. "And the same misspelling? Important, I agree." He shepherded her inside out of the wind. "We're talking about one vandal, even if we ignore the broken window."

Gabrio yelped as the wind re-distributed all the bits of sawdust and other detritus he had piled near the door.

Douglas shut the door on the weather and, gazing at the wind-blown debris littering the new subfloor awaiting the laying of the new vinyl, called out, "Sorry, mate."

Someone called from the kitchen.

"Probably the electrician. He's prowling around somewhere seeing what's to be done," Douglas said, walking out of the utility room, "or Tina, of course."

Tina? Maddie froze. Not about their offer? Should she follow Douglas to protect him from having to handle Tina directly? She stepped along the corridor.

"I said I was looking at it." Douglas's voice had raised from the murmurs earlier.

Maddie took another step closer.

"Can't discuss it with you, Tina. You know that. Talk to Madeleine Brooks. That's her job."

Maddie paused. Douglas was handling it fine, and not admitting that Maddie was at this moment here at the Manor. Maddie turned back to the utility room and grabbed the dustpan and brush to help clean up the mess they'd made.

"Chuck it into my pail," Gabrio said. "Otherwise, if someone opens the door again, it will happen again."

Maddie did as she was told.

They paused. Voices could still be heard.

"But you can't have a bench top of wood, Douglas, dear. Too, too rustic. It must be granite. Or marble, but granite is much more trendy. Throw out this tatty piece of old terrazzo and do it properly, for heaven's sake. If you ignore everything else I recommend, at least listen to me on this one."

Gabrio met Maddie's eyes and winked. "She's one determined lady," he said. "Now the bank has okayed the repairs, she's over here every day. Twice, sometimes. She had a fit about the vinyl floor in here. Wanted real stone." He opened up a big pot of dark gloop and spooned out a glob onto the freshly swept floor. Glue for the offensive vinyl, presumably. "I told her this 'Manor' is coming up a respectable two hundred years old, not eight hundred. It is not medieval and never has been."

Maddie smiled. Tina already lived in a medieval set of cottages which far outdated the Manor. She'd shown real talent in their restoration but she couldn't replicate what she'd done there; the eras were totally different.

"Do you know who started calling it the 'Manor' rather than 'Cherry Tree House'?" Maddie asked, fascinated by Gabrio's rhythmic strokes which left patterns of wavy lines in the glue. At the same time her ears were tuned to the kitchen down the hallway.

"No idea, but it fits with old Mrs Fanshaw's delusions of grandeur, don't you think?"

"I suppose that's why she didn't sell, even though she was so hard up... this house was her last vestige of opulence." Maddie was leaning against the new bench top. When the vinyl was laid, the utility room would look like the invitingly bright and clean workplace it was meant to be.

More voices.

"Please, Douglas, do let me," Tina's penetrating voice said.

Douglas mumbled something in reply.

"Of course he won't mind. He doesn't care what I do."

The voices were coming closer. Maddie kept her eyes on Gabrio as Douglas entered the utility with Tina, who started slightly on seeing Maddie.

"Maddie! I didn't know you were here. Do let's have that coffee soon," she said. She nodded at Gabrio and touched Douglas on the hand before hopping over the working area to the doorsill to crack open the door to the gathering storm. Maddie saw Gabrio frown.

"Can't bear to see this floor cheapened with vinyl," Tina said dramatically, "so I'll take myself off." She smiled at Douglas. "See me home through this stormy weather?"

"Only a blow. No rain forecast," Gabrio said to the floor where he was working. "But time is money and I have jobs for him here. No use two of you being blown to pieces."

Douglas shrugged.

"Ta da, then," she said and she was out the door.

"We've work to do, hombre," Gabrio said gruffly.

"No problemo," Douglas said. "What's next?"

Maddie caught a glimpse of Tina as she walked across the window towards the farm track. Her head was down facing into the wind which was blowing her mane of hair in all directions. A workman with a notebook in hand looked up as she passed by, his eyes following her. How did some women manage to look attractive even in the most unfriendly conditions?

The man appeared at the utility door. "Come take a look at this, would you please, Gabrio."

"Still contemplating the offer?" Maddie asked Douglas when Gabrio left.

"Nothing to contemplate," he said. "They think just because I'm not working and don't have the readies without the bank being involved, they can pick this place up for a song."

Gabrio came back shaking his head. "The plumber will have to make a mess of the wall under the window," he said. "Old fashioned piping that's got to be changed. Sorry, Douglas, more expense."

He stepped into the corridor and heaved a roll of vinyl into the utility room. It was laid in a jiffy, instantly completing the room.

"Looks great," Maddie said and meant it. Period features were not necessary in a room like this. Practicality wins in such a space. "Buyers love utility rooms. I love utility rooms. And having the ironing board permanently up? Such a good idea."

"Mine," Douglas said with no false modesty.

"What will you tackle next?" Maddie asked, expecting them to say the kitchen.

"The conservatory people want to start straight away," Gabrio said. "We were supposed to be taking the dining room window out today. Or at least, that was the plan. But it's a no-go with this wind."

A conservatory. Maddie was delighted. Douglas had taken her advice on a major addition. Quite a heady experience.

"Did I tell you we're putting in French doors between the dining room and the conservatory? Taking the window out completely, of course, but we'll have much more light coming in," Douglas said. "On good days, the dining room and the conservatory will almost be one room; in inclement weather, we can seal the conservatory off." He turned to Gabrio. "We can still do the dining room table today."

Gabrio nodded.

"Maybe the guys can lend a hand," Douglas said. "The electrician is upstairs somewhere and the plumber needs a break from looking at sewerage pipes outside in the wind."

"I'll get them," Gabrio said.

Douglas nodded and turned to Maddie. "I'll show you what we're going to do. The problem is, we need room to work in the dining room. My idea is to take the leaves out of the table to bring it down from enormous to merely bloody big."

"I'll help too, of course," she said.

In the dining room, he explained, decades ago the table most likely had been permanently set to this its largest size. "We tried but couldn't shift it on our own. But with help, we might just be able to do it. If Gabrio is right, each extra leaf will have dowels set to interlock into the next leaf. Whatever, they're well stuck together and the more hands on deck the better."

Maddie stood for a moment looking at the dining room window with its obvious repair. She had no problem visualising a full set of French doors opening into a sun-filled conservatory. What a selling point! Moreover, what an asset to an already lovely house.

The table was grand as she'd noted the first time she'd seen it. She passed her hand over the old wood, walnut, probably. It could be the same age as the house or even older. She couldn't imagine bringing it into the room through the door. Maybe the dining room was constructed around the table? Four wide leaves had extended a large oval table into a massive one. Each leaf extended the table a further three feet wide; all were constructed from the identical walnut.

Gabrio returned with the plumber Maddie had seen earlier and an older man she assumed was the electrician. Douglas positioned Gabrio with the electrician at one end of the table and himself with the plumber at the other, with Maddie in the middle. "On the count of three, we'll each pull like crazy. Maddie, watch for any movement, then try to push it apart. Don't strain yourself. We'll be doing the majority of the grunt work. Ready?"

Maddie glued her eyes to the crack between the leaves. Douglas counted to three. They heaved. But nothing. Another count of three. No opening of the crack.

"Yank, everybody, really jerk it," she said.

On the count of three, they wrenched it.

"Again," she said with some enthusiasm. "I think I felt something give."

They did so and a tiny gap appeared in front of her.

"A crack! I can see a crack," Maddie said. "We're almost there."

"Once more," Douglas said as he counted, "and again!"

Finally one of the leaves was pulled sufficiently apart to allow fingers to be inserted. Maddie stepped aside as Gabrio and Douglas tugged on the leaf itself to increase the gap while the other men continued to heave on the ends.

They repeated the exercise to form the next gap, leaving one leaf free. Douglas hoisted it up, tipping it over until he could carry it upright to the wall. The leaf itself was a full inch and a half thick with dowels along one edge and holes for dowels on the other as Gabrio had suggested.

"You can't believe how heavy it is. There's no way Aunt Beryl could have changed the table's size," he said, making certain the leaf was propped squarely against the wall.

The table had been constructed with a cleverly designed space immediately under the table-top for storage of the extension leaves. Part of this hidden compartment was now visible. Maddie spotted something in the gap. "What's that?" she asked.

"No idea. But I can guess it's been here a while." Douglas reached his hand in and under and pulled out a thick dossier, reddish brown in colour and tied with a white string. "You don't think this is...?" He untied the string and pulled out a sheaf of yellowing papers of an odd size. "No way," he muttered.

Maddie peered over his shoulder.

"What are they? Certificates?" she asked.

"No idea. Are bearer bonds certificates? Share certificates?" Douglas asked. He rifled through the stack. "My god, maybe they are! Have we found it! Aunt Beryl's horde?" He grinned at the others. He grabbed Gabrio's outstretched hand and shook it vigorously. Then each of them in turn.

"I'll get my phone and record this for posterity," Gabrio said, dashing out of the room.

Douglas turned to Maddie and enveloped her in an enthusiastic hug.

"Ahem," said Tina from the doorway. "Am I interrupting something?"

Douglas turned to her. "Hi Tina – you're back. You'll never guess what's happened. I might have found Aunt Beryl's hidden booty! I mean, we *have* just found her hidden booty!" At Tina's querulous face, his enthusiasm waned. "Of course it may be worthless. Who knows." He gave her a hug too.

"But that's wonderful, darling," she said, her face softening. She hugged him back. That's two, Maddie thought. But who's counting.

"Congratulations," Tina said. She then turned to Maddie. "No tennis this morning so half way home I thought I'd come back to where the action is. Woman's intuition that something's up!"

Gabrio burst back into the room bringing enthusiasm with him, taking photographs of the hiding spot, of Douglas holding the dossier packet, of the bonds themselves fanned out on the table, of Douglas, his arm around the shoulders of a grinning Maddie and a coolly smiling Tina, of the lot of them using the trigger delay with Douglas in the middle, his hands displaying the bonds.

They crowded around the phone as Gabrio played back the photos.

"Got to run; I'm out to lunch in Pangbourne," Tina said when he'd finished. "Congrats again, Douglas." She pecked him on the cheek. Douglas coloured, his hand going to the spot; his eyes flicked to Maddie.

"Bye. I'll think about that granite. Maybe this will be the ticket," he said, brandishing one of the bonds.

After Tina left, Douglas carefully replaced the bonds into the dossier. "I'll take them into the bank for advice," he said, "first thing tomorrow. Maybe get a safety deposit box."

The electrician and plumber left to continue their assessments of what needed doing to the Manor and Maddie had to get going too. Odd that Douglas checked to see if she'd spotted Tina kiss him.

As she turned down the drive, her phone rang. The de Milles. She almost sighed. Too much was happening on one day. She headed home for a quick sandwich before meeting up with the de Milles.

Maddie thought again of her spontaneous hug from Douglas. Nice.

Chapter Twenty

THINGS ARE GETTING WAY way out of control. Sneaky is way way into the problem. You'd think she'd get the message. You'd think she'd know to get out of Dodge. Anyone with half a brain would leave. But, oh no, little Ms Sneaky is wriggling her wormy way into life here and affecting everything. Our precious, beautiful, traditional life here. But she doesn't know what she's up against.

Me.

Love it. Wriggling her wormy way into way way out of control.

Yes!

Can't stop laughing.

Chapter Twenty-One

"THINGS ARE REALLY MOVING," Maddie said to the de Milles as she pulled her notebook out of her commodious handbag. "We have some serious buyers here." She smiled broadly, hoping the image she was portraying was one of confidence.

Louise and Antoine both had expressions of intense interest. No children were around, presumably tucked up in their beds for an afternoon nap.

Maddie put the Campbell offer on the table, turning it so both of the de Milles could read it.

Antoine smiled at Maddie. "Now we're talking," he said. "Great, ay, Louise?"

"Not great," she said flatly. "What do they think they're playing at? We're not fools."

Maddie took a deep breath. She concentrated on Antoine. "Yes, I agree with you. It's a very fair offer, Antoine. I think we can tweak it one more time perhaps, but it's looking good. It really is, Louise."

"Don't you tag me onto this conversation," Louise retorted. "I said it was pathetic. I mean it. We're not anywhere near where we need to be."

"Don't react like that, love," Antoine said. "This is ballpark, maybe not quite there, but near. Listen to Madeleine. It will go up once we tweak it."

"Tweak it? I want more than a tweak." Her mouth was a thin line. She crossed her arms in front of her in the classic defensive pose that Maddie recognised from a lifetime of seeing it in her former career.

"Please, Louise, let's wait until we have a new figure. Please," he said, putting his arm around her shoulders. She jerked herself away as if she'd been touched with a red hot poker.

Maddie was acutely embarrassed.

"How far do you think we could move it, Madeleine?" he asked.

"I think it's safe enough now to do the 'split the difference' request." She kept her eyes on his, not daring to give Louise any encouragement.

As soon as Antoine produced the new figure, Maddie grabbed it and left. As the door shut behind her, she heard Louise yelling at her husband. Maddie hoped he'd be able to calm her down. What a temper!

Maddie reminded herself that these were ordinary folk and she needed to empathise rather than criticise. She let herself imagine being in Louise's circumstances. She well remembered a time when Olivia was not yet in school and Jade a newborn a long yesterday ago. Could she have coped in a tiny terrace house where the sitting room doubled as a playroom? Where their bedroom had no space between the bed and the walls? Could she have dodged wet laundry strung across the kitchen on cold winter days? She thought back to that time. All she could recall was how tired she was. Forever exhausted. Olivia was demanding during the day and Jade during the night. Olivia wouldn't play by herself and it seemed whenever Maddie sat down with her, Jade would let out a howl.

Was she ever angry underneath like Louise? Sometimes, she had to admit. Yes, sometimes, definitely. She'd have to be more tolerant with Louise. Selling and buying were stressful events and, she reminded herself, events which would be taking every cent not only of their own savings but mortgage money that needed to be paid back, and then some. Louise could easily be as tired as she herself had been all those years ago. Did Louise's mother help with babysitting like she had done with Olivia's two?

That thought gave way to a surge of guilt. She'd moved away from Olivia and her family. She was no longer available to babysit on weekends or to allow Olivia and her husband an occasional evening out, just the two of them. And she missed her grandchildren.

Maddie sighed. It was so very difficult doing the right thing. Olivia had encouraged this change of direction in her mother's life. Until this moment, Maddie hadn't fully comprehended her daughter's self-sacrifice. She would call Olivia when she reached home.

• • • • • • • • •

Maddie was shattered from both the event-filled day and the heat, plus the lingering aftermath of Douglas's good fortune and what it could mean. She was keeping all fingers and toes crossed the bearer bonds were worth something, at least enough to contribute to the renovations of the Manor.

As she walked across the wind-swept back garden of Briar Cottage, questions swirled in her mind … was it Freddy who hid the bonds in the old table? Maybe Beryl didn't ever know they were there. Or was it Beryl who had hidden them years ago from Freddy when he was being profligate with their dwindling resources? Did she forget where she'd hidden them? Or was she content with living simply and getting a kick from stealing a treat from *Jenny's Kitchen* whenever she wanted? Maybe those bonds were her rainy day savings and she never grasped that for her, rainy days had already arrived. Such an elusive character, Beryl. How she wished Beryl had taken those bonds and left for some holiday resort. She'd enjoyed thinking of her relishing the consternation her leaving would cause. But no. Beryl didn't take her fortune and leave. Beryl was forced to leave. Wandering off still seemed uncharacteristic.

There was nothing for it; Beryl must have been murdered and her body concealed in someplace unknown. But why would she be murdered? No, even though she'd been a little old lady who enjoyed playing practical jokes on one and sundry, she was not the stuff of a murder victim.

As Maddie sipped a cup of tea in her little conservatory after a long and satisfying talk with Olivia – and an apology – she found herself wondering again about Louise and Antoine. Their relationship reminded her of someone's. Not herself and Wayne. Never. Not Wayne and Chrystal either. Not Olivia and her Bradley. Not Gabrio and Jenny. Tina and George? Yes, that's it, although she couldn't quite grasp why. Tina and her veiled annoyance and George handling it? Could be. Only Tina's moods weren't as apparent as Louise's and besides, the Higgins didn't have the stress of a young family. Tina's moods were the suppressed kind, controlled. But the underlying emotion was similar.

***

When Maddie had returned to Briar Cottage her landline phone had been blinking which meant a message had been left on the voice-mail but she'd ignored it in favour of a late supper. Just too much in one day. She remembered to listen to the message before taking herself upstairs to bed. Douglas. Calling on the landline at the cottage so he wouldn't interrupt negotiations or other estate agent business. "Give me a ring when you get home," she heard on the message he had left. "I won't be turning in for hours yet."

Curious, she rang his mobile.

***

Don't know. Maybe," he said. "You know I'm renting in Streatley? My flat's been trashed."

"Trashed? Like in a break-in trashed?"

"Don't know. Probably."

"What do you mean? Did someone steal the bonds?" Her voice rose in panic. His inheritance, maybe his key to making the Manor really his.

"No," he said loudly to still her alarm. "No, Maddie. They didn't get them. I'd put them in Gabrio's safe."

Relief flooded through her "Thank goodness," she said. "But the thief didn't know that, obviously."

"That's what I figure," Douglas said. "We went to Gabrio's home office to scan the bonds. We wanted to make a record as soon as possible, so we saved them in a pdf file which I sent by email to my lawyer and the bank. Trying to be as open as I could. But the bonds themselves are in Gabrio's safe."

"I should have known you'd take precautions," she said feeling relief flood through her.

"Gabrio suggested it. I didn't consider they'd be in any danger just overnight. How wrong I was."

"When did it happen?" She couldn't think there would have been much time between finding the bonds and his arriving back at his flat.

"While I was having a pub meal in Goring, I suppose," he said, "unless the break-in has nothing to do with the bonds, of course. Then it could have been any time during the day because I hadn't been home since breakfast."

"I don't understand. You left the Manor to go to the Flores' house, then you went home to clean up before dinner—"

"Sorry, no," Douglas said. "I'm confusing you. I went from the Flores' place to grab a bite in Goring in my work clothes. It's on the way. I went home afterwards."

"And found the place had been burgled?"

"Burgled? Don't know. An unholy mess, but not much missing that I can see. The television's here, sound system too. Microwave. Even, believe it or not, my laptop. The only thing missing is the twenty quid note I'd left on the side. It's gone. But every drawer in the place has been upended, my bedclothes strewn about the floor, my underwear and socks everywhere, books too. Even the food in the freezer was on the kitchen floor."

"Sounds as if they were looking for something all right," Maddie said. "It has to be the bonds, doesn't it?"

"What about the missing twenty quid? Maybe it was only kids on the hunt for cash and booze."

"Or the person searching for the bonds took it opportunistically. Maybe so you'd think it was kids."

"I have one colossal mess here. Hard to figure out ... no, it has to be the bonds. If so, it's all happened between leaving the bonds in Gabrio's safe and arriving home after my meal."

"The food from your freezer ... was it defrosted?" Maddie asked.

"Good point," he said. "No. It had hoar frost on it, so I shoved it back into the freezer, still rock solid. It can't have been out too long before I arrived home."

"Not very many of us knew about the bonds, did they? You and Gabrio went straight to his place from the Manor?"

"Directly, with the bonds in their packet in the car beside me. I didn't stop. When we got there, we went straight into ... no, we saw Jenny and ... yes, their son Mel and his pals who were in the sitting room eating pizza in front of telly. I told them the amazing news. Then Gabrio and I went into his office where we scanned all the bonds. I sent emails to the bank and my lawyer and attached the file to each email. I suppose it's just possible they know about the bonds by now but it's damn unlikely. Business emails are rarely read on a Sunday night." He sighed. "We copied the file onto a memory stick which I now have in my pocket ... hang on ... yes, it's still there. I stopped at the pub to eat and then home to find this mess."

"That means nobody in the Flores household is our likely culprit, I presume," she said. "They all knew you'd put the bonds in the safe?"

"Probably," he said slowly. "No, not really. Although the lads heard my good news, they were in the lounge. We were in the office; we put the bonds in the safe there. Gabrio might have mentioned it to the boys after I left, of course. Only Jenny was in and out."

"Jenny? No way would she be involved," Maddie said, aware she was using gut instinct only. "And two of the boys are still the nice kids I eliminated from my vandalism suspicions." She couldn't imagine them hearing about the bonds, waiting for Douglas to leave, presumably with the bonds, going to his flat to discover he wasn't there, then breaking in and searching wildly. Improbable, especially if they had no idea if he had even been back to the flat to hide the bonds and, more importantly, when he'd return. "The boys – do they know where you live?"

"Mel does, yes. He brought me the plans of the conservatory from Gabrio one time when I needed them for the bank."

"Still, so unlikely. But what about the plumber and the electrician?"

"I hate this, Maddie. We're talking about decent folk."

"I know; I know. Sickening. But trashing your place is more sickening and any of these people – any of them – could have spread the news. Friends, family, strangers ... it's an intriguing story."

Douglas sighed. "Tina, of course knows about my find this afternoon, and she would have told George," Douglas said. "I really hate this." He sighed once more.

Maddie remembered Tina first leaving then arriving back at the Manor when they made the discovery. Why had Tina come back? Intuition, she said. Probably simply snooping. No, she could think of a more probable explanation for her return – Tina wanted to keep an eye on Douglas, especially with another woman there.

She brought her thoughts back to the subject. "Yes, the electrician or the plumber. Can't see the connection. Then George or Tina, they're unlikely, I agree. Can't figure it. Maybe we should let it go for a bit. Sleep on it."

"Besides, could you imagine George wrecking my place – with what? A cattle prod maybe? Or the beauteous Tina with a tennis racquet? Because they couldn't find the bonds? Hardly." He paused. "It looks as if a tornado went through here."

"Should I come over and help tidy up?" she asked. Offering but hoping he'd refuse. She was beat.

"No, but thanks for volunteering," he said. "I'll clear a path to my bed and leave the clean-up for the morning."

"If you're getting discouraged at any time, give me a bell," she said. "I mean that."

"You're a star, Maddie," he said. "Sweet dreams."

· · · · • · • · · ·

Maddie did not have sweet dreams or any dreams at all for some time because she was wide awake. Her mind would not let go; the facts concerning the strange burglary went round and round her head. Gabrio and Jenny didn't do it because they knew the bonds were in their own safe. That only left Mel, Bart and the other young man. Or Tina and George. Who was that third young man? She'd have to find out. All so unlikely, but they were the sum total, excepting the email contacts, who knew about the bonds. Or somebody any one of them had spoken to, of course. Or it was coincidental. She didn't believe in convenient coincidences. Damn, it went on and on.

Douglas had used the term 'tornado'. A storm. A furious destructive tempest. In human terms, not a tempest but a temper. Was his flat destroyed in anger?

She went to sleep with the image of the calm and collected George coming into Douglas's flat with a vengeance, strewing his clothes, books and food everywhere. She smiled at the absurdity of the image. Straight-laced businessman George? Uh uh.

Her eyes opened briefly. A tiny thought: did George resent Tina's flirtation with Douglas? No doubt she was the most attractive woman in the three villages. And then those brooding eyebrows...maybe they hid dark thoughts she couldn't read.

Jealousy?

The Campbells were considering the de Mille's new price. Two couples – much the same age yet so different – Maddie didn't want to contemplate what was happening within the de Mille couple; Louise was a loose cannon if there ever was one. Suppressed anger. Or not so suppressed. Which brought to mind her musings about the parallels between the young matron Louise and the elegant tennis player Tina. She threw that theory into the bin. Musings, only. She wondered if George had a temper too.

"You know George and Tina better than I do," Maddie said to Douglas. She'd called into his Streatley flat in the late morning to see if she could help with the clean-up. He'd already been to the bank and deposited the bonds into a safe-deposit box. He'd asked if the financial people there could find out their worth. He'd also heard from his lawyer who was bemused more than anything, but wanted to be kept in the loop.

"I know Tina much better than George. Yes. She was the first person I met here," Douglas said. Maddie had found him re-assembling the kitchen in his little rented flat. He was busy rescuing cutlery and crockery from all over the place and Maddie was now elbow deep in sudsy water washing whatever had been on the floor, whatever remained useable, that is. "She was friendly and encouraging me to do something about my rights to the Manor. She kept on at me to get a lawyer and the lawyer started the court cases. She kept reminding me I was Aunt Beryl's only living relative. I appreciated Tina's interest ... kept me going. I wouldn't be where I am today without her. I owe her a lot." He bent to pick up cutlery scattered along the wall under the table. "She was a friend of Beryl's, did you know?"

He clambered up from under the table and Maddie accepted a fistful of cutlery from him. "Yes, she told me. She said she was promised first refusal on the Manor should Beryl decide to sell. Or maybe a deal involving the cottages."

"Tina certainly loves the house, but first refusal? Don't know about that," he said as he reached down behind the stove. "Gotcha." He held up a butter knife.

"Their offer? Have you had a decent look?"

"Come on, Maddie. Honestly, do you think I should treat an offer that low as serious? Even if the bonds prove to be not worth the paper they're printed on, it's still damnably cheeky."

She nodded. "I thought you'd react this way, but I did have to present it. What do you want to do in reply?"

He shrugged. "I can't be bothered. If they want to re-open discussions, they're going to have to be a great deal more realistic." He grimaced. "I don't have to consider promises made in the past. I mean, do you honestly think I should be influenced by whatever friendship existed between Aunt Beryl and Tina?"

"Of course not," she said. "This is business. Probably the most important contribution to your financial well-being in your entire life."

He grabbed a pile of kitchen knives from the table where he'd been collecting them. "Do you want the sharp things now?"

"Yes, please," she said, reaching for them. "The friendship between Beryl and Tina amazes me, to be honest. An old lady – going senile according to Tina – not interested in the things Tina holds dear like her tennis, her interior decorating, her socialising ... what did they see in each other? It seems Aunt Beryl got her kicks from tormenting other people." She glanced at Douglas. "Oops, sorry, that popped out without due care."

Douglas smiled. "My mother would have agreed with you. Only she was under the impression she was Aunt Beryl's sole victim."

"I don't know who else, but Jenny Flores was certainly another, although I still haven't got to the bottom of that," Maddie said. "Gabrio is still furious at Beryl on Jenny's account."

"And the greengrocer in Woodley Bottom. He banned her from his shop."

"Really?"

"So I heard. She was not the well-loved or even well-tolerated old eccentric Tina likes to portray. She's far too kind to Aunt Beryl."

"The other way around is strange too. I mean Beryl accepting Tina as a friend," Maddie said turning to the stack of plates, those that weren't cracked or broken, and put them into the hot soapy water.

"I was wondering that too," Douglas said as he swept the kitchen floor. "Some things Tina's talked about make me think she's garnishing the truth a tad."

Maddie raised an eyebrow.

"She told me she'd rarely been anywhere in the house but the kitchen. That's unlikely if they were great friends, don't you think?"

"Hmmm," Maddie murmured. "I take your point, but your aunt Beryl wasn't usual. Or maybe they only had friendly cups of tea at the kitchen table."

"Friendly cups of tea? Hardly. You didn't know Aunt Beryl. Besides, the kitchen at the Manor is on the cold side of the house. Not too hospitable."

"You have a point. But maybe Beryl usually popped over to Tina's instead of entertaining at the Manor."

He shook his head. "She never mentioned Beryl visiting her at the cottages. Not once."

"Are you suggesting they weren't such bosom buddies?"

He shrugged. "I can find Tina a bit much sometimes especially if she's set her sights on something. Look, I'm not complaining. She's good fun and she prodded me into doing the right thing. But the Aunt Beryl I knew as a child was much less tolerant than I am."

Maddie shot him a glance. That comment explained a lot. "Can you tell me something," she began, "about Tina? Does she have a temper?" Just a little supposition on her part.

Douglas barked a laugh. "Temper? My god, woman, does she have a temper! Poor old George must cop it often enough. Never directed against me, luckily."

"Directed against what? Or whom?" Maddie asked, letting out the sudsy water before grabbing a tea-towel.

"I've ducked out of her way several times. Once she had dropped in at the Manor, as is her wont, and her car wouldn't start. She tried again and again until she ran the battery right down. I tried to persuade her to call the car rescue people but she kept grinding and grinding the starter motor. When the battery started clicking, she got out of the car and kicked it. Really kicked it. Not once but three or four times. Each time she left a dent in the car door."

"A proper temper tantrum," Maddie said with a grin.

"Like a two-year old," he said. "She didn't say a word to me, just stomped off down the farm track. Later George drove over, connected up the battery on his car and started it. He bent down to look at the kick marks and apologised for Tina's behaviour."

"Hmmm," Maddie said again. She glanced at Douglas. "I'm thinking nasty thoughts, Douglas. This chaos, this wanton destruction..."

"You're thinking ... someone was way out of control?"

She nodded once, stricken. She wanted to grab the words back again. Douglas obviously thought a lot of Tina.

"But why? I haven't done anything to her. I haven't even replied to their silly offer on the house. She likes me; she's always all over me." His mouth became a thin line. "I don't believe it."

"Forget what I said, Douglas. I had no right. I have open-mouth, insert-foot disorder and I'm suffering badly today. Please, let's say no more about it."

They dried the remaining dishes in silence. Maddie left soon after, kicking herself for speaking her thoughts aloud.

• • • • ● • ● • • •

At the office, she sat for several minutes with her eyes shut, letting her muscles relax. Insert foot indeed. She'd make it up to him by persevering in their quest for information about Beryl. That weird allegation about Beryl, motherhood and Jenny of all people....

"Bad time, Jenny?" she asked when the phone was picked up. She knew Jenny baked at home in the mornings.

"As good as it gets in this hothouse," she said. "How I wish the weather would break. It's like a sauna in here."

"Not good being a baker in a summer like this one," Maddie said. She took a deep breath and launched into why she'd called. "I'm still stuck on figuring out old Beryl Fanshaw. And I heard she'd sent you off to some school or other when you were a child."

"That she did," Jenny said. "I should have been properly grateful, but even at the time I thought she was doing it for some purpose. Now I am appreciative; I gained from it and to this day I'm reaping the benefits from a good education. But it was a difficult, complex situation between Beryl and my mother."

"Not something to discuss over the phone?"

"Pop over for coffee? I'm due for a break. Has to be fairly short though."

"At your shop?" Maddie asked.

"Here, at my place, if you don't mind. Mel is minding the shop. I'll fill you in."

Maddie looked up as soon as she put the phone down. Nathan was hanging over the partition that divided her space from his. It provided a modicum of privacy, visual but not auditory, at least. He looked serious.

"What's up?" Maddie asked.

"Bad news, I'm afraid. Your clients have been gazumped for the Anson place."

Maddie stared at him confused. Gazumped?

"There's another buyer who's come up with an extra chunk of money. Sorry, love. Unless your people are willing to up the ante, they've lost out."

Maddie didn't need this, not today of all days, and not given the precarious state of her finances. "I'll ring straight away. But honestly? I'd bet they can't. They were precariously close to overextending with their own offer."

"Give them the opportunity, yeah?"

"Yeah." The last thing she wanted to do, but she immediately picked up the phone. Nathan grimaced and left her to it.

As she predicted, Mr Reynolds accepted they'd lost the house with equanimity, Mrs Reynolds with cries of despair. But they both agreed, something substantially above their offer was well beyond their resources. She told them she'd get right onto looking for something else. Their response was lukewarm, not surprising given the circumstances.

It was Maddie's turn to lean over the partition. "No new offer, Nathan. Sorry."

"These new buyers have more money than sense," he said. "They loved the outdoor space. I think it was the veggie garden that clinched the deal."

"Congratulate the Ansons for me, will you?" Maddie asked. "And give them my best wishes." No sense displaying her own irritation. Not even to Nathan.

She sat back down on her side of the partition and brought her bank balance up on the screen. She'd have to cut down spending on anything but essentials. She really would have to gird her loins and hassle Wayne about the divorce settlement. Not a fun prospect.

• • • • • • • • • • •

Jenny ushered Maddie outside into the shade on the terrace at the back of the Flores' kitchen. It looked over a long back garden; lawn and flower beds were in the immediate vicinity of the house and further back were fruit trees, herbs and vegetables. Quite a plot.

"Long story," Jenny began. "I was a pretty child, bright and reasonably self-possessed. I knew the Fanshaws because my mother worked there. General maid." She sipped her tea. "Other kids also had no fathers like me so I didn't feel different. I walked to the Manor after school instead of home, but even that wasn't all that odd. Other kids went to their grandparent's or a neighbour's if their mothers worked. I had to sort of report in to Mrs Fanshaw, to tell her what had happened at school then she'd send me for milk and cakes in the kitchen. I didn't mind her questions and I liked the cakes. She started buying me little dresses, new shoes, a leather school bag, things like that. My mother protested, but not too vigorously. Every little girl likes presents. She never wanted me to kiss her or anything like that, thank goodness. Mum started saying she was my fairy godmother but I know she resented it a bit. I wasn't bothered. I saw it as only a slight variant of normal life."

"Was she interfering in how your mother was bringing you up?" Maddie relished the excellent coffee Jenny had provided but surreptitiously glanced at the time as she placed the mug on the wooden table. This was taking longer than she'd bargained for.

"In hindsight, yes, probably she was. Mum growled at the flounces and general fanciness of some of the dresses. High maintenance clothing; all would need ironing. The situation deteriorated when I was ten. Mrs

Fanshaw wanted me to go to St Helen's, which is a good school, top notch academically and they don't take just anybody. If they did accept me, she promised to stump up the fees. Quite a gift, really." She smiled ruefully. "I loved it. Made good friends. So when the Fanshaw's money ran out, the consequences were quite dire. My mother lost her job and, of course, I had to leave school. Pretty devastating, all in all. Little snot that I was, I was angry at Mrs Fanshaw instead of old Freddy, who was really to blame." She smiled at Maddie. "See, I was just a stuck-up little brat privately educated beyond my station."

Maddie shook her head at the old-fashioned thinking. "But later you worked for her on the book?"

"That blessed book. Yes, eventually. I finished school locally and, yes, I did find the transition difficult. When I left school, she hired me and suddenly I was the brunt of her inner frustrations. She felt I owed her. Which I did, but try telling someone that age to be grateful for something they'd taken for granted. I started hating going to work. And she was complaining she was overpaying me. It was all going down the gurgler."

"So you took that European holiday, met Gabrio etc."

"Eventually, yes." She drained her mug. "And I told you the rest the other day."

"Thank you so much, Jenny," Maddie said, reaching for her bag and standing up. "I have a much deeper understanding of Mrs Fanshaw now. So sad she deteriorated so much at the end."

Jenny nodded. "She was basically a controlling person. Eventually I couldn't be controlled. And I never really told her how I did appreciate being sent to St Helen's. By the time I realised I should tell her, she was making my life miserable."

Maddie had a thought that shot through her mind like a hot knife through butter. "You're not...I mean, William and Beryl Fanshaw were...are you adopted?" It had come out all wrong.

Jenny laughed. "Not you too! All my life I've had people think that."

Maddie gave her a wan smile through her embarrassment. "Sorry, Jenny, that was an insert-foot moment. Too fanciful for my own good."

"Just to make it clear, for sure Mum is my mother. For sure Beryl Fanshaw never had a child. For sure my father, may he rest in hell, was my biological father; in spite of being female, I'm the spitting image of him."

"Please forget it," Maddie mumbled. She hoped her blush wasn't horribly obvious. She wished the ground would open up and she could disappear.

A loud buzz sounded from the kitchen.

"Got to run," Jenny said. "Bread rolls need to get into the oven."

Maddie felt a huge wave of relief. Saved by the buzzer. Besides, she had to contact Fiona and Clive Campbell. She shouldn't have stayed so long with so much going on.

Once back in her car, she squirmed yet again at her outburst. Still, it would fit so neatly. Beryl getting pregnant by William, not able to keep the baby, adopting it out to her personal maid.... By the time she was on her way back to work, she was laughing at herself.

Should she ask William if he'd heard the rumour and see how he reacts? She shook her head. Not now anyway. She had to get back to business. She rang the Campbells suggesting they meet.

"We were only this minute wondering if we should tweak the offer once more or just accept their price," Fiona said. "Yes, let's all have a coffee. Maybe flip a coin?"

Maddie laughed, wishing she wasn't already buzzing from too much caffeine. "See you at the *Coffee Clique* in fifteen minutes?"

The day was heading towards prodicing another record-breaking hot afternoon. The drought was obvious to all now. Farmers were complaining and municipalities were making noises about a hosepipe ban. Global warming. But on this June morning, it was certainly pleasant sitting in front of the little café in the shade of an umbrella.

"You have a compelling reason for accepting the de Mille's current price," Maddie said once they'd settled with their coffees, hers an iced decaf. "The vendors are really trying to meet you in a place where both parties feel good." She kept Louise's bad temper and unpredictability to herself. Another tweak and Louise was liable to explode. Maddie had heard stories where clients were pushed beyond endurance and a deal so close to agreement suddenly fell apart.

"My argument," Clive said. "We're not talking much here."

"I'm not arguing against acceptance," Fiona said. "I want to know where we are in this dance."

"It is a dance," Maddie said. "You've successfully brought the price down to the point where we're in danger of spoiling the deal. And, believe me, a danger exists." She suppressed all thoughts of gazumping and other estate disasters.

"Okay, so that's where we are. We're fine with this new asking price, aren't we, darling?" Clive said. His eyes glowed. He could see that back garden completed, the two of them sitting there, drinks in hand, watching the sun set over their own fence line.

"If you think it's okay," Fiona said to Maddie, "then I'll go along with it."

"Let's get this thing confirmed." Maddie dug into her bag for her mobile and rang the de Milles. Antoine answered immediately, as if he'd been waiting for her call.

The conversation was short and very sweet. Maddie raised one thumb to the Campbells. At the other end, Antoine was overjoyed. Maddie was relieved she was talking to him rather than Louise. He could handle his wife after the call.

"I think you've bought yourself a new house," Maddie said with a relieved grin as she put her phone away. She raised her coffee mug. "To it all going smoothly from here on in," she said. They clunked mugs.

"We did it!" Clive said.

"I can't believe it!" Fiona joined in, her face shining.

With their thanks ringing in her ears, Maddie left them to it. She had paperwork, always paperwork, to organise. But her step was light as she re-entered the office. She could almost see her part of the commission filling the growing hole in her bank account.

Yes, maybe she'd made the right choice in this change of career.

• • • • • • • • • • •

In the afternoon, Maddie forced herself to ring the Higgins. Tina, as expected, answered. "If you can fit me in, I'd like to see you both," Maddie said, "to talk about your offer for the Manor. Do you want to meet for coffee at the *Coffee Clique* here in Goring?" She took a deep breath. "Or I could come out like last time."

"Come over here, Maddie dear," Tina said. She'd heard Douglas call her Maddie and started using the diminutive as well, in spite of Maddie's intension to restrict it to close friends. "I'll see that tardy old George is on time today. Five? I'll have the wine cooling."

An appointment at five meant Maddie had time to go home before tackling the Higgins' problems. The heat was oppressive and she needed a cool shower to be able to contemplate the prospect. And it was debilitating even thinking about managing George and his dilemma about his offices and Tina with her enthusiasms. Or maybe George was simply luke-warm to the idea of buying the manor and this was a way of dragging his heels. Tina, she had no doubts about. Tina wanted to be mistress of Cherry Tree Manor, no matter what.

Maddie thought through Douglas's reaction to her idea that the vandalism had to be carried out by someone with a temper. She shouldn't have implied it could be Tina. Not a good idea – maybe there was something going on between them after all. She felt a pang, which she quickly suppressed.

Certainly Tina was a character, but, actually, Maddie had never seen her being violent in thought or action. She wriggled uncomfortably when thinking about what she'd suggested. She shouldn't have become so carried away. When was she going to learn to keep her own counsel?

The shower did its trick and Maddie donned fresh clothes – the cropped beige slacks from the trouser suit she'd worn to the barbecue and a white sleeveless top – feeling moderately refreshed. She was looking forward to that cold white wine. She hoped it would be the same one; fingers crossed. She'd knock on the door with her hand outstretched. The thought brought a smile to her face. That wine was truly exceptional. She could almost taste it.

By now the Higgins must have figured their offer for the Manor had been declined. Maddie arrived at the cottages again right on time and, unlike the last occasion, George met her at the door.

"We're on the terrace in the back garden," he said, ushering her through the hallway and out the kitchen door. Tina was sitting in a cool blue and green sun-frock at the terrace table, her long tanned legs stretched in front of her, a glass of white wine at her elbow.

"Tina tells me you enjoyed this white," George, ever the host, said. "Nicely cold for such a scorcher of a day." He took the bottle from a bucket of ice and poured her a glass.

Maddie took a sip. Crisp and fruity. Perfect. She enthused about it aloud.

The view from the terrace had changed in the few days since she'd been there; now the field of hay was taller and she could see a flower or two undulating in the faint breeze. But the bank of roses was drooping.

"Oh dear, your poor roses," Maddie said as she sank into the chair George held out for her. "I heard a hosepipe ban is in effect now."

Tina's lips formed a closed-mouth smile. "No one would see if I gave the poor darlings a drink, but George is the original goodie-goodie." She paused, her glass at her lips, watching how George reacted to her latest provocative statement.

"You're merely lazy, darling," he said with good humour. "We're in the fortunate position of having a working well, Madeleine. We have water for Africa, perfect for this type of heat."

"That's a real well?" Maddie asked. "I honestly thought it was only a picturesque 'garden feature'." She laughed. "A working well. I should have known a set of cottages this old would have had a well."

"It was a dangerous hole in what was a wild bit of pasture when we moved into the cottages all those years ago," George explained. "Then Tina did her magic to produce the garden and she found this mock Victorian 'garden feature' that did the trick. We sited it over the real well and we fixed two problems at once: we'd covered something dangerous in our back garden and we now have a bucket to pull water up whenever we have the need to do so. This drought is the first opportunity." He got up from his chair, wine glass in hand and walked down the steps to the lawn. "Come see it, Madeleine. I love to show it off."

"Don't be a pain, George darling," Tina said. "Maddie has hardly arrived and you're dragging her out into the heat."

"Won't be a mo," he said heading down the garden steps.

Tina stayed where she was, slightly frowning and shaking her head. With a nod and smile at Tina who seemed to be looking beyond the well over the sea of rippling hay, Maddie, also taking her glass with her, followed George. The wine was as delicious this time as last. And just the thing before some unpleasant negotiations.

She and George walked down the lawn which could also use a drink, as Tina had put it. What a lovely garden with its far vista beyond the roses, the stone wall and the hayfield. She took a deep breath of countryside air. Yet again she congratulated herself on her decision to move to the countryside.

George balanced his glass on the edge of the 'garden feature' much where Maddie had left the bottle of wine after the barbecue, and pulled up two hinged doors covering the interior of the well. A bucket hung from a rope coiled around a pole that stretched under the tiled canopy. A crooked lever wound the bucket up and down.

"I'll give you a treat," George said. "A drink of beautifully cold water from our very own sweet-water well. Hopefully sweet ... I haven't checked since we put in the well-top several years ago."

"You had it re-dug?"

"Heaven's no. Probably this well was put in about three hundred years ago and it's still going strong. Access to good water was valuable. This would have been a desirable place to live in those days. Watch how it works."

"Fantastic, George," she said with true delight. An ancient well with cool, fresh water. Lovely.

He leaned over to unclip a bracket. As he did so, his elbow knocked against his wine glass, balanced somewhat precariously on the rim of the well. It teetered slowly before toppling inside, striking something on its way down and shattering. George and Maddie glanced at each other. He was obviously thinking what she was thinking. The glass didn't fall into water; it fell first onto some hard surface and broke. A split second afterwards, several pieces had splashed into the water below.

"Damn, I'll be in trouble," George said.

"It must have hit the side somehow," Maddie commented. They both peered into inky blackness.

"Maybe a brick sticks out from the wall down there," George said. "Clumsy of me, anyway."

"Will it stop you giving me a drink from this ancient well of yours?" Maddie asked to ease any awkwardness.

"Of course not ... oh, just had a thought. Will any splinters of glass still be in the water?"

"I can't imagine so. Glass is heavy. All the bits will be at the bottom of the well by now."

"George," Tina called from her seat on the terrace. "Madeleine is here on business. Stop avoiding the issue and come here." She waved her glass at them. "More wine anyone?"

"Be there shortly, darling," George called back to her, as he winked at Maddie. He unwound the bucket and lowered it down into the black depths of the well. Almost immediately it clanged on something. "Damn," George said. "Something is down there after all." He jiggled the rope and the bucket banged repeatedly against whatever it was. "Possibly a stick jammed across the opening." He pulled the rope to one side, jiggled it again and so freed the bucket to descend down to the water. "Sorry about that. I'll have to clear it." He bounced the bucket until it tipped enough to become heavy with water. He tested its weight and reversed the handle so the bucket was now being pulled up. On its way, it struck whatever the obstruction was, as Maddie had expected it would. George did the jiggling act, finally jerking the rope hard. The bucket came free with a graunch.

"It's like catching a fish," he said with a grin. "I'm hauling both the bucket and whatever was stuck down there with it." He wound the rope a couple of more turns, the obstacle scraping the irregular walls of the well. "It's not far down." He reached into the well with one hand.

"I'll hold the handle steady," Maddie said, "so you can use both hands."

They could hear Tina remonstrating with George yet again. He ignored her.

George leaned over, his thighs hard against the outside of the little 'feature'.

"Be careful, George," Maddie said, wondering what she'd do if he tipped in headfirst. It didn't bear thinking about.

He yanked and yanked at whatever it was, half his body down the well. Suddenly, with a screech of metal on stone, it came free. "Got it," he said, hauling up a stick that quickly revealed itself to be a rifle. "What in hell is this doing here?" he asked, more to himself than Maddie as she wound the bucket up to the top.

She glanced at what he had in his hands. "It's a gun," she said, securing the rope and stating the obvious. But a split second later, it hit her. "Who would throw a gun down your well?"

George held it in his hands, turning it over and over. It was damp and the metal parts sported a coating of rust. But the stock was a burnished walnut. In spite of the rust, the gun looked well cared for.

"My god," he muttered, "not the old man's?" He turned to Maddie. "Get behind me, Madeleine. This thing could be dangerous."

Maddie scuttled behind him, troubled, feeling as if things were out of control. She hated guns. What old man? Why on earth was it lodged in the well? They walked in single file towards the terrace, the rusty rifle in George's hands, the drink of cold well-water forgotten.

"What in heaven's name have you got there?" Tina asked from her seat behind the table.

George didn't answer her. His face was white and his lips clenched. He carefully placed the rifle on the terrace floor pointing away from them all, using the terrace's bricked floor as a work surface. Maddie peered over his shoulder. He unclipped the magazine and looked at it before placing it with care on the bricks. He opened the breech.

"It's loaded?" Maddie asked, horrified. Why was a loaded gun more terrifying than the presence of the gun itself? Something about purpose and danger, she supposed.

"Not any more," he muttered as he bent over it.

Maddie climbed the steps to collapse on a chair beside Tina.

"Leave it, George," Tina said. "I've brought you another glass of wine. You were damnably careless, knocking one of my best glasses down the well. If you'd only—"

"Shut the hell up," he said.

Maddie blinked. George said that?

Tina's face flushed. She turned away to compose herself for a second, then grinned at Maddie, mouthing 'men' silently as she rolled her eyes.

George left the rifle and joined them at the terrace table. He picked up the new glass of wine and downed it in two swallows.

"George!" Tina protested.

He turned to Maddie. "Would it be all right with you if we postponed our discussion about the offer on the Manor to a more appropriate time?" he asked in a strangled voice.

Maddie swallowed her last sip of wine. "Of course." She smiled, saying 'fluffy, fluffy' to herself.

George opened the kitchen door for her.

"I'll see myself out," she said quickly and made perfunctory thank-yous. She scampered through the kitchen, hallway and front door without breathing. It wasn't until the front door was firmly shut on the disturbed atmosphere behind it that she dared take a deep and cleansing breath.

What had just happened there? Why? Maddie felt so agitated she almost ran to the car. Must have been the undoubted tension between George and Tina.

So, George had a temper too. Interesting. She started her car with shaking hands and found herself driving towards Beech Cottage and William's calm good sense.

At his door, William took one look at Maddie and offered food and booze to calm her down. Soon she was sitting at his table being served up a thick pea and ham soup and a glass of rich red wine.

"So much has happened, I don't know where to start," she said, willing her hand to stop trembling as she took a gulp of wine.

"You start by appreciating that Aussie Shiraz you're drinking," he said. "Then you dig into my special pea soup. It's been cooking all afternoon."

"I don't know about hot soup," Maddie started to say.

"I'll hear nothing about eating hot soup on a hot day, young lady. It will give you a healthy sweat and that's cleansing."

Maddie wondered at the logic but dutifully put a spoon into her bowl.

"Pure nourishment," William said, unfolding his paper serviette.

Maddie felt as if she was a child who'd managed to outrun some torment in the schoolyard. William's dining room felt like a haven of calm normality.

The first mouthful, delicious as it was, brought sweat to her brow. The second to her neck followed by every square inch of skin on her body. If it was designed to make her sweat, it was wholly successful. She dabbed her serviette against her face.

The story tumbled out. Finding the bonds, Douglas's burglary, her helping him clean up the destruction and her comment about a temper being behind it.

"Too close to home?" William asked when she told him that she'd implied the person with a temper could have been Tina. But that was before she'd seen the cold anger displayed by George today. Nevertheless, it was Tina's temper she'd been thinking about then.

"Douglas wouldn't have a bar of it," Maddie said. "Yet there we were surrounded by evidence of someone gone mad. That someone was furious, furious they couldn't find the bonds, probably. Nothing to do with Tina. Or George for that matter."

"Or simply furious at Douglas?" William asked. He cleared their soup bowls away.

"That's what he thought I was saying," she said. "I suppose that's what was at the back of my mind. Either/or."

"Evidence for fury, yes," William said in his calm voice. "You know what it was, don't you, Maddie?"

She turned her eyes onto him.

"It wasn't a burglary at Douglas's flat," he said. "It was yet another case of vandalism."

Chapter Twenty-Two

VANDALISM. MADDIE NODDED, IN immediate agreement. Her mind cleared itself of the irrelevancies to concentrate on that one concept. "We've instances of vandalism in three locations. First in time is the graffiti at Beryl's place plus the possibly vandalised broken window. Second was my car door. Third is Douglas's so called 'burglary'," she said. "Of all the people involved – and given we're only looking for one perp – who could have reasons for each instance?"

William, the old insurance investigator that he was, shook his head. "Perp?" He laughed. "First time I've heard you use jargon, my dear."

"Sorry," she said, forcing herself to finish the hot soup.

"We don't know about possible motivations yet," he said. "An easier place to start is with opportunity. Besides, I'd like to leave Beryl to last."

"To my car, then. We said it was most likely to be someone from the barbecue. That's a pretty broad category. And the message was explicit to me. I was an interloper and the vandal wanted me to know I was not welcome. In spite of the village appearing to be so friendly."

"You're back to motivation, Maddie. Forget it for a while. Confine your thoughts to opportunity."

"Okay," Maddie said with a sigh. It was typically male to think about factual circumstances rather than the human psyche. And she was itching to tell him about her jealousy theory. "Lots of people with opportunity. Of the people I know, eliminating anybody who I'd merely been introduced to, leaves us with only a few. George and Tina as hosts have to be included, Gabrio and Jenny, plus the good folk I talked to there like the judge and Adrian, and then there was Douglas. I think that's the entire list of people with any sort of opportunity who also have a connection to me. That's not counting someone I haven't even met who's taken against me for some reason." She looked at him. "How am I doing?"

"For a first cut, very well," he said. "Go on."

"Then Douglas's trashed flat. Opportunity? Not many people at all knew about the bonds."

"Forget the bonds," William said. "They're a distraction. For this exercise, anyway."

"Okay," she said in some frustration. "The only people with opportunity include me, Douglas himself, Tina, George, Gabrio and his household which includes Bart and the other young men, and a distant last, his lawyer and some bank officials. Opportunity because they were the only...oh, yes," she said with a sigh, "nothing to do with the bonds." She sighed. "Those with opportunity? Anybody who knows where he lives, I suppose, and somebody who Douglas has irritated, as you so succinctly pointed out with my own vandalism episode. Irritated big time."

"Workmen? Contractors he hadn't paid? Lovers? His ex-wife?"

"Good list of possibles," Maddie said, trying to be fair. "From the way he was speaking he's on relatively good terms with his ex-wife. They have a legal agreement on their assets and he's forever helping her out with DIY jobs."

"But maybe she's resentful the Manor came to him after they'd legally separated? When she has no call on it?"

"You have a point." But Maddie didn't believe it, not the way Douglas was speaking of his ex-wife. From her own days of being a Probation Officer, Maddie had observed the gamut of emotional reactions displayed by divorced clients – from easy to murderous. "And lovers? None I've seen or heard about, except...." She remembered his flirtation with Tina. "Maybe I wasn't so far off the mark with Tina. She seems to have an ongoing playful, if coy, relationship with him," she explained.

"Does she? I mean, is it a relationship? Does he respond?"

Maddie thought back to the times they had not known they were being observed. "Flattered. What man wouldn't be?" she said and rushed on. "He likes her, certainly. Grateful to her. And a gorgeous woman like that? He's bound to have some ... some sexual interest." She gulped some air. "Now Tina – I don't know how sensitive Tina is to other people's emotions. You've come across that sort of person?"

"I've met them. Go their own way. Hurt other people and never know or care."

She nodded. "And then there are these people who see life as a screenplay; they act, sort of play a role; they portray what they want someone to observe." She felt a frisson of excitement at her own words. "Faking it. Maybe Tina does, maybe not. But why?"

"That I don't know. Has she any great passions?" William asked.

"I wouldn't say her relationship with George is based on a grand passion," Maddie said. "He's a good provider, as my grandmother used to say. Although that's quite possibly unfair."

"She lives in a lovely old historic house—"

"Which George's business now shares." Maddie interrupted his observation. "I can understand her aggravation at losing a sizable proportion of her home; any woman can. George hinted that she feels resentful."

"And she has the perfect solution: buy the Manor."

But Maddie's mind had bopped back to vandalism. "Beryl's graffiti?" she asked, "She'd be able to see that insulting message every time she looked out the back windows. How do you think she'd have reacted to it?"

William poured them each a tall glass of water. "We have to give our bodies some replacement fluids after such a hot soup," he said from the kitchen. "You'll see how beneficial this regime is when you wake up tomorrow."

"I believe you, though thousands wouldn't," Maddie said, again quoting her grandmother. She grabbed the water eagerly, stifling the impulse to rub the dewy glass all over her face and neck.

"Beryl would have been livid," William said, back on topic. "She was another who became angry when she didn't get her own way, much like Tina, I expect. And such an offensive message? She'd have been outraged. Especially since it had more than a grain of truth in it." He chuckled. "I can just see Beryl's reaction. Fuming. If someone wanted to wind her up, this was how to do it. Wish I'd thought of it."

"Did you do it?" Maddie asked him over the glass of water she was clutching in both hands. "I mean, did you send her that message?" She raised an eyebrow at him.

"Far too crude for me," William said easily. "Let me see ... yes, a Shakespearean quote would be more my style."

"Unless you were bent on disguising your style, my friend. Seriously though, this is not your signature at all. Not my style either. Nor Douglas's. Not Gabrio or Jenny's, although I've seen Gabrio's face when he talks about Beryl. But he gets on very well with Douglas and me too. George? I don't know him all that well, but it seems highly unlikely. And very likely not Tina except...what do you think of the theory that she lost her temper with Beryl?"

"A message is calculated. It may be given in irritation, but not in the heat of a temper."

"So the only person not crossed off our list is the unknown young man," Maddie said although she didn't believe it and she knew William didn't either.

They sat sipping from their water glasses.

"If we really stretch things, can we put even a tentative question mark beside anyone's name?" she asked.

William shook his head. "Is anyone we know capable of vandalism on such a scale? Come back to the young men for a moment. Maybe your boys were having some nasty fun even though basically they're good lads. Modern youth."

"You're an old curmudgeon," she said with a smile. "Besides, what about that misspelling? They're all far from illiterate."

He smiled. "I've always thought it was intentional, my dear. A big misspelling but a correctly placed comma? The misspelling was deliberate as a mock red herring; the comma was automatic and not seen...because it was correct."

Maddie recalled the message on her car door: 'Your not wanted here. Go away, bitch!!!' "You're absolutely right, William," she said with some delight. "I completely missed the comma!"

Maddie's phone rang from the depths of her handbag.

Douglas. "George has had an accident," he said, his voice stressed. "I was invited over for a drink – probably because they'd wanted to talk to me about the offer on the Manor. But when I arrived, I walked into chaos. George was bleeding and slipping into unconsciousness; Tina was hysterical and still is. I called an ambulance which has taken George to Reading and there's no way she can drive herself. She's, well, she's out of control, Maddie, screaming, crying. I can't calm her down and drive at the same time. Are you available? If you can support her – maybe in the back seat? – I can be free to drive relatively safely."

"Of course," Maddie said, appalled. "I'm at William's. Where are you?"

"At the Higgins'. The ambulance has already gone ahead. They wouldn't take her; she was making such a commotion."

"Where is she now?"

"Getting her handbag ... there you are," he said, obviously to Tina. Maddie could hear gulping sobs "We'll get you a drink of water first then we'll be on our way." He paused. "Bye," he whispered. "See you in a couple of minutes?"

"I'm leaving now," Maddie said.

She hastily explained to William what was happening and dashed to her car.

Once she was outside the cottages, Douglas came out supporting a weeping Tina who protested even more wildly when she saw Maddie.

"Oh, Maddie, you don't have to...oh, it's so awful...." Her voice ended in a wail.

"Get in the back of my car, Tina, with Douglas. I'll drive." She looked at Douglas who nodded. Tina would certainly prefer it that way and might, as a result, be more likely to settle down.

When the two were safely in the back with seat belts on and only the briefest of thoughts about the glass of wine she'd drunk with dinner, Maddie headed towards Reading on the B4546, driving as quickly as she could to be safe. "I'll take the 4074 down to Reading, right? Should take something less than half an hour. But which hospital?" she asked.

Tina was now collapsed against Douglas, crying still and beating her hands against him. "Just like...just like...nooooooo. Not again. Not again. Oh god, not again. Do something. Stop this. Stop it, stop it, stop it...." and so she kept on, a continual stream of consciousness that made little sense.

Tina's voice occasionally rose high enough over the road noise so that Maddie could hear some of what she was saying. At other times she would quieten again as she spoke only to Douglas.

At one point Tina wailed, "I shouldn't have let him do it. It's all my fault."

Her fault? Maddie flicked her eyes to the rear vision mirror to see what was happening. Tina was clutching Douglas's shoulder, her head on his arm. But Maddie could see her face. The words were there; the weeping and wailing were on-going but for a second, the expression on her face was cold. Utterly devoid of the passion of her words, then it collapsed again appropriately and Maddie doubted what she'd observed.

"What am I going to do?" Tina howled. "I can't...I mustn't...noooooo."

"Which hospital?" Maddie asked again, louder. Reading had several.

"Which one, Tina?" Douglas asked.

"The Royal Berkshire," Tina said clearly enough. It seemed to help, relaying that little fact. Her wailing was interrupted.

"What happened to George?" Maddie asked but again no answer was forthcoming. Tina was still awkwardly hanging off Douglas's shoulder. Maddie watched Douglas pat Tina's back. The seat belts were holding them a person's width apart which necessitated the pose, Maddie figured. Tina must want comforting. Need it. And Tina was a physical sort, judging from her previous behaviour with Douglas.

Maddie checked herself; she was being coldly clinical, sceptical, a bit of the old Probation Officer demeanour reasserting itself. She needed to get back in touch with being a caring human being who takes things at face value. George was injured. Tina's husband. People react to adversity in unique ways. Who was she to judge this particular response?

As her car ate up the miles, Maddie became aware the two in the back seat were quieter again. She could no longer make out any words but she could hear a constant murmuring. She caught Tina stroking Douglas's neck, her head turned up to his in the classic adoration pose of seventeenth century religious paintings. Douglas appeared to be staring into the middle distance, not moving.

Maddie steeled herself to keep her eyes on the road, only occasionally peeking into the mirror. Once, Douglas met her eyes and raised his eyebrows for an instant, reconnecting in this bizarre situation.

The long summer evening was drawing in and Maddie turned on her headlights. As the sky faded into oranges and yellows, it was more difficult to see the two in the back, and it was certainly quieter. Maddie was tired and wished the journey over as soon as possible. Such emotion was draining.

When they hit the outskirts of Reading, she asked Douglas to direct her to the hospital, her voice loud in the stillness.

"Oh god, oh god," Tina said, her voice again raised.

"Hush and go back to sleep," Douglas said as if speaking to a child. "There, there." Maddie could see him rub Tina's back slowly and rhythmically.

At the hospital, they were told George was in intensive care in a serious but stable condition. No visitors but family. Tina was whisked away to a private conference with the doctors while Maddie and Douglas were left kicking their heels in a badly furnished waiting room without any direction about whether to stay or leave. Maddie sat on a plastic chair and let her head fall back against the wall.

"Do you know what happened to George?" she asked.

"Gunshot wound to his chest," Douglas said in a flat voice that betrayed his exhaustion.

Shot? Not with the rifle they'd found in the well? "Whose gun?" she asked, straightening up.

"No idea. George found it. He took out the magazine but it accidently went off because a bullet was ready to be fired, evidently. Shot himself in the chest."

She was suddenly wide awake. "A rifle? You know we found a rifle in their well."

Douglas frowned at her. "What do you know about a rifle?"

"We fished it out of the garden feature – it looks like a little well and it really is. A real well, I mean. The gun was stuck down a little way, across the opening. The barrel was covered in rust but it's a modern rifle. Semi-automatic with a magazine. But, Douglas, George made sure the gun was unloaded. I know. I was there."

They stared at each other.

"Tina said it was an accident," he said. "She blamed herself for not checking a bullet wasn't up the spout. That's what she called it. Up the spout. She was horribly distressed. You saw her."

Maddie nodded miserably. He was still defending Tina. But Maddie was certain no bullet could have been left in that rifle. Almost certain. George had been ultra careful, ultra cognizant about the danger. No way would he have removed the magazine and opened the breech without checking for another bullet.

Douglas stood up, looking years older than his age. "I'll find out whether we're needed or not. Even if Tina stays, maybe we can go home."

"I hope," Maddie said. "But I don't want her waiting alone if there's bad news."

Douglas nodded and left the room. He returned with Tina, as beautiful as ever now she wasn't constantly crying. Tina said George was doing better and the kind people here had organised a cot for her to spend the night at George's bedside. She was amazingly calm.

"I'm hugely pleased for George." Maddie gave her a little hug. "And I'm pleased you're feeling better now, too." She held Tina's hands. "I'm so sorry about it all. I gather it was the gun we found earlier today?"

"Isn't it terrible, Maddie? So hard to believe, but you saw that horrid thing. Someone threw it into our well and it's injured my darling George." Her voice started to rise again. "It could have been me – or it could have been you – lying in intensive care with a bullet in your chest, fighting for your life!"

"It could indeed," Maddie said trying to keep her voice even. Yeah, right. She had no intention of attacking Tina's story at this point. In fact, she had a great deal to think about before talking to her about wells, guns or bullets.

Douglas offered to drive home and Maddie gratefully accepted. Night had fallen by the time they descended to the level of the hospital carpark; it was still and warm, almost tropical. They headed back up the highway towards their part of South Oxfordshire.

"What else did Tina say on our way here?" she asked when they left the street lamps behind and were travelling through dark countryside.

Douglas stretched his neck and shoulders, his hands on the wheel. "She was going on and on about grabbing the gun, an accident, her fault, the stupidity of it. She was really bothered by it all. And the well and the roses. I've never seen her like this. Hell, I've never seen anybody like that in my entire life."

"'Stupidity of it'?" Maddie repeated. "Not George. I saw a man who was dumbfounded that a rifle had appeared in his well, who took due care in handling it, making sure neither Tina nor I were anywhere near, who immediately removed the magazine and, moreover, must have ejected the single bullet that was ready to be fired."

Douglas shot her a glance. "Must have? The bullet up the spout? You didn't actually see it?"

"I saw him open up the gun. I saw him replacing a bullet into the spring loaded contraption in the magazine and lay it onto the terrace. I saw him leave the chamber open. If the gun is open, you can see whether or not a bullet is there. He's no fool, Douglas, and he's obviously handled firearms before. As far as I'm concerned, to fire that gun, someone had to put a new bullet in, or else put the magazine in, close the mechanism and cock it ready to fire."

"Maybe you only saw a spare bullet, one he could have removed from the magazine to see the calibre."

"Of course any of that's possible, but my impression ... oh, I don't know anything, really. But I was right there, Douglas, behind George, and I saw him being conscientious and safe, warning me about the danger. I think I know George wouldn't take any chances. I've been around rifles too. My dad had one for years. I know what a magazine does; I know the size of a .22 bullet; I even know the term 'up the spout' and what it means. George would have removed an unfired shot if it was there. He *must* have retrieved it because I saw him replace a bullet into the top of the magazine."

Douglas didn't reply at first to her lecture. Then he spoke. "It's okay, Maddie. What you're saying is logical. But it doesn't jibe with what Tina told me. However, I agree with you that anyone who knows how to remove a magazine would check whether a bullet was ready to be fired." He was driving steadily, his face expressionless.

"You can see the base of the bullet when you open the gun," Maddie said. She told herself to be quiet. All had been said that needed to be said.

They rode in silence. The night was dark. Clouds must have moved in while they were inside the hospital.

As they neared Cherry Tree Cottages, where Douglas had left his car, he thanked Maddie for coming to the rescue. "There's an awful lot to think about, isn't there?"

"Time enough in the morning," Maddie said. "Give me a ring, won't you, and we can go over the ramifications."

When she opened the kitchen door back at Briar Cottage, the phone was blinking its silent communication that a message was waiting.

"Ring me when you come in, Maddie," said William's voice. "I won't be able to sleep until I hear the next instalment."

She dutifully rang and the phone was picked up immediately. "How's the long-suffering George?" William asked.

"Hanging in there," Maddie said. "He's in intensive care and they've stabilised him. He was shot."

"Shot?" William's voice portrayed the same shock Maddie had felt when she'd heard.

"Shot. An accident. We deposited Tina into the welcome arms of the Royal Berkshire and skedaddled home." Maddie gave him an abbreviated version of what had happened, keeping to herself her own observations of George's carefulness with both ammunition and the gun itself. She was too worn out to go over it all.

Chapter Twenty-Three

MADDIE PUT THE PHONE down, leaning heavily on the bench top as she did so. The silence of the little cottage should have been comforting, shutting away all the ugliness of the evening, but she was distraught. Shootings; such things belonged to her old life in tales from her crims. A shooting of someone she knew? That was foreign to her, horrible, not to be contemplated. She shook her head. She felt unsettled, nervous. She checked the doors. Both locked. She made certain all the ground floor windows were secure. She still felt uneasy.

She looked around the little kitchen, searching for something to calm her nerves, to bring her back to normality. Cup of tea? Whisky? Cocoa? In the end, she made herself a hot chocolate drink with added cream. Comfort food. She and Wayne used to have late night cups of cocoa when things had gone wrong during the day – the children being fractious, stress at work, or, she remembered, being overwhelmed by circumstances like the 7/7 terrorist attacks on the London Underground. They'd talked softly in the dimly lit kitchen of their south-west London house before wandering up together to bed, often hand in hand, to sleep, warmed by the presence of each other.

She carried the cocoa up to her bedroom alone, tears pricking her eyes. At first it was George she was concerned about; she couldn't bear to think of him lying in hospital fighting for his life. Instead, she forced her mind onto happier times ... Wayne and the girls when they were little; family picnics; Christmas mornings; her first promotion in the Probation Service; her deep felt joy when she knew she'd helped a habitual crim go straight. But she found she couldn't bear to think of the good times when she was so agitated; she knew good times far outweighed the bad, even at the end of her marriage, but it didn't help.

Maddie hated going to bed alone, always triggering sadness and regrets. Could she have done things differently? Tears ran down her face unchecked now. Somehow she felt dreadful, as if her world was crashing.

She sipped her cocoa, first one sip, then another and another until it was finished, the warmth transferred into her very being, melting her heart and soothing her troubles. Her tears dried as she appreciated how stressful the dramatic events concerning the Higgins were and the impact of that stress on everyone involved, including her. No wonder tension like this brought up other bits of unfinished business in her life ... like Wayne and her lost marriage and even the demise of a career that had provided her with an opportunity to contribute to society.

No. It was better to be starting afresh, maybe even better to be sleeping alone. She grabbed the lightest, prettiest and sexiest set of pyjamas she owned – tiny scraps of satin trimmed in lace – and climbed into bed. Somehow that period of weakness, the crying and, yes, the cocoa had drained her of the latent negativity. Finally she was sleepy even though the hour was not late. Within a minute of pulling up a single sheet on this warm night, a fresh breeze wafting through the open window, she was asleep.

Maddie struggled awake. Something was very, very wrong; her sleep-soaked brain pushed aside the shrill call of an eagle in a flying dream. Not the screech of an eagle. The screech of an alarm! That piercing WHEE, WHEE, WHEE sound which was designed to violently snatch a person from sleep.

She sat up. What, where? Why was an alarm sounding?

Smoke! Her internal alarm scared any remnants of sleep away.

Smoke?

Fire!

She leapt out of bed towards the door of her room which she'd left slightly ajar. Clouds of thick smoke poured in and the noise was deafening. The smoke detector! Starting to cough, she slammed the door shut, figuring the smoke was coming up the stairwell where the smoke detector was located.

She spun around. The window?

Oh no.

She spun around. Door? absolutely not. Window? Only the window was available for escape. Nothing else. Small, in a little dormer high above the roof. Dangerous.

No choice. The window.

She ran to it and pushed aside the curtains. On such a warm night she'd left it fully open but it was protected by a fly screen. She scrabbled at it, not knowing where the fasteners were, finally, in desperation, punching her way through it. When she could grab the torn screen, she yanked it towards her and away.

She leaned out of the open window, alternately coughing and gulping fresh air before putting her hands through the window, feeling for the roofing outside. Steep. Slightly damp from dew. She was horribly frightened of skidding and falling uncontrollably. She glanced at the door where smoke was pushing its way under and around the ill-fitting old frame. No way out. Through the window or face the smoke and flames? No alternative. But she really, really did not want to go out that window.

She took a deep breath, coughed and leaned further out. If she panicked, she'd slip. Instead of going through the window head first, she grabbed the bedroom chair and knelt on the windowsill, feet out but facing inside so she could keep a good grip on the window surround.

She eased one knee down to the roof, then the other, holding on tightly. Once outside, she stopped, holding on tightly, coughing. She was suddenly giddy, and told herself to calm down. She held her breath and willed herself to the epitome of a panicky situation. She took a couple of deep breaths, and coughed the final bits of smoke from her lungs. Oh, that sweet, fresh air.

Oh no! Her phone. She couldn't see it through the smoke, but knew it was on her bedside table. There was no way she was going inside again. She'd just have to get down as quickly as possible.

Once she turned her thoughts fully on the problem, she figured her best way was towards the conservatory, over its roof and down. It was almost, but not quite, directly below her. The moonlight reflected in its glass roof making it look even more insubstantial than it probably was. Her eyes darted around. No close trees. No handy down-spouting. Her only choice was ease herself down to the conservatory or jump from the edge of the roof. Conservatory it was. Now, how to force herself away from the dormer window to which she was still desperately clinging?

She leaned a bit heavier on her toes, now firmly planted on the tiled roof.

Steady. But the thought of letting her fingers go from the window surround was thoroughly unpleasant, to say the least.

She extended one foot down a bit. It held onto the surface of the roof. She let her weight down onto that foot and extended one arm onto the damp surface of the tiles, the other still holding on for dear life.

It seemed firm enough. A billow of smoke came through the window and set her coughing again. She had to get off this roof. She lowered her knees to the tiles to increase contact, so both legs were touching at knees and toes, plus one hand was flat on a tile keeping as much friction as possible.

Finally it was time to release the hand clutching the window surround. She took a deep breath and slowly slid her fingers down to the sill and finally onto the roof. She was now thoroughly frightened. Another deep breath later, she carefully lifted one foot and knee and moved the leg lower down. Good. If she kept three limbs on the surface of the roof, she could move one. Next was a hand. Then the other leg. Another hand. The leading leg touched something below her vision.

She swivelled her head. Yes! Her foot was on the edge of the gutter. Would it hold? She put pressure on it. It wobbled and she hastily withdrew it. But there was nothing else to do. She took a deep breath extended her foot to the gutter again and gripped it with her toes. She cautiously put pressure on it. It bent but didn't crack away or break. She did it again and it seemed okay so she carefully moved a hand closer, then the other foot and knee. As she was gaining confidence, suddenly the first leg gave way, sliding down until her toes hit the far side of the gutter.

Maddie yelped, and she froze. She forced herself to breathe. In and out. In and out. The guttering wobbled then steadied. How much strain could it take? Surely not the weight of a person. Her weight. She kept as little pressure on that foot as possible, merely steadying the rest of her body.

She then felt with that foot for the glass of the conservatory roof. No, it was more to the left. Was the smoke coming through the tiles? She had to get down as soon as possible. What would happen if she slipped? Maybe she'd hang onto the gutter until it slowly gave way and she'd drop to the ground. The very solid drought-hardened ground.

Using the gutter as little as possible, she inched to the left, probing with her bare toes. Finally, finally, they hit glass and her toes found the edge of the panel which was faintly raised. A tiny toehold. She moved first one hand then the other before stretching out the second foot. It, too, felt more secure on the moulding holding the glass panels together than on the slippery roof tiles, but could the conservatory glass roof take her weight? She lowered herself down to spread her weight over the glass as much as possible, not only hands, knees and toes, but her entire body now touched the cool glass. She inched downwards until her hands were on the gutter and her feet stretched along the glass to the edge of the conservatory roof.

At that point, her progress improved as she descended the glass roof which was not as steeply pitched as the tile roof above, and less slippery. She edged downwards until she was holding onto one of the mouldings by her fingertips with her legs hanging down towards the ground. One foot felt something that frightened her so much, she almost lost her grip on the tiny moulding. What was there? She forced her mind to imagine sitting in the conservatory and looking through the windows. Bushes. But which bushes brushed the glass?

Yes. Hydrangea bushes with their large cool blue heads of flowers that must be eight or nine inches across. That's what her toes felt – cool, soft-as-silk blossom. Could she drop into the hydrangea? Would it have any substance to break her fall? She smelled smoke and the decision was taken from her.

She took a deep breath, shut her eyes and let herself go, falling the rest of the way into the bush. She landed unceremoniously on her bottom with a few scratches but nothing major. She was extricating herself from the bush when she heard the distant wail of a fire truck closely followed by the howl of a police car.

Relief flooded through her, as much for the arrival of the authorities as landing relatively unscathed. By the time she'd dashed into the front garden, firemen were running towards the front door which had smoke pouring from around it.

The fire hose was trained inside the door and smoke and steam billowed into the night. A frantic ten minutes later, the fire was out and the diagnosis had been made. Someone had lit a fire on the stone floor of the front porch, then, when it got going sufficiently, shoved burning twigs and extra paper in through the mail slot. The front hall was scorched, the hall table sported burnt legs and the rug, now pulled from the house, still smouldered on the front lawn producing intermittent swirls of smoke. The firemen said the flooring would have been damaged but the fire had been confined to the front hall. Most of the smoke was from the old woollen rug. But in another few minutes, the hall table would have been alight and there would have been a different end to the story.

The firemen let her go upstairs to change from her scanty pyjamas – her only embarrassment – and she descended in jeans and t-shirt to make cups of tea for them all.

The firemen were full of praise she had a working smoke detector (thank you, Caroline) and about her skill in extricating herself off the roof so competently (she was mentally patting herself on the back for this too). She could have been overcome, they said, if she'd tried descending the stairs due to the acrid smoke produced by the smouldering front hall carpet. Smoke kills more people than fire does. She accepted the praise but felt a false heroine. She had been ridiculously frightened by it all and it was only by good fortune she managed her escape.

A neighbour across the lane had been up for a call of nature and heard a car spin its wheels as it drove off in a hurry. He'd glanced out and seen the small fire on the front porch and maybe a faint glow through the window of the front door of Briar Cottage. He'd rung the fire brigade, thereby gaining precious minutes.

They all ended up enjoying stories of fires and idiocy told by the firemen as dawn spread its glow over them all. Tea and toast, the perfect antidote to fear-driven adrenalin.

The police, in the form of two young policemen, had turned up with the fire engine to cordon off the road. Detectives would be along later to question her, one of them told her. She stared at him.

"Have we met?" she asked.

"Almost," he said with a wide smile. "I'm PC Fergus Waters. You might not remember but we almost bowled you and Mr Dingle when you were going into the Flores house one evening. Me and Mel and Bart."

The third young man. A policeman.

Maddie smiled back. "Nice to meet you properly, Constable Waters. And you can tell the detectives that I may have a hunch who might have motivation to do this. It could be linked to the shooting last night."

The young policeman immediately lost his smile. "I'll tell him, Mrs Brooks. DS Katz, it will be then. He's handling the shooting. He'll be in touch this morning."

Chapter Twenty-Four

Once her kitchen had been cleared of people and her dishes done, Maddie rang a concerned Caroline, then the insurance company, leaving a message about what had occurred overnight. She had no intention of going into work until things were more settled at home.

Besides, she could rest on her laurels a little with the de Mille sale. She definitely had the impression Louise wanted to stay on the same estate. Soon she would follow up the de Milles to see if they wanted her to show them larger homes there, but not today. Not that Maddie particularly wanted to have to deal with Louise again, but she reminded herself that estate agents don't have to like their clients. Only pretend to. Besides, Antoine was okay. And the Reynolds needed a breathing space, which was exactly what she herself needed.

Amazingly enough, Maddie felt totally revitalised in spite of a shortened night's sleep and all the excitement and huge apprehension of the fire. Maybe William's sweating regime had something going for it after all.

She tried to ring Douglas to discuss her suspicions with him, but it flipped to voicemail. Had he again been summoned to Liverpool? Or, perhaps he'd gone to the Manor. She grabbed her handbag and drove over, just in case.

Douglas's car was parked in front. Good. She tried his mobile again, but still no answer. It felt excessively quiet; she was aware of that blank feeling that empty houses exude when nobody is home.

She sat in the sunshine on the front step, deciding what to do when she had a devastating series of thoughts and possible answers to many of her questions: Why did George's face go white? The gun in the well? Did he really recognise it? The shot that Adrian the vet's colleague heard all that time ago? Even the roses wilting in the heat yesterday.

Was Douglas thinking along the same lines? She needed to talk to him.

She rushed down the farm track towards the isolated cottages in sudden certainty Douglas had headed that way already. Before she was half way along, it hit her.

Ohmygod, George.

She stopped, rummaged for her mobile and snatched it from her handbag, poking in those three vital numbers as she continued on her way. The operator answered immediately and Maddie started her story, asking for DS Katz, the policeman in charge of the shooting in South Oxfordshire. The operator calmly told her to ring the police number, not the emergency services. Maddie interrupted her. "You don't understand. Someone is in grave danger. Immediate danger. It's an emergency of the first order," Maddie said putting as much urgency into her voice as she could.

She could hear the sounds of a farm machine coming closer. Were they mowing the hay crop?

"Connecting now," the operator said. She proceeded to ask for Maddie's details.

Maddie was in a state of intense frustration. How could she not have thought of the danger to George last night? She paced along the small patch of the farm track in her frustration. If something happened to him.... She didn't finish the thought.

"Ms Brooks?" a voice said into her ear. "DS Katz here. You're worried about Mr George Higgins being in danger?"

"Thanks for talking to me," she said feeling a wave of relief, "It's only that we believe—"

"'We'? Ms Brooks?"

"Sorry, I believe...." She took a deep breath. "We were in the hospital last night, Mr Douglas Fanshaw and myself, but neither of us realised the possible danger George may be in—"

"We're onto it. And we know of your fire this morning. Thanks for ringing. We're gathering information as we speak. Could I please ask you – the two of you – to come in? We'd be most interested in speaking to you both."

Maddie agreed and arranged to call into the station after lunch. With Douglas, if possible. She stopped walking as she put the phone away, feeling flat, staring out through the bushes to where the sun was shining on the rippling field of hay. The machine was closer, louder.

The police were onto it, DS Katz had said. What did that mean, really mean? The police would have been involved, she knew that, because when a person is shot, the police are informed and their duty is to investigate. But, onto it? Onto what? She cursed herself that she hadn't elicited more information.

She continued walking along the track towards the back of the Higgins' cottages, turning her mind to her original thought that Douglas had figured it all out too.

The mowing machine noise increased with every step she took. It must be working this field even though, to her city-slicker eyes, it was nowhere near the golden colour she expected at harvest. She peered through the branches out over the sweet smelling hay but nothing was in sight.

As she turned a final bend in the path, she could just make out Douglas through the foliage of the hedgerow bushes. She stopped, sensing something was very wrong. She peered through the foliage, touching none, making as little movement as possible. Yes, he was exactly where she expected him to be, smack dab in the middle of the bank of roses. But something was certainly awry. He wasn't digging. In fact, he wasn't moving.

The machine was making a deafening racket now.

Douglas was staring back at the cottages, a shovel in his hands. He hadn't noticed Maddie, intent on something happening well beyond her vision. He was speaking to someone but she couldn't make out anything with the din made by the mower. And Maddie couldn't see what he was looking at, either. Her heart was beating frantically.

Maddie hunkered down in case her shadowy figure still appeared humanlike through the leaves.

The machine slowly passed and the noise started to abate.

"It was an accident, I tell you." Tina's voice. She was screaming over the mower.

"How, Tina? How did it happen?" Douglas's voice was raised as well, but he sounded relatively calm, at least in comparison to her.

"Things started out so well," Tina said, her voice breaking into a sob. Douglas didn't answer. "I offered to do some gardening; I brought over some homemade biscuits." Her voice broke again. "I laughed when she told me about how she never had to pay for things."

Maddie flinched. She wasn't talking about George; she was talking about Beryl.

"I sympathised when she said how she was going to get back at William Dingle," Tina said. "She was a horrid old woman, and I was so understanding, so supportive. You have to know I gave it my best!"

"I have no doubts you did," Douglas said. "So why have that gun in your hands, Tina? Put it down, please."

Maddie held her breath and tried to still her heart.

The gun.

"I'll have this gun in my hands if I want to," Tina said, her voice rising again.

"Okay, okay," Douglas said. "You were saying it was an accident?"

Maddie reached for her phone and dialled emergency services again. This time she whispered the facts immediately: the location, the gun, Tina Higgins and Douglas Fanshaw. She was told to leave her mobile on and connected. Seconds later the operator said they'd dispatched police but it would be some minutes. Maddie was to keep on the phone and in hiding and not to interfere.

"She wouldn't sell to me, Douglas, you have to understand," Tina was saying. "No matter how pleasant, how friendly I was, she wouldn't let me have the Manor. Then even when I did the other things, the nasty things, I was so sympathetic. I told her again and again it was a sign she should leave. But would she go? No. She should have, shouldn't she? Any sensible person would leave when harassed like that. She was in danger, for god's sake."

Maddie rolled her eyes. Danger? From whom, pray?

"But you tried one more time?" Douglas asked.

No! Don't provoke her, Douglas, for heaven's sake! Leave it. Slowly back off. He stayed where he was, not receiving Maddie's silent commands. She still couldn't see Tina. But she presumed she was on the terrace, the heavy gun resting on the railing, pointed down the garden towards Douglas.

The mower was well away now, its roar a mere purr from somewhere in the distance. Except for the roaring in her ears, Maddie could hear more clearly now.

"She'd guessed the harassment was me. She came out of the utility room with Freddy's gun. It was kept chained up, she told me, precisely for this type of emergency. An intruder." Tina's voice held another sob. "Me, an intruder?"

"And?"

"Who's frightened of an old gun in the arms of an old lady, a gun unused for a dozen years or more? She was bluffing, right?" Tina's voice regained its momentum.

Douglas didn't answer.

"She was bluffing," Tina said, brooking no argument, "so I walked right up to it and grabbed it from her."

"You then turned it onto her?"

A pause. Maddie held her breath, imagining Tina making a non-verbal communication, nodding or shaking her head.

"I wanted her to feel what's it's like to be opposite the business end of a gun. I pointed it at her and the damned thing went off."

"So, it was an accident," Douglas said. "Put the gun away now, Tina. We certainly don't want any more accidents."

"The police are turning into Cherry Tree Farm Lane now," the calm voice of the operator said in Maddie's ear.

"Tell them to continue past the cottages to the farm buildings," Maddie whispered, frightened her voice would be audible in the now still morning air. "On the right is a track that leads to the back of the cottages. They'll be able to see Douglas Fanshaw after a dozen yards or so. Tina Higgins is talking to him. She has a gun. She's on the terrace with the gun, the terrace behind the cottages. I can hear her but I can't see her. Tell them to be quick. Things are deteriorating."

The operator suggested she find some protection and be still. Get down. Don't stand or run. And stay connected.

Maddie slithered back along the track until she came to a turn where the path made a slight depression. She could finally see Tina from beneath the bushes. She was dressed in the same clothes as yesterday, her hair dishevelled. As Maddie watched, Tina, using her tennis-strengthened arms, steadily raised the gun to sight along its length, pointing directly at Douglas. Maddie was mesmerised, impotent. Her heart thumped erratically. Her breathing stopped. Where were the police? Tina was ready to shoot. What could she do? She had to do something!

A stick? Nothing but twigs. No stones or rocks. Nothing useful was on the track.

Her phone.

Maddie pitched her phone as hard as she could towards Douglas. It crashed through the bushes well short, as she'd known it would, but the gun swung towards the noise.

A gunshot rang out.

"Down, Douglas," Maddie yelled. "Get down." She obeyed her own command and pulled her head below the edge of the track. She gasped what air she could into her lungs, her hands over her head pushing her face into the sharp grasses of the track.

Another shot hit the stone wall.

A third and a cry.

No! Tears sprang to Maddie's eyes. Douglas?

Suddenly the police had Tina, holding her arm where the police marksman had shot her; seconds later Douglas was helping Maddie up, hugging her.

"My phone," Maddie said. "I threw my phone." Laughing a little hysterically, they searched for it and found it with its screen reflecting the blue sky.

The operator was still connected. "It's okay, thanks. It's okay. He's okay," Maddie said breathlessly. "The police are here and it's all okay."

"The whole time Tina was talking to me, I was worried about you," Douglas said, his hands on Maddie's shoulders. "Why didn't I realise earlier you'd be in danger? It wasn't until Tina trained that gun on me I knew. If she could shoot me, she certainly would be out to get you. After all, you'd seen George's carefulness with the gun; you knew George would have removed that last bullet." He hugged her again. "When you created the diversion, she shot at it; that's when I knew she was for real. She must have had her finger on the trigger. On a gun pointing at me! Thank you, Maddie, so very much. I owe you my life."

"It gave you time to get behind the wall?"

"I took a flying leap like a cat at a rat. I was safe behind that stone wall even before you'd finished yelling at me."

"And the police shot the gun off her." Maddie reached up and brushed his face. Given the dirt on his face and clothes, his flying leap must have landed him in the hayfield with a thump.

A policeman in Kevlar armour approached them.

Douglas extracted himself from their embrace. "I came across something where I was digging," Douglas said to him. "Some blue cloth. Maybe a woman's dress?" He shot a quick glance at Maddie.

Maddie trailed along after Douglas who led the policeman to the rose bed. He pointed out the patch of dirty blue fabric at the bottom of his small trench.

Douglas and Maddie were immediately ushered back from the rose garden onto the back garden and told to wait for the detective. They had quite a story for him.

Douglas turned his attention back to his failure to realise Maddie's danger. When he heard about the fire, he was even more distressed.

"But I'm all right, Douglas, and so is Briar Cottage," Maddie said in an attempt to ease his guilt. "It's not only you. Last night I didn't give personal danger a thought. Worse, even with all the excitement of the fire this morning, I still didn't think about George lying helpless in hospital."

"With Tina right there," Douglas said. "And murder in her heart."

• • • • • • • • • •

The next two days went past in a blur. George was in a critical condition for twenty-four hours. Tina had tried her best to ensure he didn't regain consciousness and thus be able to tell his tale. The doctors figured Tina had leaned her full weight on his injured chest again and again, destroying the fragile healing and starting the internal bleeding again. She then turned up the drip going into his veins to maximum, not knowing the nature of the substance pouring into his blood, but reasoning an increased dose of most intravenous drugs would wreak havoc. But George stubbornly refused to die.

As it turned out, the drip was delivering an antibiotic and nurses discovered it on a routine check before any harm could take place. But they also noticed George's breathing was ragged and his heartbeat up, with fresh bleeding on the bandage over the wound. A scan quickly diagnosed the extent of the internal bleeding. Medication was administered and he was monitored carefully. Scans apparently now replace exploratory surgery when doctors want to see what is happening inside, much less messy and certainly easier on the patient.

The second day, George's condition was changed from being 'critical' back to 'serious' and finally 'stable'. He was kept in a state of semi-consciousness to keep him as immobile as possible to aid the internal healing, a mercy, given all that had happened to him, and by whom.

Tina had been taken into custody, not for injuring George nor even for threatening Douglas, but for murder. The police, after continuing to dig Douglas's trench in the rose bed, found the blue fabric was indeed a dress. Beryl Fanshaw's dress. There, deep under the garden, they found her remains, one skeletonised foot within an old lady's shoe, the other clad only in the tattered remnants of a lisle stocking, a bullet through her chest, probably her heart. It didn't take long to identify the shot that killed her. It was a .22 bullet belonging to the rifle found in the well, a rifle once registered to Mr Frederic Fanshaw.

After the police questioned Tina about the smoky smell still on her clothes and in her wild mane of hair, she confessed to setting the fire at Briar Cottage and, surprisingly, to Beryl's homicide, which she continued to declare was an accident. She had no intention of shooting Beryl, she claimed. The disposal of both the gun and Beryl's body was pure panic.

When Maddie heard, she sniffed. It must have been a long-lasting panic. And George? Surely one 'accident' with that gun too many.

Chapter Twenty-Five

DOUGLAS AND WILLIAM WERE sitting with Maddie in the conservatory at Briar Cottage enjoying a cup of tea and, not cream buns, but an equally delicious date slice from *Jenny's Kitchen*. The day was warm but rain was slashing down, thoroughly soaking the fields and village gardens. The whole of Oxfordshire was smiling because of it. Thunder rolled in the distance.

"William," Maddie said carefully, "you never had any children?"

"Now what brings that up?" William asked with a sidelong glance at Maddie.

"Oh, just that you and Beryl ... all those years ... and then Beryl, who was such a skinflint, spent such a lot of money on Jenny...."

William took a sip of his tea, partially concealing a smile. "I've always had a soft spot for Jenny." He leaned over the table and helped himself to another date slice. "But to focus on a more pressing issue, why do you think Tina turned on you? A shrewd guess?"

"Tina may not have known if I'd seen or hadn't seen George eject the last bullet from the gun but she couldn't be certain," Maddie said, giving in to the change of subject, "and she had to do something about it." Her back was to the broken hydrangea bush where she'd slithered more or less gracefully off the roof.

"But George knew he'd taken due care," William said. "She had to finish the job on him or she'd be in big trouble – looking at a divorce and probably a gaol term. Goodbye Manor as well."

"My guess is the whole past history became crystal clear as soon as he found the gun in the well," Douglas said, "much like happened to both Maddie and me. I was kicking myself I hadn't clued in when George was shot."

"Same, same," Maddie added, reaching for a paper serviette for her sticky fingerd.

"It had to be all about Tina," Douglas said. "And what, I asked myself, was happening at the Higgins' house when Aunt Beryl disappeared? George was away on business and Tina ripped up the pathway and put in a substantial rose bed complete with stone wall. All in the five or so days George was away? Something like that usually means weeks of thinking about it and certainly consultation with your partner. So I had a series of bad thoughts about what was in that rose garden. That led to my trek over there with a spade."

"Clever you," Maddie said. "I hadn't got that far."

"We were woefully slow on the uptake, weren't we? Putting it all together. I guess it was when Tina hadn't taken advantage of their well water for her precious yellow roses that things dropped into place in George's mind. He'd figured it out, all right. He must have told her it was one cover-up too far."

"She's still claiming Beryl's death was an accident," Maddie said.

"It was no accident," William said firmly. "You don't take the trouble she took to cover up an accidental death."

"It's complex," Maddie said with a frown. "It makes you wonder why she didn't leave Beryl's body down the well. Easier, certainly. Poor old Beryl was in there, we know that, because the police found a few of her hairs caught on the bricks on the inside of the well walls."

"Agreed. Beryl's body was there. But Tina couldn't leave it there. Eventually it would smell," William said.

"Nothing would have covered the stench of rotting flesh right there in the back garden."

Stench? Rotting flesh? Maddie gave him a look. After all, Beryl had been a living person who was dear to him at one time.

"The Higgins' back garden was used regularly," William continued. "Drinks on the terrace, their annual barbecue – it must have been about that time of year – I can imagine it, eating those special steaks to the smell of something decidedly rotten."

"Yuck. Stop it, William. Enough, already."

"I bet she would have used the well for a ready-made grave if she could have," Douglas interjected, helping himself to another date slice. "My take on it is that she threw the rifle down the well and, unbeknownst to her, it wedged where the garden feature ended and the more narrow opening to the actual well began. Then she heaved in Beryl's body, her head scraping along the bricks and depositing the hairs at that time. But that's when it all went belly up. Beryl was stuck right there, prevented from descending to the water level by the jammed gun." He grinned. "I can almost see Tina's face when she realised. Success when getting rid of the gun into the old well, hooray. Next, throwing the body after it and disaster. It caught, supported only a matter of feet down from the lip. What could she do? Beryl was probably staring right up at her with sightless eyes. Now, that's when she'd panic. What could she do with the body now? Leave it to rot? No way."

William was enjoying this. "She'd have slammed those shutters tight shut above the body and thanked her lucky stars George was away on business. She had to hope like hell he wouldn't come back and decide to peer down the well before she could implement Plan B. I bet she organised the digger that very day. She badly needed a grave so she had the trees from the track dug up and Bob's your uncle," William said, using another of his old fashioned sayings. "Loosened soil. Perfect for

Beryl's body. Then a couple of loads of topsoil over the top. And, luckily for Douglas, she'd had the stone wall built."

Maddie smiled, thinking of his dive over the wall.

"To turn the grave into a garden, all she needed," he continued, "was a load of plants. The body would be hidden forever under a bank of much-admired, sunshiny yellow roses."

"Still, some days must have gone by before she could put the body in the grave. I bet dear Beryl had begun to smell quite ripe," William said with a chortle. "I hope so, anyway."

"You're an old ghoul," Maddie said, passing more of the date slice. The wind rattled the rain against the conservatory glass.

"Did you both independently realise George was in danger?" William asked.

"Yes," Maddie said.

"No," Douglas said at the same time.

Maddie looked at him. "Why 'no'?"

Douglas turned to William. "I was so intent on proving my theory about Aunt Beryl, I didn't give a thought to more recent events. As I started to dig up those rose bushes, my thoughts came closer, ranging from George admiring Tina's garden design ... then to him being careful with the ammo and then, dammit, how Maddie was there. She knew about it, too. Maddie was in danger." He shook his head. "Then it occurred to me ... maybe Tina wasn't finished with George, poor devil. The worst thing was, we'd left her right beside him in hospital."

"I bet George knew about some of her earlier shenanigans at Beryl's place," Maddie said. "Someone painted over that graffiti on the shed and it wouldn't have been our glamorous Tina. And somebody skilled in DIY – well, semi-skilled anyway – fixed the broken window in the dining room. George had covered for her."

"But he didn't know she'd killed Beryl," Douglas said. "Maybe suspected, but not known until he saw Freddy's gun."

"Must have been galling for Tina to have shot George exactly like she did Beryl and he didn't die in the same way," William said, clearly having thought his opinions through. "But Beryl's murder? In my book it was one murderer knocking off another." He scrunched his face into a grimace. "I would bet my last quid Beryl managed to kill Mary Beth all those years ago, cancer or no cancer. And it makes you wonder about old Freddy. He died when he's lost almost everything – everything but the bonds – it had all been spent. Convenient timing."

Maddie held her breath. Couldn't be.

Yes, it could.

Douglas had a wry smile on his face. "No love lost between Aunt Beryl and you, I gather," Douglas said to William.

"I was a young fool," William said. "Then a middle aged fool, but eventually I became a wise old man."

"Are you sure you didn't knock off Beryl?" Maddie teased.

"Never quite got the chance, that's all," he said. "Now Tina – seems she had plenty of opportunity except she wasn't very good at this killing business. Success with Beryl, but she botched shooting George. Imagine the cold blooded effort it must have taken to compress poor George's chest and to turn up his drip. Stupid woman, even that didn't work. But then what? Coolly takes a taxi home in the middle of the night? Picks up her car and heads for Maddie's place?" William asked. "She botches that, too."

"Due to my cunning ability to cling to roofing tiles," Maddie said. "Which reminds me, I must ring Caroline and thank her properly for putting in that smoke alarm. Without it, we certainly wouldn't be sitting here together now."

"The word is out you wear nice pyjamas," Douglas said with a smirk.

Maddie smirked right back at him. "Eat your heart out," she said. On such a warm night thank goodness she hadn't been sleeping in the nude. She needed to change the subject. "Now the case of the reappearing will ... I figure Tina found it after she killed Beryl, appropriated it in case it was to her advantage, causing quite a delay while she figured out another plan of attack in her quest for the Manor," she said. "Flirting with you, Douglas, all that sort of thing. Then when she felt somewhat secure in her relationship with you, and, probably when it looked as if you'd win the court case as sole heir anyway, she replaced the will under the mattress. Hey, presto, I find it, exactly where you thought it would be all along."

"And it introduced doubt in my mind about you," Douglas said. "But what I can't figure out is the vandalism. Tina explained all about the graffiti directed against Aunt Beryl, but why did she scratch up your car? Or vandalise my flat?"

"Jealousy," Maddie said, pleased she'd identified the emotion earlier, conveniently forgetting her theory about which characters were involved. "At the end of the barbecue she spotted us going off arm in arm together as you escorted me – supported me – in the direction of the Manor instead of towards my car. She snooped around, found my car sitting in glorious isolation, was incensed about it all and scratched the daft message. She had a crush on you, a silly schoolgirl's pash."

Douglas shook his head. "I don't know about that," he said. "I always felt she was play-acting. Nothing serious."

"Exactly," William said leaning forward and waggling his finger for emphasis. "She wanted the Manor. Everything is consistent. She was a monomaniac with one passion and only one. To be mistress of the Manor. If her husband wouldn't cough up, she could divorce him and marry Douglas. The flirtation was a preliminary move. After all, she had every right to have confidence in her attractiveness and its power over mere men."

"She's a vixen, albeit a stunning one," Douglas agreed.

"First our Maddie leaving with you in the middle of the night, then going out for a drink with you not long afterwards?" William continued, as if Douglas hadn't spoken. "Tina would have seen red both times. Not because of romantic jealousy, but because Maddie was interfering in her little plot. All to do with gaining the Manor. And trashing your flat, Douglas? Nothing to do with searching for the bearer bonds, as I suspected."

"Fury at their turning up? At being foiled?" Maddie asked. "Douglas might no longer be forced to sell?"

"Precisely." He drained the last of his tea and turned to Douglas. "A question from a curious old man. Have you had your bonds valued yet?"

"A few days ago now, yes," Douglas said. "Not a fortune, but it will leave me comfortable. It's now possible for me to live in the Manor, for a while anyway, to see how I like it. My kids are excited about that prospect; they're already talking about a swimming pool, tennis court, weekend parties and their student pals coming to stay, the materialistic little rotters. Early days yet. I'll see how it goes."

Douglas looked slightly awkward. Maddie guessed that 'comfortable' was his way of being modest. He had no pressing need to sell the Manor now, and was keen to do the renovations at his own pace.

"So, you're going to do me out of my commission," she said with a smile.

He gave an exaggerated shrug, smiling in return.

Maddie was pleased he'd not be leaving any time soon. Pleased, in spite of losing the opportunity for a solution to her money worries. Douglas was becoming a good friend.

Maybe, only the slightest possibility of course, more than a friend.

Afterword from Tannis Laidlaw, author

The second book in the Madeleine Brooks Mystery series is Death at Valley View Cottage. The first part of the book is here:

Death at Valley View Cottage, by Tannis Laidlaw

Chapter One:
Can't breathe.
Chest heaving but no air enters. Try again. Nothing. And again.
Panic.
Eyes tear away from the body lying in the middle of the floor. Blood pools under his head.
Instead, look out of the window. A gust. Coppery leaves of the beech trees dance in the wind.
No air. Just distress. Dizzy. Dying, just like him.
Poetic justice...

Fresh air? Fresh air.

Leap for the door; swing it open.
Crisp breezes.
Gasp. Autumnal air.
Lungs fill.
Finally.
Stand. Just breathing. In and out. Letting the panic slowly dissipate into the wind. Watching the leaves. One detaches itself and lazily spins to the ground and skitters across the drive. And another.
Slowly turn.
He had not moved. Would never move again.
Why so angry?

Chapter Two:
Madeleine Brooks glanced at the digital clock on the dashboard. She should have known to avoid the A4074 this close to rush hour. After a millennium-like wait she swept off towards Courtneyside in relief. A new client wanted to sell his country bungalow and she was to meet him shortly. Her ex-husband had referred him, and, for a myriad of reasons, Maddie wanted the contact to go smoothly.

She brought her car to a halt in front of a steep drive. Walk? Or risk having to back the car down? One glance at the traffic sweeping past the foot of the drive and she opted to park on the verge and slog uphill on the concrete driveway. Lucky she did make that decision as a small car swooped down the steep drive past her trudging figure, dangerously wove into the traffic and sped away. She blinked, and more cautiously continued her way up the drive, keeping a sharp lookout for any other vehicles, but all was quiet. The drive might be steep but the property was in a nice setting within a forested hill even though just off a busy road; the trees likely absorbed a lot of the traffic noise.

She needn't have worried about parking. At the top, a vast turning area spread out in front of a cheaply built modern multi-car garage, suitable for parking a whole fleet, what appeared to be a recent addition to the thirties bungalow. She wasn't sure it was a selling point. No curb appeal, a steep drive then a concrete yard without a hint of the cottage itself. It was an odd layout and a charmless one at that.

She paused at the edge of the huge parking area. Where was the front door? She'd seen photos of Valley View Cottage. Although an older twentieth century bungalow like this was not without interest, it was hardly the charming centuries-old classic she'd hoped for when she was asked to take it on.

She walked past the three enormous garage roller-doors adorning the tin garage then spotted a person-sized door which was ajar. She peeked inside to find an immense, undivided space. Empty, smelling of fresh concrete. Totally clean and neat; at least that.

She ignored the back door of the bungalow set in a wall at right angles to the front of the set of garages because she could see a brick footpath leading around the side of the house. And it was the front door she wanted to see. With the sales photographs of the bungalow in mind, she was looking for a front porch replete with climbing roses which had been blooming in profusion when the photos were taken. Maybe not so prolific now it was August.

She skirted a beautifully restored classic car parked close to the footpath. She was to meet the client, David Sparling, here at the cottage. Probably the car belonged to him. Each step along the path revealed more of the extensive view promised by the cottage's name: fields stretching below her with copses of woods and lanes that wound in and out of view west across Oxfordshire towards the distant River Thames. Valley View Cottage had been well named. A real selling point.

As she rounded the corner of the bungalow, now seeing the rose-covered front porch, she gasped. Someone was lying awkwardly at the foot of the brick steps in a pool of blood. She dropped her business bag and raced over. A man's body, a very large body, was draped over the front step with blood dripping from a head wound. His breathing was noisy, proving he was alive, if nothing else. She tried, but could not move him; he was grossly overweight. She fumbled for her phone and dialled 999.

After seeing the man into the ambulance, Maddie felt as purposeless as a person who was left standing on an emptying station watching a train disappear around the next bend. She took a couple of deep breaths, waiting for the remaining tension to dissipate. Her bag had landed awkwardly when she dropped it, spewing papers over the footpath. With shaking hands, she gathered them up and shoved them back. She slowly walked down the steep drive towards her car. Lucky for David Sparling she had arranged to meet him at Valley View Cottage when she did.

She took some care driving through the still thick traffic. As soon as she arrived home, she rang her ex.

"Some bad news," she said to Wayne. "Your pal David Sparling?"

"You met him?"

"I'm not sure," she said. "When I got there, I found a man had slipped on the front steps and cracked his head against the brickwork. A nasty accident, Wayne. He was out cold and still only semi-conscious when the ambulance arrived. It might not be your friend, though, because when I asked him who he was, he mumbled an unfamiliar name. Clyde? I think it was Clyde."

There was a small silence. "Bald? Fifties? Big guy?"

"Very big. Kind of blubbery lips."

"David," he said. "His name's David Sparling. Okay, I'll find out what's happened and let you know."

Typical Wayne. Taking over. Presuming she'd called him for just that purpose when she was only being polite. Sparling was his friend, so she'd thought he should be told.

Maddie didn't fight it. Just gritted her teeth and hung up. But she came off the telephone agitated. Nobody in the world could get under her skin or wind her up as much her 'darling' ex-husband. Especially given she'd heard rock music in the background. Wayne was a classical fan like she was or he listened to his own avant-garde type of music; his new dolly-bird obviously was into the top hits of her generation. Maddie couldn't suppress a sigh. She'd supported the creation of his music their entire marriage, one of the things she and Wayne had in common. Obviously not as important a factor in their relationship as she'd thought.

A couple of days later, Wayne left a message on her voice mail to say David Sparling had been discharged home to the Oxfordshire cottage and he'd be pleased if she called around as he was feeling much better. Maddie rang Wayne back, got voice mail, and thanked him for the referral once more. She set off, once again, to meet her new client.

The same man, now sporting a large bandage on the side of his head, opened the door to her knock. "My rescuer," he said with a wide smile. "I can't thank you enough." He shook her hand with both of his. "You saved my life."

Maddie smiled but privately thought how unlikely that was, given his quick discharge from hospital. "Blind luck I arrived at the right time. How did you fall?"

"Can't remember a thing," he said with a wink.

"That's what they all say," she replied, remembering to keep smiling. How true. As a former Probation Officer who dealt with criminals – crims – day in and day out, she'd heard many an excuse about memory failure. For the most part, lying through their teeth. Interesting he avoided telling her, though. More to the story, undoubtedly.

David Sparling was a large man who bought his clothes from an excellent outfitter, one who could transform obesity into sleek substantiality. His suit was made of the finest materials and his pure white shirt appeared to be handmade. Obviously he spent money on his clothes. A lot of money. A little detail she filed away: appearances counted for Mr Sparling.

She forgot all that when she saw through the cottage. He had upgraded the kitchen and the bathroom; he had repainted throughout and the floors were dressed with bright rugs over wide floorboards. She loved the newly painted black exposed beams overhead in the front hallway and sitting room. This was how a modernised bungalow should turn out. And she was well aware of the amount of money and effort it could take to end up with a result like this.

She made all the right noises about the renovation as they sat in chairs placed to take advantage of the view over the valley.

"Can't you give me a ballpark figure?" David Sparling asked her when she prevaricated on the asking price. She promised him he would be the first to know. She was too new at the game to hazard a guess.

Armed with a list from her colleagues at the Goring branch of *Green Acres Estate Agents*, Maddie visited every detached freehold bungalow for sale in the area – all part of her education in this new profession she'd taken up. Her plan was to assess the listed price with what she could observe as she inspected each property and then see how it compared with Valley View Cottage. It was part of the steep learning curve she was on, and a vital part at that.

The next day, David Sparling ushered her back into his kitchen-diner with its new bench-top and shiny white tiling, a good choice for a room with the typically tiny kitchen windows of the era.

They discussed the business end of things over a cup of tea and some sweet cakes. Maddie was sure the bungalow, south-facing with such outstanding rural views from its elevated position, would fetch 'top dollar', as they called it in the estate agent correspondence course she'd taken. The cottage was small but beautifully refurbished and it would be a pleasure to show to prospective buyers.

She told him the median price for the four rural cottages similar to his. "Ballpark, but maybe on the high side. I'd love you to get about that," she said, "but I'll need to check any figures with my colleagues back at the office. If we did aim there, then I'd suggest we list it as 'offers over' about twenty thousand lower, something like that."

"How about only ten lower?" he asked with a smile. "I could use the extra dosh."

Maddie hesitated then nodded. "It might take longer to sell."

Sparling shrugged.

"But we can always drop it if it doesn't fly." The customer was always right. Sort of, anyway.

"For a short time, yeah? But I do want to move it as quickly as I can. As you can," he said, again smiling. He was good at smiling, although Maddie noticed it didn't always reach his eyes. She was just a tad cautious about Mr David Sparling. She'd met smilers like him often in her previous career.

As she got the paperwork out of her business bag, she reflected that she was probably safe enough with his figure. She had priced a few houses now and her confidence was growing. The price could be dropped later if she was wrong. She was quite sure Valley View Cottage was not in the same league as the two rather more upmarket places she'd seen. But its comfortable modernisation beat the two which had not been modernised recently. This place had the additional advantage of an enormous garage and parking for a veritable fleet of cars; Sparling could park half a dozen off the road, should he have need to do so. It could be a selling point, particularly to men.

While David Sparling was reading the various bits of paper containing their joint estimation for a selling price, Maddie gathered the tea things and took them into the immaculate kitchen. She opened the pedal bin to drop in the used paper serviettes and she found it almost full. Tossed on top of the rubbish was a soft plastic wrist band, the kind usually provided for each patient in hospital. She stared at it. 'Clive Holloway'. Clive? Clyde? Was that what he'd said when concussed?

Footsteps.

She let the lid down quickly and half turned to face towards the bench.

"Don't go to any trouble," he said. "I'll tidy up afterwards."

The serviettes were scrunched in her fists. She smiled, smoothed the serviettes and left them by the tea things, thinking furiously. Two names for one person had raised a red flag, a bright red flag. Sparling had seemed calm when she'd turned around. Enough to presume he hadn't seen her looking into his bin with its hospital wristband.

So which was it? David pretending to be Clyde/Clive or Clive pretending to be David? She'd find out. Not idle curiosity; it might mean the forms were made out with a false name. Worse would be a sale using the false name. Thank heavens she'd opened that bin.

"I'll make copies of everything back in the office and drop off a set for you," she said.

"You don't have to do that," he said. "I have a photocopier in my office."

He came back with two copies, one for each and he gave the original back to Maddie. "When can we set it into motion?"

"I'd like to hold the first Open Day on the weekend after next," she said, pushing the Open Day date later because of the uncertainty with David/Clyde/Clive's identity. "Can you have the bungalow looking like this?

You've presented it beautifully. Clean, organised and tidy."

"My pleasure," he said with a genuine smile.

She had to admit she was faintly repelled by him, in spite of his impeccable manners. Was it his protuberant lips, always moist and that bit too red? Or how his eyes bored into hers? She'd known eyes like that in her former career as a Probation Officer. Inevitably possessed by shifty crims. The plain fact was, she didn't trust Whatever-his-name-was. Nothing to do with her natural inclination, drummed into her by years of experience, how unwise it was to take anything anybody said at face value. She didn't know David was really Clive, but she strongly suspected it. Or Clive was really David.

Maddie processed the paperwork as soon as she arrived back into the *Green Acres* office in Goring. She stuck her head into the boss's office.

"Just listing that rental outside of Courtneyside, Rupert; he's decided to sell. A very nice little modernised bungalow," she said.

"Now we're talking," he called back to her and gave her a thumb's up.

She looked for Renata, the rentals expert in the office. She would be the person most in the know about Valley View Cottage, given it had been a rental before the renovations. Perhaps she could shed some light on the David/Clive business. But Renata was busy with a client in the Glass Cage, their shared office that gave privacy, auditory if not visual. She waved at Renata who nodded at her through the glass. The nod said they'd catch up soon.

She walked back to her cubicle against the wall of their open plan office. The vendor had two names. Something wasn't quite right. She tried to put her apprehension out of her mind, tried to dismiss it as fanciful.

She failed.

Would you like a free copy of the prequel novella to the Madeleine Brooks Mystery series? It's called *Death at Grenstead House* and here is the link :
https://dl.bookfunnel.com/28cqf6w7vb

Feel free to contact me at: tannis@tannislaidlaw.com. I'd love to hear from you.

Books by Tannis Laidlaw

The Madeleine Brooks Mystery series:
Book 1: Death at Cherry Tree Manor
Book 2: Death at Valley View Cottage
Book 3: Death in Lachmore Wood
Book 4: Death at the Olde Woodley Grange
Prequel: Death in Cold Waters (also in paperback)
Prequel Novella: Death at Grenstead House

The Darkwater Lake Mystery series
Book 1: A Writer is Dead
Book 2: A Swimmer is Dead
Book 3: The Nanny is Dead
Book 4: A Neighbour is Dead

More crime novels:
Marcia's Dead (also in paperback)
Bye Baby Bunting (also in paperback)
The Pumpkin Eater's Wife
Half Truths and Whole Lies
Thursday's Child

Non-fiction:
Full Stop: Eat until you're full and stop gaining weight

About Tannis Laidlaw

Nowadays, Tannis writes mostly fiction instead of academic papers – well-researched psychological crime books: thrillers, suspense or mysteries - utilising her background as a research and clinical psychologist. She has five stand-alone novels available, this mystery series featuring Madeleine Brooks, plus two collections of short stories. She is currently working on another murder mystery series set in the wild lake country of Canada called the Darkwater Lake Mysteries. The first in this four-book series is *A Writer is Dead*, available in both paperback and Kindle.

Most of the time Tannis lives with her husband in New Zealand alternating between Auckland and an adobe house high above an isolated beach in Northland. They also spend time each year in an off-the-grid cottage on a remote lake in the Canadian wilderness in NW Ontario (now you know why she's located her Darkwater Lake series in a similar place). All are wonderful places for writing.

Her website is www.TannisLaidlaw.com

Printed in Great Britain
by Amazon

56048550R00148